Thursday Morning Breakfast (and Murder) Club

Liz Stauffer

SARTORIS
LITERARY
GROUP

A traditional publisher with a non-traditional approach to publishing

Sartoris Literary Group, Inc.
Jackson, Mississippi
www.sartorisliterary.com

To Todd Stauffer with love,
Mom

1

"Clare's dead!"

When she spoke the words, her voice was so low it was barely above a whisper. With the phone still ringing on the other end of the line, the sturdy woman with short, curly red hair dropped the handset back into its cradle and began to pace.

Lillie Mae Harris stopped at the front window, taking no notice of the white buds that were just opening on the two Bradford pear trees in her front yard, or the spring flowers peeping through the freshly hoed soil in the close-by flower bed.

Her thoughts were of Clare.

She had the best view in Mount Penn from this window. On a winter's morning she could see for some thirty miles out over the valley with the big blue sky as the backdrop. The night view was even more amazing, offering a shower of dancing lights in the distance, competing only with the brightest stars.

It was now early spring and the vista had already begun to shrink even though the trees were just beginning to bud. Once the trees were filled out with big green leaves the view would pull in even more until fall, when the colors exploded and the view once again took one's breath away. But today the scenery did nothing to still Lillie Mae's pounding heart or quell her shaking hands. She couldn't stop worrying about Clare. Rushing back to the phone, she scooped it up, and punched in a familiar number.

"Hello," Alice Portman answered in her sweet Southern drawl, after just one ring. Her Jack Russell terrier, Alfred, barked in the background.

"Clare's not answering her phone this morning," Lillie Mae said. "I'm so worried about her, Alice. I'm not sure what to do."

"Settle down, Lillie Mae," Alice said, shushing Alfred. "Why are you so concerned today?"

"You were at the water meeting last night," Lillie Mae said. "You saw how Roger was acting. Yelling and screaming like an idiot. When he's gotten that riled up in the past, Clare's been his punching bag."

"Well, yes," Alice agreed, deliberately slowing the pace of the conversation. "But, Roger was just being Roger last night, dear. Just showing off. I didn't see anything unusual in his behavior. Certainly nothing to make you so worried this morning."

"He was acting worse than usual," Lillie Mae insisted, still pacing the living room floor. "And I'm sure he drank himself crazy when the meeting was finally over. That's the real reason I'm worried, Alice. You know how he is when he drinks. What he does to Clare."

"Roger playacts, you know, when it suits him, Lillie Mae," Alice said, her voice still soft and cool. "He knows he's going to make a lot of money hooking people up to the public water in a few short months, but he wants to come across as the good guy to his neighbors, not the money grubbing fool that he is. He'll use every wile that he has to seduce the community. If the project fails, which it won't this time, he looks like he's the man who stopped it. If it passes, he wins big time."

"You're probably right, Alice," Lillie Mae said, calming a bit. "I know Roger is shrewd. If he wasn't always out there trying to make a deal, he wouldn't be Roger, I guess."

"So, stop overreacting, Lillie Mae. What's brought all this on anyway?"

"I've been calling Clare's house all morning and nobody answers the phone," Lillie Mae said. "It's stupid, I know, but I picture Clare lying on her kitchen floor, needing my help. Dead, even."

A sigh escaped Alice's lips. "You're way over dramatizing this morning, Lillie Mae," she said. "Roger's not even home. He drove by me in that stupid yellow Hummer of his while Alfred and I were out on our early morning walk."

"That's good to hear," Lillie Mae said.

"Stop imagining the worst, Lillie Mae. Clare's probably out, too. It's such a warm spring day. Doesn't she usually go grocery shopping on Wednesday mornings?"

"Maybe," Lillie Mae conceded. "Or she could be in her garden, I guess."

"She'll call you back when she gets to it," Alice said, a hint of impatience in her voice.

"I doubt if she does." Lillie Mae's voice broke. "She rarely calls me anymore. We've been such good friends for so many years and I miss her, Alice. I wish I knew what I did wrong."

"Clare's changing, Lillie Mae. She's getting stronger. Give the girl some space."

"I've noticed a change, too," Lillie Mae said, "since Billy went off to university. She does have more confidence, I'll give you that."

"Have you written your article on the water meeting for the *Antioch Gazette*, yet?" Alice asked. "I thought it was due today."

"Not yet," Lillie Mae confessed. "I've been too worried about Clare."

"Maybe being busy will take your mind off things that are not really any of your business," Alice said.

"I guess you're right. Clare is a big girl and can take care of herself."

"Did you hear that Clare and Dale Beavers are going to sing a duet in church on Sunday?" Alice asked, deliberately changing the subject. "They're practicing for the county competition next month. They're entered, you know."

"No, I didn't know. That is good news." Lillie Mae smiled for the first time that morning. "Roger stopped her singing for way too many years, except for the church choir, and he didn't really like her doing that very much."

"Let's hope Clare and Dale win the competition," Alice chuckled. "That should piss off Roger rather nicely."

"Alice!" Lillie Mae exclaimed, laughing. "I don't think I've heard you say anything like that before."

"That's because you can't read my thoughts."

"Are you going over to Janet's for supper?" Lillie Mae asked, remembering the pot luck dinner was this evening.

"Yes," Alice said. "Janet's throwing quite a party. She's invited half of Mount Penn to view Pete's new truck. Are you?"

"Harriet and Kevin are picking me up, promptly at five forty-five."

"Don't be late," Alice warned. "When Harriet says five forty-five, she means five forty-five."

"I know that well," Lillie Mae said, then suddenly turned serious again when her thoughts returned to Clare. "I'm going to walk down to Clare's house and check things out before I start on the article. I need to make certain she's all right, or I won't be able to concentrate on my work. Do you want to come along?"

"No, you go on, if it'll make you feel better," Alice said. "You can fill me in on the details at dinner this evening."

* * *

Lillie Mae walked outside a few minutes later, and the cool, crisp mountain air hit her full in the face. Taking a deep breath, she glanced toward her small flower garden by the side of the patio. The daffodils had ballooned overnight. Yesterday they were just starting to open. Now they were stunning, the bright yellow blooms and the rich green stalks swaying like a colorful wave in the bright sunshine. Several tulips had popped out of their bulbs overnight as well, merging pink and red into the yellow sea.

"I'll take Clare a bouquet," she said to herself, knowing full well that Clare's flowers were as plentiful as her own. But it would give her an excuse for the pop-in visit.

Ten minutes later Lillie Mae set off on her journey carrying a vase filled with tulips and daffodils. Turning the corner at her back yard, she looked at the wrap-around porch on the two-story traditional house directly across the street from her own and thought of Sam and Margaret Jenkins, the nice young couple who had been her neighbors since they moved to the mountain five years ago.

The house looked deserted that morning. Either the Jenkins had gone away or Margaret was having one of her bad days. She'd find out later how Margaret was doing, she thought as she walked down the small hill they shared and turned onto the smooth unlined blacktop of Chestnut Lane.

"Lillie Mae, over here" someone called.

Twisting her head, Lillie Mae saw Joyce and Carlos Castro, both tall and lean, and rather exotic looking, walking towards her. In sync the pair threw their hands in the air and waved. Lillie Mae nodded, the vase of flowers preventing her from waving back.

"What a lovely spring bouquet," Joyce said, as she and Carlos drew closer.

"It's for Clare," Lillie Mae said, knowing it sounded silly since Clare's gardens were the envy of the town. Her round cheeks turned a pale shade of pink.

"Really," Joyce said. "Clare?"

"Frankly, Joyce I'm worried about her," Lillie Mae said. "I'm using these flowers as an excuse to make sure she's all right this morning."

"Is she sick?" Carlos asked, a look of alarm on his handsome Roman features, his accent more pronounced than usual.

"No, not sick," Lillie Mae said. "It's just that I phoned her house earlier, and nobody picked up. Not even the voice mail."

"Why are you so worried?" Joyce asked, her British accent a contrast to her husband's Spanish tones. "Carlos and I are so out of the loop. We've been frightfully busy since Carlos started working on the new documentary film, you see. Do tell us what's going on in Mount Penn."

Lillie Mae told them about the water meeting the night before and Roger Ballard's suspicious behavior.

"Wish you'd been there to see all the drama yourself. You see things more objectively than the rest of us Mount Penn folk. I guess it's because you haven't lived here very long, and you're not as emotionally attached to this place as the rest of us."

Carlos stepped back as if avoiding a punch. "We bought this house over ten years ago, Lillie Mae. We're as much a part of this community as anybody else on the mountain. Sam and Margaret Jenkins are the newcomers, not us. They've only lived here five years."

"But you've only been in your house, what four years full-time. The first six years you were just weekenders, and we don't count that," Lillie Mae said, failing to notice there was no smile on Carlos' face.

Joyce noticed that Carlos was none too pleased with Lillie Mae, and interceded. "Of course, Lillie Mae, everyone who wasn't born and raised in this area is a newcomer to you. But we love it here, and we consider Mount Penn our home."

Joyce held her arm out and swirled her body around, a move that showed off the dancer she used to be. "How could you not? Look how lovely it all is."

Lillie Mae's eyes followed Joyce's movement. Budding pear trees glowed white in most every yard, pink Japanese maple buds were ready to burst, the forsythia was in full bloom, and the

11

rhododendron ready to pop. Joyce was right. Who wouldn't want to live on this mountain?

"Of course you're a part of this community," Lillie Mae said. Thinking it best to change the subject before she stuffed her foot any deeper into her mouth, she went on. "Speaking of Sam and Margaret, have you heard any news about them? I just passed their place and it looks deserted."

"I haven't heard anything," Carlos said, silently checking with Joyce.

"Sam usually lets us know if he and Margaret are going somewhere," Joyce said.

"Margaret could be having one of her bad days," Lillie Mae said, a frown deepening the crease in her forehead. "The change of season probably affects her more than the rest of us."

"Poor Margaret. Too young to be housebound so much of the time."

"At least she has some good days," Lillie Mae said.

Carlos broke out in a laugh. "Look who's coming down the road."

The two ladies turned to see Sam Jenkins, some thirty feet away, walking down the mountain road. Not quite tall, but still lanky, his sandy hair ruffled, he was taking long strides, a walking cane in his hand, his eyes focused on the road, and seemingly lost in his own thoughts."

"Hello, Sam," Carlos called. "Over here."

Sam raised his eyes toward the trio. "Can't stop now, Carlos," he said as he continued his stride down the hill. "I have to get home right away. Margaret's been alone far too long this morning."

"How is she?" Joyce called.

"It's not been a good day," Sam said. "But I'll tell her you asked about her."

"I'll bring a casserole over later today for your dinner," Joyce called back.

"Don't go to any bother," Sam said. "You've been so kind already, and we haven't reciprocated."

"It's no bother," Joyce called back. "I have an extra casserole in the freezer and don't worry about reciprocating. They'll be plenty of time for that when Margaret's better."

"See you at breakfast in the morning, Sam?" Lillie Mae called. "We'll be there, if we can."

Sam waved his hand again as he walked on.

"Sam has a lot on his shoulders for such a young man," Carlos said, watching him near his own house. "Margaret is damn lucky to have him. Not every husband would take care of his wife the way Sam takes care of Margaret."

"Let's hope she feels better soon," Lillie Mae said.

Joyce nodded her head, but remained quiet, her eyes still focused on Sam's path.

"I've gotta go, if I want to be at Clare's before lunchtime," Lillie Mae said, turning toward the street. Stepping into the road, she noticed a truck speeding toward her. Before she could move out of its way, it blew by, missing her only by a few inches. Loud rap music spewed from the open window of the older, ragged, black Ford pickup. Lillie Mae jumped back onto the curb, her stomach turning flip flops.

"Any closer that guy would have hit me!" she yelled, twisting to catch her balance.

Carlos rushed toward her, Joyce at his side. "That truck must have come out of Carl Lewis' driveway. I didn't get a good look, but I'd guess it was a couple of kids by the sound of the music."

"Are you all right, Lillie Mae?" Joyce asked.

"I'll live," Lillie Mae said, her eyes burning holes in the back of the truck. "But no thanks to those two young people."

"I've seen several cars go up that way this morning," Carlos said, turning toward the entrance to the driveway of the local drug dealer's trailer. "Something's going on up there, and I doubt if it's any good."

"How that man continues to peddle drugs when everybody knows what he's up to is beyond me," Lillie Mae said, hugging the vase of flowers close to her chest. "Surely Charlie Warren could put a stop to it."

"Charlie can only do what he can do," said Carlos. "I hear whenever the cops raid the place, it's clean. Somebody in the know has to be in on it all."

"Not Charlie!" Lillie Mae said, shocked.

"Of course not Charlie," Carlos said. "No more honest cop ever existed. He's a great guy and a good neighbor."

"Follow the money," Lillie Mae said, "and you'll find the real culprit."

Carlos laughed. "With all the traffic that goes up to Carl's place each week, you'd think he'd be the man with the money. Instead he lives in a broken down old trailer. Maybe vice doesn't pay."

"Somebody's making money."

Lillie Mae nodded in agreement.

"But it sure ain't Carl Lewis."

"It's too bad our closest neighbor is a drug dealer," Joyce said, her former high spirits doused. "I just hate that man living here in Mount Penn. It's just not right."

"Now I really have to go." Lillie Mae clutched the vase of flowers to her chest, and looked both ways before stepping into the street again. "Are you going to Janet's for dinner this evening?"

"We'll be there," Joyce said. "And, we'll be at breakfast in the morning, too. Take care until then."

*   *   *

Roger Ballard's yellow Hummer was not in the driveway when Lillie Mae arrived at Clare's house a few minutes later, but Clare's Ford Escort was. That was good news on both fronts.

Lillie Mae walked around to the back of the large white two-story house trimmed with neat green shutters, to see if Clare might be working in the garden as she often was at this time of the day. She paused when she heard Clare's voice through the open back door. She sounded angry. Or was it scared?

Lillie Mae couldn't tell for sure. As she neared the back of the house, Lillie Mae could see through the screen door that Clare was on the phone, her back facing the door. Ready to call out a greeting, Lillie Mae stopped when she heard what Clare said next.

"No, don't come over here. I'm fine."

A brief pause.

"There is nothing for you to worry about. It was an accident. Really. Roger didn't touch me. I told you the truth about what happened."

More silence.

"We have to be careful," Clare said, her voice quivering. "If anyone finds out what we've done, it would be a disaster for both of us. Roger would kill us if he knew or even suspected."

A stab of guilt pricked Lillie Mae's conscience. She stepped back around the side of the house and then called out a belated greeting in her loudest voice. "Clare, are you home? Lillie Mae here." She moved again toward the back door.

"Just a minute Lillie Mae," Clare called back. "I'll be right there."

Lillie Mae could hear rustling in the kitchen and what could have been Clare whispering and then hanging up the phone. Clare's big black tomcat was at the door mewing to get out, making it impossible to hear the rest of the muffled conversation.

Clare stood at the door a few seconds later, flushed and anxious. "Thanks for stopping by, Lillie Mae," she said, brushing a strand of dark-brown hair behind her ear as she pushed the door open with her other hand. The slight smile on her lips was not in her bright blue eyes. "What a beautiful bouquet you have with you."

"It's for you." Lillie Mae stretched the vase out toward her friend.

Clare took the flowers from Lillie Mae, then ushered her into the large country kitchen. "Come in and tell me the news," Clare said, without much enthusiasm. "Would you like a cup of coffee?"

"That would be nice," Lillie Mae said.

Clare busily arranged an impromptu coffee while Lillie Mae took a seat at the table. Watching her friend as she prepared the table, Lillie Mae was struck again at how attractive Clare was despite her years with Roger. A large-boned woman, Clare could easily be a plus-size model with curves in all the right places. Although she must be in her mid-forties by now, Lillie Mae thought she could pass for a younger woman. Only her son Billy, now a freshman at the university, gave her age away.

Clare set the table with raisin-nut muffins, butter and jam, and a plate of strawberries and fresh pineapple, then poured the coffee in the mugs at each of their places. She had set the flowers in the center of the table. Sitting opposite Lillie Mae, she passed her the plate of fruit, "These are the first strawberries out of my garden. I picked them this morning."

Lillie Mae took one of the deep red strawberries from the bowl Clare had passed her, and popped it into her mouth. "That's good," she said when she had swallowed. "So sweet for an early spring berry."

15

"Sweet berries always come after a cold winter." Clare picked up a berry and tasted it.

It was then that Lillie Mae saw the bruise on her left cheek.

"That bastard!" Lillie Mae said. "What did Roger do to you?"

"Roger didn't do anything to me, Lillie Mae," Clare said.

"Right!" Lillie Mae exclaimed. "Roger never touches you, does he? In all the years I've known you, you haven't had one bruise or broken bone, thanks to Roger Ballard, have you, Clare?"

Clare looked Lillie Mae squarely in the eyes, and said very slowly, enunciating each word. "Roger did not do this to me, Lillie Mae. It was a stupid accident I did to myself."

"Right," Lillie Mae said again, this time muttering under her breath.

Clare blushed. "I'll tell you what happened if you give me the chance. You're so judgmental, Lillie Mae. You jump to the worst conclusions with very little information, and you always have to be right. I'm not a needy little girl anymore. I can take care of myself."

Lillie Mae stared at her friend, shocked by the outburst. "I'm sorry."

"Do you know what I hate the most, Lillie Mae?" Clare said, ignoring her friend's apology. "The pity. I can see it in your eyes and I can't stand it. Why do you think I've been avoiding you lately?"

Tears sprang to Lillie Mae's eyes.

"Clare I didn't realize—again, I'm sorry," she said, truly repentant. "Tell me what happened last night, and I promise I'll believe you."

Clare looked at her friend for what seemed like a full minute.

"It was so stupid," she finally said, as if the earlier conversation hadn't taken place. "I went to bed around ten o'clock and went straight to sleep. It had been a busy day and I was tired. When I woke up around midnight and Roger wasn't home yet, I got worried. As you know, when Roger stays out late, he usually comes home drunk."

Clare glanced at Lillie Mae, who was nodding, but didn't wait for her to say anything. "Most of the time he falls asleep on the sofa in the living room, but, on the rare occasion, he wants to talk to me. All I have to do to avoid him is to hide in Billy's room.

Roger never thinks to look for me there. So, last night when I was moving to Billy's room, I didn't turn on the lights in case Roger came home just then, and I tripped on an old pair of his boots that he had left by the landing. I fell and hit my cheek on the wall. That's what happened, Lillie Mae. As I told you before, Roger didn't touch me."

"So it really was an accident," Lillie Mae said, thinking that indirectly Roger was as responsible for the accident as he would have been had he made the blow himself. "Is there anything I can do for you?"

"No, Lillie Mae, there's nothing I need from you or anybody. I've told you it's not a big deal. I'm fine. I'm fine. I'm fine. Please, let's not talk about it anymore. Okay?"

"Okay," Lillie Mae said, wondering who else Clare had been trying to convince it wasn't a big deal that morning.

The phone rang, the shrill noise blasting through the tension in the air. Clare turned pale. She looked over her shoulder at the phone, than back at Lillie Mae. "I'm not going to answer that," she said with a nervous laugh. "I've been getting so many crank phone calls lately."

Lillie Mae moved her eyes from Clare to the phone, but remained quiet.

The ringing stopped as quickly as it had begun. Clare inhaled deeply and clasped her hands, but Lillie Mae could see they were shaking.

"Let's go outside, Lillie Mae," Clare said, jumping to her feet. "It's way too pretty a morning to be sitting in the house. Besides I want to show you my garden. The onions, carrots, and the spring lettuce I planted last week are already peeking through the soil." Clare picked up a bowl off the counter. "Let's pick some strawberries for you to take home."

Lillie Mae glanced back over her shoulder at the phone as she followed Clare out of the house.

2

Lillie Mae washed her lunch plate by hand and stood gazing out the window by the sink, thinking of her morning with Clare, when she heard a tap on her back door window. Turning, she saw her next-door neighbor, Hester Franklin, gesturing wildly. Lillie Mae wiped her hands on the tea towel hanging from the stove, and rushed to answer the door.

"Oh, Lillie Mae," Hester said, her pale hazel eyes glaring and the boney fingers of her hands wringing together as she stumbled into the room. "You've got to help me."

"Hester, come in and sit down," Lillie Mae said. "You look terrible." She guided the shaken woman to a chair. "Take a deep breath, pull yourself together, and tell me what's wrong."

Trying to choke back a sob, Hester covered her face with her hands. "It's all so awful, Lillie Mae. I don't know how to tell you what's happened."

"Don't say anything for a minute, Hester. Just settle yourself." Lillie Mae massaged Hester's shoulders and could feel her relax just a bit. "Let me get you a cup of coffee, dear, and then we'll talk."

After Hester had taken a few deep breaths, Lillie Mae walked over to the counter and poured the freshly brewed coffee she always kept available for an unexpected visitor into the two bright red coffee cups she took from the drying rack.

"It's all so awful," Hester repeated, watching Lillie Mae set a coffee mug on the table in front of her. Her hands still shaking, she slowly picked it up, and took a sip.

"Are you sick, Hester?" Lillie Mae asked. "Do you need me to take you to the doctor?"

"There's nothing wrong with me. I'm perfectly well, under the circumstances. It's so much worse than that, Lillie Mae."

Hester used her free hand to wipe away a tear.

"Whatever it is, you can tell me," Lillie Mae said.

Hester inhaled sharply. "It's Patrick," she said. "Mabel's boy. He was arrested this morning for transporting drugs. He called me a little bit ago from the Antioch police station."

"No!" Lillie Mae said, taken aback. "This is serious."

"I told you it was awful," Hester said.

"What did Patrick have to say for himself?"

"We could only talk a couple of minutes, and he wasn't making much sense, being upset like he was," Hester said. "He told me that he and that friend of his, Jerry Foster, went up to Carl Lewis' place this morning to meet Roger Ballard. They were supposed to pick up some piping for Roger, but he didn't show. Carl was there, but he told the boys he didn't know anything about any pick up. The boys waited around Carl's place for almost a half hour for Roger to come, and then left in none-too-pleased spirits. They were driving toward Antioch when the police stopped them."

"Were they driving an old black pickup truck?" Lillie Mae asked, remembering her near miss earlier that morning.

"Sounds right," Hester said. "Jerry has this beat-up old Ford truck he drives around."

"Do the boys like loud music?" Lillie Mae asked.

"It's horrible. They play that awful radio so loud all the time."

"That's what I thought," Lillie Mae said. "So, what happened after the police stopped them?"

Hester choked back another sob. "According to Patrick the cops checked the bed of the truck and found a large package of drugs under an old blanket."

"Oh, dear," Lillie Mae said. "Is Patrick into drugs?"

"No, never!" Hester exclaimed, her face now a beet red. "He swore to me he knew nothing about the drugs. He was shocked when the package was found. He swears it wasn't there when he and Jerry took off that morning."

"What happened then?"

"The police took the boys to the Antioch jail, Lillie Mae. Patrick's going to be locked up like a common criminal." Hester eyes were now the size of saucers. "And he's asked me to come and get him out. He begged me to help him."

"Where's Mabel?" Lillie Mae asked.

"Mabel's on another business trip this week. She's always out of town on business these days, Lillie Mae. Ever since she got that new job with that big computer company all she does is travel and work."

"What about Patrick?"

"Patrick's stays at home by himself. He may be almost nineteen, but he's still too young to be left alone so much. And, I'm too old to be responsible for him. He's way too much for me to handle."

"What did Mabel say when you called her?"

Hester hesitated. "I haven't called her yet."

"You have to call Mabel and tell her what's happened," Lillie Mae said. "You better do it right away."

"I just can't—not yet," Hester said, her eyes welling up again. "You know how Mabel is, Lillie Mae. She flies off the handle at the slightest thing. I'll call her tonight once I know more. I can't take care of Patrick and deal with Mabel at the same time."

"So what are you going to do now?" Lillie Mae asked.

"I've never been to a police station in my life, and I'm scared. I don't even know where it is in Antioch. I need your help, Lillie Mae. Will you drive me?"

Quickly thinking what else she needed to do that afternoon, Lillie Mae decided nothing was more important than helping Hester. "Of course, I'll drive you, dear."

"Thank you, Lillie Mae. Thank you so much."

"You should call Sid Firth," Lillie Mae said. "He's the best lawyer in these parts."

"I called Sid before I came over here," Hester said, pushing her coffee mug back and struggling to her feet, suddenly in a hurry. "He's going to meet us at the police station in an hour."

"Then let's go. I'll get my purse and keys and meet you by the car in ten minutes. And Hester," Lillie Mae said, when the frightened older woman turned back to her' "Everything will be all right."

Lillie Mae's heart did a flip when Hester attempted one of the saddest smiles she had ever seen.

*　　*　　*

"Pull yourself together, please," Lillie Mae said, as she guided a flustered and disheveled Hester into the Antioch Police station. "You've got to be brave for Patrick."

For the first half of the trip down the mountain and into the town, Hester seemed fine, but the closer they got to the police station, the more frantic she became. By the time Lillie Mae drove into the parking lot, Hester was a bundle of nerves, squirming like a small child. It took all Lillie Mae's patience to get the older woman out of the car and into the small, yet forbidding building.

Sid Firth, a stocky, balding man of indeterminate age approached them as they entered the large stark room that served as the lobby.

"Thank goodness you're here," Hester said. Transferring her arm from Lillie Mae's to Sid's, she gazed up at him with glassy eyes, and asked in a voice suddenly old and frail. "Have you seen our Patrick?"

Sid looked down at Hester, his face stoic but comforting, and patted her hand. "Get a hold of yourself, my dear. I have seen Patrick and he told me what happened. Now it's time for us to talk. Let's go find an empty interview room."

As if noticing her for the first time, Sid nodded toward Lillie Mae. "Thank you for driving Hester here, Lillie Mae. I know how difficult this is for her, and your being here helps make it a little easier for her. She needs to sign some papers. Will you come with us please?"

Sid guided Hester across the large room to a small office. Lillie Mae followed. The room contained a small round conference table and four folding chairs. Sid helped Hester to the chair closest to the door. Lillie Mae took the chair across from Hester, and Sid sat between the two ladies.

"Where's Patrick now?" Hester asked.

Sid glanced at Lillie Mae, a look that pleaded with her to keep quiet. Taking Hester's hand into his, he said. "I'm afraid the news is not good, Hester. Patrick has been taken to a holding cell and will have to stay here for now. He's to be called in front of the judge tomorrow morning at nine o'clock for the arraignment. I'll be there with him. I want you in the courtroom, too."

Hester winced. "Please don't make me come back here tomorrow, Sid. I can't face it again. I'm an old woman."

Squeezing Hester's hand, Sid remained quiet for a few moments. It was only after he felt her relax that he said. "I promise I'll stay with you during the arraignment."

"You will do that for me?" Hester stared at Sid, the color returning to her face.

"This is Patrick's first offense, Hester, so I'm certain we'll be able to get him out of jail on bail by tomorrow afternoon. My assistant is making the arrangements. But, I need you here in the morning to show the judge that Patrick comes from a good family who support him."

"Why can't he come home with me now?" Hester asked.

"The situation is more serious than we first thought. Apparently the Alpine police have been watching Carl Lewis' place for a couple of weeks, getting wind of some major drug deal expected to happen there. This morning the Alpine police called for a backup crew from Antioch to set up a road block, having been informed that today was the day the drug parcel was going to be passed. As you know, Patrick and Jerry were pulled over at the road block. When their truck was checked, a package was found under an old blanket in the back."

Sid paused and inhaled sharply, then continued. "The package contained marijuana, cocaine, and several different kinds of prescription drugs."

The blood drained completely out of Hester's face and her head fell to one side. Lillie Mae, having kept her eyes on Hester during Sid's speech, jumped out of her chair and caught her just as she started to fall.

Sid was out of his chair. "Bring us water, now, please," he called out the office door to the tall, uniformed attendant standing outside the room.

"You gave me a shock, Sid, but I'm better now," Hester announced a couple of minutes later after sipping from the glass of water that was brought into the room. Lillie Mae moved back to her chair when Sid pulled his chair closer to Hester, and draped his arm across her back. "Please finish what you were telling me."

"The charge against Patrick is very serious," Sid said, his face close to Hester's, his arm holding her steady. "But, I want you to also know that after talking to Patrick and Jerry, I am convinced that they are innocent."

Hester leaned toward Sid, color returning to her face. "That's wonderful news, Sid."

"But it's not enough for me to believe they're innocent, Hester. The boys are still in serious trouble with the police."

Hester slumped back into her chair. "Please, Sid. Tell me how Patrick is doing."

Sid sat up straighter, but kept his hand close to Hester's shoulder. "Patrick's confused and angry. He claims to know nothing about the drugs, and as I said before, I believe him. His story is simple enough. He and Jerry Foster went up to Carl Lewis' place to pick up some plumbing supplies for Roger Ballard. Roger was to meet them there and pay Carl, and then tell the boys where to deliver the supplies. But when they arrived at Carl Lewis's place, Roger wasn't there. Carl said he knew nothing about the pickup and had not talked to Roger about it. Patrick said he called Roger's cell phone, but got no answer. When he called Roger's house, Clare told him she didn't know where Roger was."

"What's Roger got to say about all this?" Lillie Mae asked.

"No one knows where Roger is," Sid said. "The police are looking for him. They want to talk to him as much as I do."

"How about Carl Lewis?" Lillie Mae asked. "Surely he must have put the package in the back of the boys' truck."

"Carl Lewis is missing, too, although Charlie Warren did speak to him briefly, shortly after the incident occurred. He must know the police want to talk to him again. I suspect that's why he can't be found."

"Can I see Patrick?" Hester asked.

"No, Hester, I'm sorry, but you won't be allowed to see Patrick today."

Hester nodded as if expecting Sid's answer.

Twitching in his chair, Sid rubbed his hand over his bald head. "There's something else I think you should know, Hester."

"What?" Hester asked, sitting straighter in her chair, her hands grasping the seat as if trying to forestall the next disaster.

"I'm representing Jerry Foster as well as Patrick at the arrangement tomorrow."

"I don't understand," she said, confused.

"I just didn't want you to think I wasn't giving my all to Patrick. I am. And to be honest, I think it's better for the two boys to go in front of the judge together. Shows uniformity. Just wasn't sure how you'd feel about it, or to be honest, what Mabel will say when she hears."

Hester stared at Sid as if considering what Mabel's reaction might be. "Oh, dear," she said, and then quickly brightened. "You're our lawyer, Sid. We have to trust your judgment."

"Thank you, for that, Hester," he said, the first hint of a smile on his face since meeting the ladies.

"What else did Patrick tell you?"

Sid's smile faded. "Patrick believes he was set up, and frankly, so do I. The boys were shocked when the officers found the drugs in their truck. And the shock wasn't faked. We all know those two boys have been in enough mischief over the years, but never anything really serious, and never anything pertaining to drugs. And, Carl Lewis is a bad one. I wouldn't put anything past that man."

"What about Roger Ballard?" Hester asked. "Do you think he used those boys?"

"It certainly looks suspicious, but I'd be surprised. It's not like Roger to involve two young boys in his doings. As shady as he's been at times, he's never done anything illegal. And there's Billy. Roger adores that boy of his. Billy and Patrick are friends. Of course, Billy's away at school just now, doing well I hear, so he's not involved, but I don't think Roger would set up one of his son's friends."

Lillie Mae, who had kept quiet longer than most people would have believed possible, piped up. "I wouldn't put anything past Roger Ballard."

Sid glanced toward Lillie Mae. "Patrick would agree with you Lillie Mae. He swears it was Roger who's behind all this."

Sid turned back to Hester. "And that's why I'm worried, Hester. Patrick is angry. He's saying Roger Ballard is to blame, and he's going to make things right. When Patrick gets out of here tomorrow, I'm counting on you and Mabel to make sure the boy behaves."

Hester's eyes filled with tears again.

"I'll try. But Patrick doesn't listen to me, Sid. He will listen to Mabel, though, when she's home. She doesn't let him get away with much."

"When is Mabel getting home?"

Hester cried louder.

"You haven't called her yet, have you?" Sid said.

Hester shook her head. "You know how Mabel is. I couldn't take any more grief. She gets so mad, you see."

Sid stood up. "Lillie Mae, you and Hester come with me. We need to sign some papers, and when we're done we're going to call Mabel together."

Hester looked over her shoulder at Lillie Mae who nodded reassuringly to her.

Sid continued, his voice more stern. "Hester, you have to promise me you'll be in court in the morning. Will you drive her, Lillie Mae?"

"Not tomorrow, Sid," Lillie Mae rushed to say. "It's Thursday morning breakfast. I haven't missed one in years."

"Then I'll come and pick you up." Sid took hold of Hester's arm and led her out of the small room. "I'll be at your house at eight fifteen."

"Thank you, Sid," Hester said.

"Will you check on Hester in the morning, see that she's up and ready, Lillie Mae?" Sid looked over his shoulder at the younger woman trailing the slow moving couple.

"Of course," she said, glancing at her neighbor. "I'll do what I can to help."

Hester turned to Lillie Mae, her face shrouded in misery.

"Mabel will kill that man," Hester said, her voice barely loud enough to be heard. "I'm so scared of what's going to happen once she hears what Roger Ballard's done to Patrick, Lillie Mae. You've got to help us."

Lillie Mae slowly nodded, too frightened to say anything.

*   *   *

Lillie Mae was working on the water meeting article for the *Antioch Gazette* at her desk in the corner of the living room, when a loud ring interrupted her thoughts. Checking the caller ID, she saw Peterson on the screen.

"Hi, Harriet," Lillie Mae said. "What's up?"

"I've been trying to call Hester all afternoon, but nobody answers her phone," Harriet said. "Janet asked me to invite her to dinner tonight, and then pick her up when we come for you. Do you know where she is?"

Lillie Mae told her the *Reader's Digest* version of her afternoon at the jail.

"I left her in bed awhile ago with her phone turned off," Lillie Mae said. "She's in no mood to party this evening."

A buzz on Lillie Mae's line interrupted them. "I have another call coming in, Harriet. Feast or famine. That's what I always say. Do you want me to put you on hold, or call you back?"

"I'll wait," Harriet said. "Maybe it's some news."

"Lillie Mae here."

"Lillie Mae, its Sam."

Lillie Mae heard the fear in his voice.

"What's wrong Sam?"

"Margaret has had an attack. It's serious this time. She's been vomiting, and she's in pain."

"Oh, dear!" Lillie Mae exclaimed, thinking *what next?*

"I've called her doctor, and he told me to bring her to the emergency room right away. He's going to meet us there, but I have no idea how long this will take, or when we'll be back home. I wanted to let someone know where we were going. We know how the neighbors worry about Margaret."

"What can I do to help?"

"Thanks for asking, Lillie Mae, but there's nothing to be done right now except for me to get Margaret to the doctor. I'll keep you updated on her condition."

"Let me know if I can help in any way, Sam," Lillie Mae offered, looking out her window at the Jenkins' house.

Lillie Mae pressed the connection on the phone. "That was Sam Jenkins on the other line," she said. "Margaret's had an attack, and he's taking her to the hospital."

"Poor Margaret," Harriet said. "She's gone through so much."

Lillie Mae suddenly felt very tired. "This place has gone crazy. I wonder what's next."

"That's not a good question to ask," Harriet said.

"You're right about that," Lillie Mae groaned.

"Listen, girl, Kevin's calling and I've got to go, too. You be ready at five forty-five, hear. We can't be late for dinner at Janet's this evening."

Lillie Mae groaned again, and hung up the phone.

* * *

The rest of the afternoon was surprisingly quiet. Lillie Mae was able to finish the article she was writing for the *Antioch Gazette* on Mount Penn's water project. Pressing the send button on her computer, she stood up and stretched, feeling a huge sense of relief now that one project was in her done pile. She moved to the window for a quick peek outside, and saw Carl Lewis' old black truck parked in front of her house.

"What's that fool doing here," she said to the air, and then watched as Carl opened the truck door, and stepped down, and looked in her direction. She stepped back from the window hoping he hadn't spotted her. When he took a step toward her house, blood rushed to her face, and she checked how close the phone was in case she needed help.

Although his eyes were covered by a pair of large black sunglasses, Lillie Mae felt him staring at her front door for what seemed an eternity, but was probably only a couple of seconds. Her heart raced when he took another step forward. Suddenly he turned around, and walked back up the street, this time stopping in front of Hester's bungalow. Retracing his earlier steps, he walked toward her house again.

He's not after me, she thought. He's pacing. Then, she noticed how nervous he seemed as he kept turning his head back and forth, as if scanning the neighborhood for something or someone.

Finally, he crossed the street and went up on the Jenkins' front porch. She watched him knock on their door, and then jiggle the knob, as if trying to break in. Glancing over his shoulder at her house again, he jumped off the porch and moved toward the far side of the house, disappearing from Lillie Mae's view. He reappeared again a minute later, obviously in a hurry. He crossed the street without looking for the rare passing car. He took a cell phone out of his pocket and punched in a number before getting into his truck.

"I wonder what that was all about," she said to herself.

Picking up the phone she called Charlie Warren.

3

Kevin and Harriet Peterson appeared in Lillie Mae's driveway promptly at a quarter to six, the horn on their new model Chrysler honking before she had time to lock her back door.

"I'm coming," she called when she heard a car door open, and Harriet yell, "Get moving, girl. Kevin's already griping."

"Janet's impromptu potluck dinner has turned into a neighborhood feast," Harriet told Lillie Mae when she had settled into the back seat of the car. "Joyce and Carlos are coming, and they're picking up Alice."

"Is Clare coming?" Lillie Mae asked.

"No, Janet couldn't get a hold of her, and the Jenkins' are still at the hospital. Poor, Margaret," Harriet said, shaking her head. "So young and pretty to be in so much pain."

"Hester's not coming either," Kevin piped in. "Rumor has it you can fill us in on all the details there."

Lillie Mae promised to tell all once they had arrived at Janet's house. "I don't want to have to tell the same story over and over," she said. Harriet and Kevin nodded.

Lillie Mae watched her friends from the back seat of the car as they rode quietly the short distance to Janet and Pete's house. Harriet looked as youthful as ever despite her gray hair, which she wore in a short bob. She was a lady with lots of energy, Lillie Mae thought. Kevin had aged since he retired from the cement company last year. A tall man, he was still lean, although lately, his shoulders sagged. Lillie Mae hoped he would find an interest to bring him back to life.

Harriet, who was driving, as usual, pulled into Janet and Pete's driveway and parked just beside Pete's new black truck. Carlos' Mini Cooper convertible was already parked behind it.

"Looks like we're the last to arrive," Harriet said as she, Kevin, and Lillie Mae opened their doors and stepped out of the car.

"Look, Harriet, at the sun starting to set over the valley," Lillie Mae said, marveling at the pink skies. "Red sky at night, sailor's delight."

"I do miss Mount Penn. But don't tell Kevin. He's so proud of our new ranch house in town."

The smell of roasting beef and baking biscuits filled the air as Pete, a compact man, half the size of his wife, greeted the threesome at the door of the white frame cottage. A gingerbread house flew into Lillie Mae's mind, as it always did, when she visited Janet and Pete's place. The house, like Pete and Janet, was right out of a fairytale.

"Come in, come in," he said, throwing the door wide open. "Janet's getting the meal on the table, and we're just about ready to sit down. So good of you to come on time. We like to eat at six, you see. Let's go into the dining room."

Moments later everyone, including Janet, was seated at the large dining room table where a generous spread was laid out before them. A pot roast surrounded by potatoes, carrots, peas, and onions was at the center of the table. A large bowl of beef stock gravy sat nearby. Carlos passed the spinach salad to Alice. A basket of fresh baked biscuits finished the table. Lillie Mae's mouth watered at the thought of Janet's biscuits with a pat of creamy butter and fresh strawberry jam.

Janet could cook and she had the body to prove it. Round and fleshy, she was as big as Pete was little. Jack Spratt and his wife entered Lillie Mae's mind, as it had many times before.

"Tell us how Hester is doing," Janet said, buttering her second biscuit.

Lillie Mae spent the next several minutes catching her neighbors up on the events of the afternoon at the police station. "Hester's a marvel," she finally said. "She took the punches today like a real champ."

"Roger Ballard's a devil," Pete said, his usual grin wiped from his face. "I'm not surprised he's involved in all this mess."

"Let me tell the story, Pete," Janet pleaded.

The grin on Pete's face returned. "You do tell a good story, Janet. Go ahead."

Janet started her tale with all the dramatic embellishments she was known for.

"Pete was outside washing and polishing his new truck this morning like he has every morning since he bought it, but I could tell right away that something was wrong. He looked sad when I took him a cup of coffee, as if he had lost his best friend."

"It wasn't as bad as that," Pete said.

"What's wrong with you, I asked when I handed him the coffee," Janet continued. "That's when he told me he had found a scratch on his brand new truck."

"I want to tell my story," Pete said, looking at Janet as if she had gotten the facts wrong.

Janet nodded and smiled.

Pete stood up by his chair, all five feet five inches of him, and began talking. "Janet and I were watching TV last evening and she remembered that we needed milk for breakfast. I said I'd go to Roops Grocery to buy it because I do like milk on my cereal in the morning. But it wasn't a good night for an errand. I was driving my new truck down the hill, feeling like a million dollars, when I heard an awful sound and the truck pulled to the left. I soon discovered I had a flat tire. What next, I thought."

Pete looked around the table to see if he still had everyone's attention. He did.

"Sure enough, after I changed it, I saw a big, old nail in my tire. That's where I went this morning," he said, interrupting the story and looking at Janet. "I had to get that tire fixed."

"Keep to your story, Pete," Janet said, nudging him.

"Sorry," Pete said, and blushed. "When I got to Roops Grocery, damn if the store wasn't closed. First, the flat tire, and then this. But, I had told Janet I'd get the milk, so I drove into Antioch for it. The Wal-Mart there stays open all night."

"When I was on my way back home, a crazy driver passed me. It was there at Casey's Junction, you know, where they're doing all that road work. Janet keeps telling me how dangerous that corner is right now, and that somebody's going to have an accident there sometime. Sure enough it was me."

"That's a dangerous corner," Carlos said, nodding. "I almost had a run in there a couple of days ago, too."

When no one else seemed to have a comment, Pete continued.

"To make a long story short, I saw this truck coming at me real fast in my rear view mirror, so I moved over to the far side of the road so it could pass. But that didn't work out so well. My truck swerved onto the shoulder and hit the loose gravel. That's when I

30

saw Roger Ballard in his stupid yellow Hummer racing past me, his taillights quickly disappearing in the distance."

Pete paused to breathe. "It was dark out, but I know it was him," he said, his jaw tensing. "I tried to steer the truck back onto the road, but I lost control of it for just a second and I swiped some bushes. I'm sure that's where the scratch came from. Those bushes."

"That's too bad, Pete," Kevin said.

"When I got home Janet was asleep, so I put the milk in the frig and went to bed," Pete said. "But, I couldn't sleep for nothing, so I got up at dawn to check the truck. Sure enough there was a scratch right down at the bottom of the passenger door."

Pete was almost in tears when he finished. "My brand new truck."

"Take it to Jumbo Auto in Antioch," Kevin said, stabbing a slice of roast beef with a fork. "They'll fix it right up for you."

Head still down, Pete just nodded. "Roger Ballard doesn't care about anybody but himself. He's a menace to our community."

"Roger will get his one day," Lillie Mae said, and meant it.

"Maybe sooner than he thinks," Pete said in a low voice.

"Don't talk that way," Janet said. "Roger is Clare's husband and a neighbor, whether we like him or not."

Pete sat down.

"I've got a Roger Ballard story, too," Harriet said, a sly smile on her face. Everyone looked her way. "Shall I tell it?"

"Yes," echoed through the room.

Harriet sat up straighter in her chair, and started her tale, talking in a clear strong voice.

"Clare called me earlier today, upset. I know I shouldn't tell tales out of school, but she didn't say not to tell."

Harriet looked across the table at Lillie Mae.

"Clare told me that you had stopped by this morning and she felt surprisingly good after your heart-to-heart. Cleansed, was how she put it."

"We had a good talk," Lillie Mae said.

"After Lillie Mae left, she told me she stayed outside working in her garden until she heard a car pull into the driveway. Thinking it was probably Roger, Clare decided to wait for him to come out to her. It was always best that way, she said. Ten minutes later

31

Roger hadn't made an appearance. Clare was curious, so she went inside the house. When she entered the kitchen, she saw Roger standing perfectly still, looking out the window.

"Not brave enough to ask him where he'd been, she thought it safest to ask what he wanted for lunch," Harriet continued. "He opted for breakfast and went to sit at the table while Clare fixed the food. He mentioned that he had made a pot of coffee and asked her to pour him a cup. It wasn't what he said that worried her. It was the way he said it. He was kind to her. And polite. He even thanked her a couple of times."

"What's come over Roger all of a sudden?" Alice asked, as aware as everyone else at the table just how rude the man could be and usually was.

"Clare knew something was wrong, too," Harriet said, looking at Alice. "She said she continued to tread lightly as she fixed his meal, since she still didn't trust him. His mood could change on a dime."

"That's certainly true," Lillie Mae said. "We've all seen it."

Harriet continued. "She said Roger leaned down to pet the cat that was rubbing against his leg, and then asked her if anyone had called the previous evening."

"Did anyone call?" Lillie Mae asked, curious.

"Clare told Roger that Patrick Goody called," Harriet said. "Apparently there were other calls that night, but she had stopped answering the phone. Too many crank calls, she said."

"Something's rotten in Denmark," Pete said. "It usually is when Roger Ballard's involved."

Harriet chose to ignore Pete's remark. "Roger stared at her, Clare said, while she was serving his breakfast, and, although she tried to keep her bruised left cheek turned away from him, he noticed it."

"The bruise I thought he put there," Lillie Mae said contritely, remembering how upset Clare had been with her. "Clare made it very clear to me this morning that she really did have an accident."

"Exactly," Harriet said. "She told Roger the same thing. It was just a stupid accident. Then the oddest thing happened."

Pausing for emphasis, Harriet glanced around the table. "Roger looked up from his plate and told her to take care of herself. Just like that. Take care of yourself, Clare, he said. She was speechless, she told me. As soon as he finished eating, he said he had to leave and wasn't sure when he'd be home."

Harriet thought for a second. "Now, how did she say he put it? Oh, yes, I remember. Roger told Clare he didn't know when he was going to make it home again. He said he had lots going on right now. Maybe, too much, were the words he used."

"Goodness," Alice said, putting her fork down on top of her plate. "You know, I saw Roger's yellow Hummer out and about twice today. Once early this morning when Alfred and I were out on our daily constitutional walk, and then again this afternoon. He whizzed past me and Alfred when we were out in the backyard. I had gone out to feed the birds, and Alfred was chasing a chipmunk when we heard the loud racket that truck makes. I looked up and saw the truck barreling at me. I thought at the time that a man with Roger Ballard's reputation might do well to drive a less conspicuous car, especially when he's speeding through small mountain towns. But then, genius and Roger Ballard are words I've never heard together.

Everyone at the table chuckled.

"I saw Roger Ballard this afternoon, too," Lillie Mae said "It must have been right before you saw him whiz by your back yard, Alice. Roger parked in front of my house just like Carl Lewis had done earlier. And just like Carl Lewis, he crossed the street to the Jenkins' house. But he didn't go up on the porch like Carl did. Instead, he turned around and rushed back across the road like a scared rabbit, got in the Hummer, and drove away. I thought it very odd. So odd, that I called the police."

"You did. How brave," Alice said, looking with envy at her friend.

"I called Charlie Warren. Sid told Hester and me when we were at the police station, that the police were looking for Roger, so, I felt I had to do my duty."

"Bet that it didn't give you a second's worth of pleasure," Harriet said, laughing. Everyone joined in, including Lillie Mae.

Joyce spoke up. "I forgot to tell you. Sam called just before Carlos and I left the house to come here."

"How's Margaret?" several people asked.

"That's what I want to tell you," Joyce said. "Margaret's doing much better, and Sam said she's coming home tomorrow. If all goes well, they plan to see us at breakfast in the morning."

"That is good news," Harriet said.

*   *   *

"I'm walking home, and nobody's stopping me," Lillie Mae insisted when Kevin and Harriet wanted to drive her to her house.

"The night is way too beautiful to ride five minutes in a car," she said. "Besides, I want the exercise. Janet's meals are amazingly good, but can quickly add inches to the hips without a daily walk. So, let me get my exercise. I don't want anyone to tell me different."

"Go," Harriet said. "Enjoy."

Lillie Mae walked briskly down the hill from Janet and Pete's house toward the Mount Penn Park, taking advantage of the clear, star-studded night to light her way. Fortunately, she had thought to bring an extra sweater so the slight chill in the spring air did not bother her at all. In fact, she found it refreshing.

Curious whether Roger Ballard finally made it home, she decided to walk up the High Mount road past Clare's place, even though it was the long way around to her own house. It felt good to be free.

When she reached Clare's house, a few minutes later, she saw Clare standing on the front porch with a man. It looks a lot like the choir director at the Mount Penn Community Church, Dale Beavers, she thought, although she couldn't be sure. His car was nowhere in sight.

Not wanting to be seen by the pair, Lillie Mae quickly turned around and headed back toward Janet's house, before scooting quickly up the hill to her own street, past the Jenkins' place, and into her own house.

Blood pumped through her brain, smudging the thoughts that were running through it. Why was Dale Beavers at Clare's house? Were they practicing the duet they were to sing on Sunday? No, that can't be it, she thought. They would practice in the church, not at Clare's house. Were they having a liaison? No, Dale would not be so obvious as to be standing on the front porch of Clare's house if that was the case. But what was he doing there? Another thought popped into her brain. Could it have been Dale Beavers Clare was talking to on the phone that morning?

Lillie Mae was stumped, but determined to find out. And she knew how to do that. Tomorrow at Thursday morning breakfast, she'd simply ask Clare what was going on.

4

Lillie Mae looked through the screen door and saw Hester standing in the middle of her living room in stocking feet, dressed in a Sunday black dress, her hair falling out of its bun, sobbing.

"Knock, knock," she said. "Can I come in?"

"Oh, Lillie Mae," Hester rambled, her body quivering and tears streaming down her face. "Thank goodness you've come. Everything has gone wrong this morning. First, the toilet flooded and I had to clean up the mess, and now I can't find my best black shoes. This is all just too much for me."

Hester hung her head and sobbed louder.

"It'll be all right, dear," Lillie Mae said. "I'm here now. How can I help?"

"Come in, come in," Hester said, gesturing toward the door as she remembered her duty as hostess.

Lillie Mae opened the door and came into the house. Noticing that Hester was the only thing out of order in the immaculate room with its frilly curtains and dainty odds and ends, she moved closer to her friend and took hold of her hand.

"I'm not going with Sid today," Hester said. "Mabel should be home before too long, and she can go. It's her job to take care of Patrick, not mine."

"Of course you're going to the courthouse today, Hester," Lillie Mae said. "Sid promised to take care of you and you promised to be there for Patrick. Now pull yourself together."

Hester looked up at Lillie Mae, her hazel eyes faded by her tears. "I'm at my wits end."

"You need to calm down, dear," Lillie Mae said, in a soft, cooing voice. "I know this is a terrible ordeal for you, but you'll get through it if you stay brave. Take one step at a time. Isn't that what you tell Patrick? He needs you right now and, if you do this, he'll remember your support for the rest of his life."

"I blame Roger Ballard for all this," Hester said. "I know it's a terrible thing to say, Lillie Mae, but I just hate that man."

"You know you don't mean that Hester."

36

Hester leaned her head into Lillie Mae's shoulder.

"Things will get better, you'll see," Lillie Mae added. "Finish getting dressed, dear, and all this will soon be over."

Hester stood up straighter, a look of resolve on her face. "Okay, I'll go," she finally said.

Moving toward the stairs, she looked back over her shoulder. "I'll do this for Patrick this one time, but never again."

"You need to hurry, Hester," Lillie Mae said. "Sid's here. He's pulling his car into the driveway."

"Tell him I'm almost ready," Hester called back. "I just need to straighten my hair and find another pair of shoes."

Lillie Mae walked to the door to wait for Sid. She watched him get out of his new black Mercedes, talking a mile a minute on his cell phone. He closed it and put it back in his pocket when he reached the porch.

"Bail bondsman," he said, nodding to Lillie Mae. "How's Hester doing this morning?"

"She's flustered, but almost ready," said Lillie Mae. "Stay with her today, Sid. She's teetering on the edge."

Sid nodded. "Any news of Mabel?"

"Hester said she's on her way."

"Well, let's hope she gets here soon," Sid said, frowning. "But to be honest, I'm not sure I want her at the courthouse today. She can be a handful, and we don't need any more drama right now."

Hester came down the steps a moment later with shoes on her feet and her hair in order.

"Ready?" Sid asked her, his tone changing. "You look perfect, my dear. Patrick will be proud of you today."

"Let's go," Hester said, her face strangely determined. "Let's get this over with."

Picking up her purse, she straightened the skirt of her dress with one hand and looked around the room as if making sure all was in its place, before following Sid out of the house. Turning back one last time to Lillie Mae, who had followed the pair outside, she mouthed a thank you.

"You go get them, girl," Lillie Mae said, smiling.

*   *   *

When Lillie Mae entered the Mountain View Inn's main dining room for Thursday morning breakfast, Clare, Harriet, Alice, and

Janet were huddled together talking at the club's usual breakfast table, coffee in front of them. All four women raised their hands in greeting as Lillie Mae made her way to the table.

Glancing at the men's table, situated across the large oak floored dining room, she saw Pete and Kevin deep in conversation. Must be talking sports, she thought, noting baseball season was just around the corner. Fantasy baseball became their favorite topic of conversation during this season.

"Clare's been telling us that Billy's coming home for a visit," Alice said, watching Lillie Mae take her large purple purse off her shoulder and settle into a chair beside Janet.

"What wonderful news," Lillie Mae smiled.

"It is," Clare said. "He's to be home in time for supper this very evening, dirty laundry in hand, I'm sure."

"You'll love doing that," Harriet said.

"I will," Clare said. "It's funny, but now that Billy's away at school, I miss doing things for him as much as I miss him."

"There is one odd thing about this visit, though."

"What is that?" Lillie Mae asked.

"Billy told me his father had called him earlier this week and asked him to come home today. Left him a message on his cell phone saying he wanted to talk to him."

Clare hesitated as if thinking whether to say any more. "Roger misses the boy as much as I do, but he's never done that before."

"What do you think Roger wants to tell the boy?" Harriet asked.

"I have no idea," Clare said. "Roger's been behaving so oddly lately."

"Look who's here," Janet interrupted.

All heads turned to see Sam and Margaret Jenkins walking slowing toward the table, Margaret's arm comfortably in the crook of Sam's. Joyce Castro was just behind them.

"Good morning," Alice said, waving a greeting. "It is so good to see you, Margaret. You look well this morning."

She did, Lillie Mae thought remembering just how ill she was the day before. But today her cheeks glowed, and her eyes were clear. She and Sam were about the same height, and even with her illness, she was not rail thin. Sam continued to hold her arm as he helped her to sit down, though she appeared able enough to do the job herself. Dressed in a pair of tailored jeans and a twin sweater set, she looked more like a teenager ready for school, than the invalid they knew her to be.

"You are too kind," Margaret said as Sam settled her into a chair. "I do feel better today. The doctor was so attentive yesterday. He's the best, and the drugs he gives me are miracles. I feel stronger than I have in a long time."

"Whatever that man gave you worked," Janet said. "Wish I could get a miracle drug to lose some of this weight," she added under her breath.

Sam patted Margaret on the shoulder, then leaned down and whispered something in her ear. She smiled. Rising again, he said. "I'm going to join the men's table, but I have my cell phone with me. Ring me, Margaret, if you need anything."

Addressing the other ladies, he added. "Margaret insisted on coming to breakfast club this morning against my better judgment. But I must say, your chats are often the best medicine for her." Turning, he threw his hand in the air, as he made his way across the room.

"Where's Carlos this morning?" Harriet asked Joyce when she sat down next to her.

"He wanted to come today, but he's got so much work right now. His documentary on migrant workers in the mid-Atlantic area is about to wrap up, and he's signed new contracts just this week for two more films. Feast or famine as Lillie Mae would say," she added. "But they're all good projects, and he's most happy when he's working."

The next several minutes were spent giving breakfast orders to the chunky waitress dressed in a plain brown A-line dress, partially covered with a white half apron. Dull hair, blotchy skin, and unfiled fingernails defined her style. Another girl, dressed in an identical outfit with similar characteristics, poured coffee all around. Only Margaret asked for tea. While the Mountain View Inn was as plain as the day long, the food came out fast and hot, so it was only a short time later when the ladies had plates of eggs and fixings, the daily special, in front of them. Margaret waited for a custom order of French toast.

"I've met the new girl in town," Alice said as breakfast arrived and the ladies hankered down to eat. "Rose Maynard is her name and she's as cute as a button. Reminds me of one of those dolls you see on folks' porches. You know the ones wearing overalls and leaning their little faces against the wall."

"I want to know all about her," Margaret said. "Sam and I have been the new kids on the block for too long. It will feel good to have the title taken away."

Although the statement was ordinary enough, all eyes turned to her in surprise. Margaret Jenkins showed up at Thursday morning breakfast as often as her health permitted, but rarely said anything, giving her the infamous title of a good listener. Lillie Mae suspected Margaret's mind was actually elsewhere much of the time.

"She's a junior high school teacher from Baltimore," Alice said, looking a bit like a doll herself. A perfectly dressed doll with lovely white hair and porcelain skin, that is. The matriarch of Mount Penn, having lived in the community since childhood, her knowledge of the area and its people, made her exactly the right person for a newcomer to seek out.

"And she's recently divorced after ten years of marriage," she added. "A very sloppy one according to Rose. Seems her husband had an affair with his secretary. Embarrassingly common was how Rose put it."

"Has she moved into the old Dexter place yet?" Janet asked.

"Not yet. She's got the Bryant boys working there, restoring much of what old Mr. Dexter let go for so long. She plans to move to the mountain once school is out."

"Did you tell her about our Thursday morning breakfasts?" Lillie Mae asked.

"I did," Alice said, picking up a piece of toast and taking a bite as if reminded that breakfast was in front of her. "She seemed pleased to find out how close-knit our community is and said she looks forward to meeting you all. She also mentioned that she enjoyed singing, so I told her about the church choir. She said she's not really religious but I told her that wasn't necessary. Just ask Lillie Mae Harris."

The women, including Lillie Mae, chuckled.

Alice turned toward Harriet. "Rose is about Barbara's age and I bet the two of them could be great friends, given the chance. How is Barbara by the way? We've not seen her at breakfast the last couple of weeks."

"Barbara's been so busy lately, helping Chip with the new business, and taking care of Chelsea, so she's divvying out her time for other activities sparingly," Harriet said. "I offered to babysit this past weekend, so the kids could go out on a date. As cranky as Kevin can get now that he's retired, he becomes a different man when his granddaughter is around. Younger, happier, more energetic. Lots more fun. Although I hadn't told Kevin that I had committed us to the babysitting, since he would have crabbed around for half the week, I knew he'd be happy once Chelsea arrived."

The ladies nodded in unison.

"Kevin was in the basement when Barbara and Chelsea arrived on Saturday morning. Once Barbara unbuckled Chelsea's seat belt, the little imp was down on the ground, waddling toward the door, her favorite doll under her arm, and a small suitcase in her hand. Grandpa, she yelled in her high pitched voice. I'm here. Kevin rushed out of the basement and gathered Chelsea up into his arms. Did I know you were coming, he asked Barbara as he nuzzled Chelsea's neck forcing her to giggle."

"What was Barbara's answer to that?" Alice asked.

"She wasn't sure what to say, so she told her dad the truth that I had volunteered her dad and I to babysit this weekend."

"What did Kevin say to that?" Alice asked, setting herself up as Harriet's straight lady.

"He looked at Barbara and told her no, your mother didn't tell me Chelsea was coming," Harriet explained. "Barbara looked so worried that he had to grin, breaking the stern look he'd been pretending."

"He's an old softie at heart," Lillie Mae said, chuckling.

"He is, but don't you ever tell him I said so," Harriet said, trying not to smile.

"Tell Barbara we miss her when you see her again," Alice said. "And we wish her and Chip the best with their new business."

Harriet nodded.

"She'll be back to breakfast soon. Once things settle down some."

"Pete and I have some big news, too," Janet said when Harriet picked up her coffee cup and began to drink, signaling she was finished her story.

41

"What's that?" Lillie Mae asked.

"We're going on a diet starting right after breakfast today."

The group emitted a collective groan. Janet's diets were notorious. Every time she and Pete started one, Pete, who was skinny enough to slip through the eye of a needle, would lose weight, while Janet just got fatter.

"We're serious this time," Janet said.

Another collective groan could be heard throughout the restaurant. Even the men turned their heads toward the ladies table, and they were across the room.

"We went out early this morning to shop for diet food," Janet said. Dressed in a bright blue two-piece crop pant outfit that she had purchased from a shopping channel on television, she looked a bit like a big beach ball. A crop of yellow, permed hair topped off her smiling chubby face.

"You know how Pete is," she continued. "Once he agrees to do something, he wants to do it right away. So we went to the health food store in Antioch for supplies early this morning, before coming to breakfast. That's why we were a few minutes late. When we get home, I'm going to clear the house of all foods with sugar and flour. If anyone wants extra supplies, or leftovers from last night's dinner, stop by."

Eyes rolled and shoulders shrugged as the ladies anticipated Janet's conversation over the next couple of days, about the time one of her diets lasted.

"But, that's not all I wanted to tell you," Janet said. "It's what Pete and I saw on our way into town this morning that's curious."

This last bit of gossip seemed to have re-captured the ladies attention since all eyes focused back on Janet.

"Pete was still smarting from that scratch on his new truck, so he carefully backed out of our driveway and drove way too slow past the park. If we had continued at that speed, it would have taken us an hour to get to Antioch."

"Is this your important bit of news?" Lillie Mae asked.

"Hush up," Janet said. "It's coming."

Janet picked up her water glass and took a sip, casting a glance at Lillie Mae out of the corner of her eye. "We were just by the entrance to the Appalachian Trail when I spotted Dale Beaver's truck parked by the gate," she said. "He's the only one I know that drives a bright red Eddie Bauer Bronco."

Lillie Mae noticed Clare's face go red.

"What's he doing out there now, I asked Pete," Janet continued. "It's a school day and he should be at work. Pete called me a nosey parker, but I could tell he was as curious as me."

A loud voice coming from the front of the dining room interrupted Janet's story. In the entrance Mabel Goody stood in a rage, all five feet of her, dressed in a business suit, her dark curly hair sticking up everywhere, looking a lot like an oversized Shirley Temple doll.

Lillie Mae sat back in her chair, her hands clinched together as she braced herself for the next drama.

"Over here, Mabel," Lillie Mae called out to the bedazzled young woman, knowing that the next few minutes were not going to be pleasant.

They weren't.

5

"It's been a nightmare ever since Sid Firth called with the news about Patrick," Mabel told Lillie Mae on the drive to Antioch. "I was tied up in business meetings all day yesterday and didn't get his message until I got back to the hotel room. That's the first I heard about Patrick's arrest. It was after nine o'clock when Sid and I finally talked."

Once Lillie Mae had agreed to go with Mabel to the courthouse, Mabel had settled down, but her tirade at the Mountain View Inn that morning would be talked about for years. Lillie Mae shuddered remembering the scene. Thank goodness it was over.

Lillie Mae turned her attention back to Mabel.

"It was too late to call Mother after Sid and I talked, and when I called her house this morning from the airport, nobody answered. Mom doesn't know I'm home, Lillie Mae, so she's still worried about me."

"She'll be relieved when she sees you, dear," Lillie Mae said, knowing her statement to be true.

"The trip from St Louis to Baltimore was awful," Mabel said, her voice breaking. "I booked the last seat on an American Airlines plane to Baltimore leaving around midnight, then sent an email to the client to let her know I had an emergency at home and wouldn't be in the office today. Thank goodness she doesn't know what the emergency is. I took a cab to the airport, but that turned out to be another disaster."

"You poor dear," Lillie Mae said, keeping her eyes on the road. "What happened on the ride to the airport?"

"It started off fine. In fact we were making good time. Then less than two miles from the airport, the taxi driver told me there was an accident up ahead. The rest of the drive was stop and go. I checked my watch every minute, but kept my mouth shut, hoping we'd make it to the airport on time for the flight. By the time we got there, I was a bundle of nerves."

"You did make the flight," Lillie Mae said.

"Fortunately, yes," Mabel said. When the taxi finally reached the terminal, I had forty-five minutes before the plane was to take off. I paid the driver and rushed inside. The line at the American Airlines desk was long, so I checked in at a kiosk, and left my bag at the self-serve station. But when I reached security, there was another long line. By the time I made it through security, final boarding was being called for my plane. I ran to the gate and felt so relieved. I handed my ticket to the agent, and walked down the gangway. I was literally the last person to get on the plane."

"It must have felt good to finally take your seat," Lillie Mae said.

"It did, but the good feeling was short-lived," Mabel said. "I was buckling my seat belt when the pilot came on the intercom and told us the flight was being delayed because of thunderstorms in the area."

"Oh, no," Lillie Mae said.

"It gets worse," Mabel said, the memory of it causing her to grimace. "We sat on the tarmac for two hours before the plane was cleared to take off. Once we were in the air, the ride was horribly bumpy because of the same storms that had delayed our takeoff. The pilot apologized for what he called the inconvenience, but I was ready to scream from the stress. Thank goodness the drinks were free. After two rum and Cokes, I felt a little better."

"Lillie Mae chuckled, 'I bet.'"

"But any relief I felt didn't last long," Mabel said. "When I got into Baltimore, I went to the baggage claim area to pick up my suitcase. I would have carried it onboard, but for the toiletries. Of course, it didn't show up."

"You poor child," Lillie Mae said, feeling genuine pity for the girl. This was the trip from hell.

"What next, I asked as I waited in line at the airport's luggage office to fill out the forms to have my luggage delivered to the house, once it arrives into Baltimore. I'll get it someday, but Mount Penn is not the easiest place in the world to get to, so I don't have much hope that day will be anytime soon. I was so glad I had my car keys in my purse and my car was parked at the airport. At least I could get home."

"You handled it better than I would have," Lillie Mae said.

"I don't know about that," Mabel said, squirming in her seat. "But when I got to Mother's house and she wasn't there, I panicked. When I finally settled down and gave it some thought, I suspected she had gone to the courthouse to be with Patrick. I should have asked Sid when I was talking to him what the logistics were for today, but I was befuddled when he called, and I just did not think of it. Then, I remembered it was Thursday morning, so I knew where I could find you. Sid told me all you did for Mother yesterday."

Mabel paused to gather her thoughts. "I'm so sorry for being a jerk this morning, Lillie Mae, but it's all been too much and I just lost it. Thank you for driving me to Antioch even though slapping me might have been the choice of a lesser person. And, thank you for taking care of Mother."

"You're welcome, dear," Lillie Mae said. "We're almost at the courthouse, and I have to say something to you, Mabel, that I want to be sure you hear."

"What's that?" Mabel asked, cautiously.

"I want you to stay calm today, girl. Your mother's been through so much the last two days and doesn't need you to be a problem, too. Especially today."

"I promise to behave," Mabel said, settling into her seat, her head against the back rest, her eyes closed.

Lillie Mae wished she could believe her.

* * *

Mabel and Lillie Mae entered the courthouse, checked their purses through security, and headed in the direction of the courtroom indicated on the roster at the front of the long hallway. Rounding the last corner, they saw Sid Firth standing in the hall talking to Patrick and Jerry. Perry and Sarah Foster were huddled around the group. Hester was nowhere to be seen.

"Listen, up," they heard Sid say to the two boys, who were dressed alike in pressed jeans, blue oxford shirts, and ties. "You're free for now. The judge was very lenient with you today, but that doesn't mean you're free for good. This was only the arraignment, you understand. There could still be a trial. I'm going to work on getting the charges dismissed against you, but you must stay out of trouble. If either one of you makes one wrong move, you'll both be back here before you can blink an eye. Do you understand?"

"Yes," Jerry Foster answered.

"Yes," Patrick said.

Looking back at Sid, Patrick spied his mother and Lillie Mae.

"We'll make certain our boy stays clean," Perry Foster said, turning his head just in time to see Mabel arrive. His wife Sarah, nodded, but said nothing to the newcomers.

Perry was a large bulky man who stood over six feet tall. He had spent much of his life working outdoors in construction before an accident a couple of years earlier had changed his life. But he was still strong. Now he worked for the state on the roads as a flag bearer.

"But, Dad, you said . . ." Jerry said, interrupting his dad.

"That's enough." Perry glared at his son. "We'll talk about all that later, once we're home."

"Patrick," Mabel yelled as she flung her arms around her son, tears streaming down her cheeks. "I'm so sorry I wasn't here for you before. I came as quickly as I could."

Patrick gave his mother a quick hug, then broke from the embrace, shaking himself as if embarrassed by the contact.

"It's all right, Mom," he said. "Glad you're here now."

"The arraignment's over, Mabel," Sid said.

"Morning, Lillie Mae," he nodded. "Patrick's free to go home for now, but I'm counting on you to be on your best behavior," Sid added, looking directly at Mabel.

"Where's Mother?" Mabel asked, choosing to ignore Sid's last statement.

"My assistant, Jane Jackson, took her to my office to lie down after the hearing ended," Sid said. "We'll go get her in a minute, Mabel. I know she'll be glad to see you."

"Wait a minute, Perry," Sid said when he saw the Fosters turn to leave. "There's something I want to say to all of you before we go get Hester."

The group reassembled around Sid.

"I do believe these boys are innocent," Sid said, with authority. "I also think there's a lot more going on here than any of us knows about. I promise I'll do everything I can to find out the truth, but you all have to keep yourselves under control. The worst thing that could happen right now is that any one of you turns up somewhere

where they shouldn't be, or be seen doing something they shouldn't be doing. Do you understand?"

Sid looked sternly at each of the three parents in turn. "I'm talking to you, the parents, as well as the boys."

"We'll be good," Perry said, guiding his family away from Sid. "Call us, Sid, if you get more news."

"I hope he keeps his word," Sid said under his breath as he ushered Patrick, Mabel, and Lillie Mae in the opposite direction.

Hester was sitting on the dark brown leather sofa staring at the door when they entered Sid's large office.

"Oh, my darling," she exclaimed when she saw Mabel. Jumping off the sofa, she fell into Mabel's arms sobbing. "Thank goodness you've come at last."

Mabel took her mother's hand, and led her back to the sofa. "I'm sorry you've had to go through all this alone, Mother. I wish I had been here with you, but you've done wonderfully, and I'm proud of you," Mabel said, holding her mother's hand. "Let's sit here together while Sid talks to us, then I'll take you home, and help you to bed."

"Lillie Mae, Patrick, come sit down," Sid said, motioning them to the chairs across from the sofa. "I want to talk to you all together before you go home."

Sid sat down on the other side of Hester."

"Mabel, I want you to go home with your mother and Patrick , and stay there. If possible, move in with your mother until all this is settled. The last two days have been hard on her, and she needs your support now. I suspect you can use hers as well. Lillie Mae, you'll drive them?" he asked.

She nodded.

"You all need a good rest today and some time to sort out what's happened here. At least Hester does. Will you promise to take care of her once you get home?" he asked, twisting his head to look at both Patrick and Mabel.

Mabel nodded, but Patrick sat firm.

"I'm so thankful you're free," Hester said, interrupting Sid to reach over and put her hand on Patrick's knee. "I've been praying for you all day."

"It's all right, Grandma." Patrick said. "I'm out of jail now, and I ain't going back in there, ever again. I didn't know anything

48

about the drugs. I wasn't lying to you." A menacing look covered the boy's face. "I was framed, Grandma, and whoever did this to me is going to pay."

"Now that's enough, Patrick," Sid said, looking sternly at the boy. "Have you not listened to a word I've said to you? You are not the first innocent person to be locked up in jail for a night."

Patrick stared at Sid, his eyes blank.

"You have to admit the circumstances are suspicious, Patrick, so don't go blaming the system for all your woes," Sid said. "If you want to stay out of trouble in the future, then you have to stay away from places where trouble happens. Carl Lewis' place is one of those. You should know that."

"We only went there because we had this job to do for Roger Ballard," Patrick said. "Roger Ballard set us up."

"You don't know that for sure," Sid said, interrupting the boy. "The best you can do for yourself right now, young man, is to let the police find out what happened. If you try to go after Roger Ballard or anyone else yourself, you're just asking for more trouble."

"Charlie Warren will take care of everything," Hester said.

"Sure," Patrick said, hanging his head. "I'll let Charlie Warren handle it from here."

"I'll see Patrick stays out of trouble," Mabel said.

Lillie Mae wondered who was going to promise to make sure Mabel stayed out of trouble. She certainly wasn't volunteering for the job.

"You all need to go home now," Sid said, helping Hester to stand up. "This woman needs rest, and I expect you to make certain she gets it."

*　*　*

Lillie Mae dropped Hester and Patrick off at Hester's house, and then drove Mabel back down the Mount Penn road to the Mountain View Inn to pick up her car.

"I'll stop in to see if Hester's resting before going on home," Lillie Mae told Mabel when she was standing by her red BMW.

"Thanks again, Lillie Mae, for everything," Mabel said. "I have a quick errand to run, but I'll be back on the mountain in a short while. Tell Mother I won't be long, and to get some rest. Sorry

49

again for the earlier meltdown." Lillie Mae shut Mabel's car door, and walked to her own car.

When she glanced in front of her, she saw Mabel look over her shoulder, and then quickly back out of the parking space, stopping only a brief moment at the entrance before making a right hand turn onto the Mount Penn road, returning the same way they had just come. She could have sworn she saw a cell phone by Mabel's ear.

Lillie Mae pulled into Hester's driveway a few minutes later, and noticed that Patrick's motorcycle was not there. Not a good sign, she thought, her heart pounding as she stepped out of her car. Where could the boy have gone?

Hester was pacing, tears streaming down her pale face, when Lillie Mae walked into her living room.

"Where's Patrick?" she asked.

"He's gone," Hester sobbed. "I begged him not to leave the house, but he wouldn't listen to me."

Lillie Mae led Hester to the sofa and insisted she sit down.

"Let me get you a glass of water," she said, worried Hester was going be sick.

When Lillie Mae returned to the living room with the water, Hester was still crying, but some color had returned to her face.

"Tell me what happened," Lillie Mae said, handing her the box of tissues she had found in the kitchen. "Where did Patrick go?"

"I have no idea," Hester said, then blew her nose. "Patrick wouldn't tell me where he was going or how long he was going to be gone. After you dropped me off, he helped me into the house holding my arm like a proper gentleman, set me down at the kitchen table, and offered to make me a cup of tea. He was being so kind, Lillie Mae. He even cut me a piece of the carrot cake I had made for his birthday last week. Once he saw I was settled and sipping the tea, he told me he was leaving."

"I'm so sorry, Hester," Lillie Mae said. "I should have been here with you."

"You can't leave, I told him," Hester said, tears welling up in her eyes again. "You promised Sid you'd stay with me."

"What did he say to that?" Lillie Mae asked, thinking it best to keep Hester talking.

"No I didn't, he told me as bold as you like. I didn't promise Sid anything, he said."

"Technically he didn't," Lillie Mae said, remembering how Patrick responded when Sid asked everyone to go home and stay home.

"I begged him to stay," Hester said. "He said he had something he had to do and nothing I said would change his mind."

"That doesn't sound good," Lillie Mae said.

"I reminded him of Sid's warning, but he paid no attention to me. Then, I thought to say that his mother would be here any minute and that she would be very angry when she found him gone. That didn't budge him either."

"I'll call Mother on her cell phone and tell her where I am, he said, but I knew he was laughing at me," Hester said. "Then he turned on the charm again, offering to help me to bed. But I told him I was too upset to sleep, and if I did decide to lay down, I didn't need the likes of him to help me."

Hester swallowed, and caught her breath. "What I need from you, I said to him, is for you to do as you're told for once in your life. Hasn't this whole experience been a lesson to you, Patrick, I asked him."

"What did he say to that?"

"He told me he was sorry I had to be involved, but this had nothing to do with me." Hester shook her head. "Go, then, I told him. It doesn't matter what I say, you're going to do what you want to do anyway. So just do it. When your mother gets here, I'm telling her I've washed my hands of you. It's her turn to control you from now on."

Hester looked around the room as if looking for something.

"Where is Mabel?" she asked.

"Oh, dear," Lillie Mae said before telling Hester the next piece of bad news.

6

Lillie Mae had promised Reverend Caven that she would clear out the flowers from last Sunday's service at the Mount Penn Community Church, and put out fresh vases for this week's flowers by today, but, with all the excitement she had forgotten. Grabbing her purse, she rushed out of her house then walked the two blocks to the small white building, knowing the front door would be unlocked and she could get in without searching for the key.

She was just coming in the back door of the church after discarding the dead flowers in the trash, when she heard someone open the front door. Peeping into the sanctuary, she saw Dale Beavers walk into the room and head straight to the organ. He was of medium height, well formed with broad shoulders, slim waist, and strong, sturdy legs. His most unusual feature was his beautiful, almost feminine hands with long tapered fingers and perfectly manicured nails. Hands designed to play music.

As he sat on the small bench before the organ, Lillie Mae watched him arrange the sheets of music, almost caressing the pages as he sifted through them. Finding the particular piece he wanted to practice, he sat up straighter, placed his fingers on the organ keys and began to play. Within moments, he appeared to relax.

Lost in the music, Dale must not have heard the door open, or see Clare Ballard enter the church but Lillie Mae did. Clare moved quietly toward one of the back pews and took a seat, not able to take her eyes off Dale. Tears streamed down her cheeks as she sat as still as a statue, listening to him play.

Lillie Mae knew she was spying on a scene she wasn't meant to see, but couldn't bring herself to announce that she was there. She watched as Dale looked up from the organ and noticed Clare. He stopped playing, stood up immediately, and looked out at her.

"What are you doing here?" he asked.

Clare sat frozen, her face a bright red.

Dale stepped off the platform, then down the steps to the choir loft, and walked toward her. "I've not been able to think of anything but you since we talked last night. Have you changed your mind?"

He reached out for her hand as he approached, but she pulled it away, putting it behind her back. As if they were doing a synchronized dance, he stepped toward her.

"No," she said so softly that she could barely be heard. "But, I wanted to talk to you, tell you why I said what I did. I thought you deserved that."

"Oh, I know why," Dale said, paling. "It's always the same reason. When are you going to stop sacrificing yourself, Clare, to a man who doesn't deserve you?" He moved closer to her, but Clare turned away.

"I'm so sorry, Dale," she said. "You know how I feel about you. And you know how happy I am when we sing together, but even that feels wrong now. I feel guilty all the time. And scared. Roger is acting so odd lately, I suspect he knows something. I don't know what he's up to or what he's capable of doing. It's just too dangerous to talk to him now. But I promise you, I will speak to him when the time is right."

"When is that going to be?" Dale asked. "It's never the right time. I don't know why you continue to protect that man. Roger doesn't need your protection. It's you that needs protecting from him. Look at your face." Dale reached out to touch her cheek. "Why do you let him treat you this way?"

"Roger didn't do anything to me. I told you that."

"Like hell he didn't!" Dale's temper flared. "You're still protecting him, Clare."

"I did this to myself," Clare said. "I'm not protecting anybody. It was just a stupid accident. Nobody believes me when I tell them the truth." She started to cry, but then caught herself, wiping the tears away with the back of her hand.

"You may have told me the truth about the accident," Dale continued. "But Roger is still to blame. If you lived a normal life, you wouldn't have to sneak around your own house in the middle of the night and hide from your husband."

Dale moved towards Clare again. This time she didn't resist when he gathered her in his arms. "Let me take care of you, Clare.

You're the most wonderful woman I know and I can't bear to see you suffering like this. We could be happy, if you'd just give us a chance."

Breaking away from the embrace, ashamed that she had let her guard down, Clare backed away from him. When he started to come toward her, she raised her hand to stop him.

"No," she said, her hand shaking. Her voice was very low. "I can't. Not now."

When she reached the door, she turned back to him.

"I will take care of the situation, Dale. I promise. I have to do something, or I'll go crazy. I want to tell Roger about us, but I also want to tell him that we have done nothing wrong. Do you understand why we have to wait?"

"Yes." Dale sat down on the nearest pew. "I do understand Clare. I've known from the start that if we're ever going to have a relationship, it has to happen your way."

Clare turned and walked out of the church.

Dale went back to the organ.

"Clare will never talk to Roger, unless I do something," he said to himself, loud enough for Lillie Mae to hear. "But, if I do what I must do, will Clare ever forgive me?"

* * *

Lillie Mae didn't have long to wait for Dale Beavers to leave. Once she was sure he was gone, she left the church by the back door in case Dale was still in the parking lot. She was determined to talk to Clare.

Lillie Mae didn't get very far before she heard her name being called. Turning, she saw Alice Portman walking toward her.

"What brings you out on this warm, sunny afternoon?" Alice asked, carrying a plate of cookies.

"I can't stop now," Lillie Mae said, impatiently. "I'm trying to catch Clare. I have to talk to her."

"Then you're out of luck, my dear," Alice said, looking at Lillie Mae suspiciously. "I passed her a couple of minutes ago, and she said she couldn't talk to me. Told me she had errands to do to get ready for Billy's homecoming. Why are you so anxious to talk to her?"

Lillie Mae wasn't going to tell anyone what she had just seen in the church. "Oh, it isn't important," she said, tossing her head back and smiling.

"Good," Alice said. "You can come with me, then. Do your good deed for the day."

Lillie Mae thought she had done quite enough good deeds for one day but didn't know how to get out of this one, so she followed Alice. "Where are we going?" she asked.

"We're going to visit Sam and Margaret," Alice said, taking hold of Lillie Mae's arm.

Lillie Mae sighed, but did as she was bid.

Minutes later, Alice and Lillie Mae were standing on the Jenkins' back porch.

"I'll knock," Alice said, making her small hand into a fist and rapping.

Sam Jenkins peeked out the kitchen window, and then opened the door. A jacket was slung across his arm as if he had been on his way out. His red plaid shirt and khaki pants looked as if he had slept in them. Even his hair, usually in perfect order, was tousled.

"Alice, Lillie Mae, it's so good to see you," he said in a hushed voice, but with his usual friendly open manner, accepting the plate of oatmeal raisin cookies Alice handed him. "These look good," he added. "I suspect they're right out of the oven. Margaret will love them. I'll let her know you brought them when she wakes up."

"Oh, is she asleep?" Alice asked, surprised. "She looked so healthy this morning at breakfast." Alice followed him into the house without being invited, gesturing to Lillie Mae to follow.

"We wanted to stop over and see Margaret before her nap, but I guess we weren't fast enough. Obviously this isn't a good time for a visit."

Lillie Mae looked around the kitchen, surprised to see it in such disarray. Dishes were piled up in the sink; clutter was everywhere. Sam usually kept the house in perfect order.

Noticing Lillie Mae scan the room, Sam apologized. "Please forgive the mess. There has been so much going on the last couple of days, I've let the dishes slip. I was going to wash them when Margaret laid down for her nap, but then something else came up. She was exhausted from the trip back from the hospital. Even breakfast tired her out. She's much better than she was yesterday, but she's still frail. She's so scared she's going to have another attack, you see. They are so hard on her."

"If we can't keep Margaret company, let us help clear up these dishes for you," Alice said. "We like to be useful, don't we Lillie Mae?" A malicious grin twinkled in her eyes.

Ignoring Alice, Lillie Mae turned to Sam. "Were you going out?"

"No, not just now," Sam said. "I took a short walk earlier when Margaret and I first got home from breakfast, but I wasn't planning to go out again until later this afternoon."

Flustered, he looked around the room. "I would appreciate your help with this mess. But first, let me go and check on Margaret one more time to see if she's resting peacefully. It will only take me a minute."

Alice walked over to the sink, rolled up the sleeves of her sweater, and started attacking the dishes, moving them out of the sink so she could fill it with water. She found the dishwashing soap under the counter. The cupboards were in perfect order, she noted as she found a dishtowel for Lillie Mae.

Lillie Mae was drying the first set of dishes when Sam came back into the room. He had changed into a fresh shirt.

"I feel much better now," he said. "Margaret is snug in her bed, resting peacefully for a change."

Sam looked around the kitchen and smiled. "Look at what you ladies have done in such a short time," he said. "Please let me help."

He took the dishtowel from Lillie Mae and picked up a wet dish.

Alice and Sam worked comfortably for the next ten minutes, sharing polite conversation while Lillie Mae sat at the kitchen table nibbling cookies.

"The oddest thing happened while you and Margaret were at the hospital yesterday," Lillie Mae said.

"What's that?" Sam asked.

"Carl Lewis stopped by your house and then an hour later, Roger Ballard was here."

"Are you serious?" Sam said. "What on earth did those two men want? Everybody in town knew we were at the hospital yesterday."

"I have no idea," Lillie Mae said. "I called Charlie Warren to let him know."

"Excellent," Sam said, picking up another dish. "Margaret and I are lucky to have you for a neighbor."

* * *

"I can't thank you enough," Sam said when the dishes were put away and the room neat and orderly. "Margaret will be so pleased when she sees how nice everything looks. It's hard for her, not being able to do all the things she used to love to do."

The ringing of the phone interrupted him. Sam rushed across the room to answer it, turning to face the wall when he picked up the receiver. He spoke so softly, the ladies only needed to move a little to avoid hearing any of the conversation. As Alice moved out of his way, she passed the door that led into the living room. Not usually a nosey parker, Lillie Mae was surprised when she saw Alice glance into the room.

Sam hung up the phone, and turned his attention back to the ladies.

"I wanted to get to the phone before it rang again, so it wouldn't wake Margaret," he said, slightly flustered. "She's such a light sleeper, you see, and she needs her rest if she has any chance of getting better."

Alice moved toward the door. Lillie Mae followed her.

"It was Margaret's brother in California on the phone," Sam explained. "He checks up on her frequently. Margaret will be so sorry she missed the call, but she'll call him back later. Michael works so hard to take care of his family and Margaret worries about him all the time. Sometimes, I wonder if it's the worry that causes her attacks." Sam absently ran his hand through his hair as if putting it in order. "I ramble on sometimes. Do forgive me."

"You have every right to ramble, Sam," Alice said. "I'd be stir crazy just putting up with the half of what you have to handle."

Alice turned toward Lillie Mae.

"Lillie Mae and I are going to go now, but if you need anything, please call us. The folks here on the mountain care about you and Margaret, and we're here to help when you need us."

"You are too good," Sam said, noticeably moved. "Margaret and I appreciate everything you do for us. I promise to call if things get out of hand again."

Sam gently ushered them out of the house.

"Do stop by and see Margaret when you can again," he said. "She'll be so sorry she missed you this time."

"That poor man," Alice said when she and Lillie Mae were walking back toward her house. "He has so much to cope with."

"I think he loves taking care of Margaret," Lillie Mae said, taking in a deep breath of the spring air. "He seems happy enough to me."

"You're probably right, dear. Men are funny creatures, not nearly as predictable as we might think," Alice said, a strange gleam in her eye.

"Some are, some aren't," Lillie Mae said, thinking of Roger Ballard.

"You can go check on Clare," Alice said. "I'm sure she's back home by now. It's been almost an hour. And thanks, Lillie Mae, for coming with me. I know Sam appreciated our help."

Alice opened the gate to enter her yard. "Hush, Alfred," she called to silence the muffled yelps from inside the house.

Lillie Mae turned to wave good-bye as she continued on her way down the hill to Clare's house.

As she turned the corner, Roger Ballard's yellow hummer passed her, traveling south toward the Old Mount Penn road. Wondering where he might be going in such a rush, she felt relieved that she wouldn't meet him when she visited Clare.

*   *   *

"Clare, are you home?" Lillie Mae called out, knocking on Clare's screen door a few minutes later. "Can I come in?"

"Of course, you can come in Lillie Mae."

Clare was on her knees scrubbing the kitchen floor.

"Oh my God, Clare," Lillie Mae said, her face ashen. "What is that red stuff all over your blouse? You look as if you just had a fight with a chicken, and the chicken won. What's going on here?"

"Roger was home—he had a nosebleed," Clare said, obviously flustered and embarrassed. "I guess I got his blood on me when I tried to stop the bleeding."

Lillie Mae didn't believe her, but she decided not to say anything.

"Where is Roger now?" Lillie Mae asked, looking at Clare suspiciously. "I thought I saw him drive out toward the Old Mount Penn Road."

"Yes, he just left." Clare laughed uncomfortably. "We got the bleeding stopped and he cleaned himself up before leaving again. He told me he had a meeting this afternoon that he couldn't miss. I asked him to go see a doctor, but he said he didn't have the time. I'm just cleaning up the mess now."

"Clare, when are you going to do something about your life?" Lillie Mae asked.

"I don't want to talk about this now, Lillie Mae." Clare's voice was sharper than Lillie Mae had ever heard it before. "I appreciate that you care about me, but I can take care of myself just fine. I don't have time right now to chat. Billy will be home soon, and I need to finish getting ready."

"You know the police are looking for Roger," Lillie Mae said.

"The police?" Clare said.

"Yes," Lillie Mae said. "Charlie Warren wants to talk to Roger about the drugs that showed up in Jerry Foster's truck."

Someone knocked on the door. Lillie Mae and Clare both jumped as they turned to see who it was.

"Clare, I need to talk to you," Dale Beavers said, standing on the back doorstep.

Clare looked at Lillie Mae, her eyes wide and desperate, her face turning red.

"Clare, do you hear me? I know you're in there. Please may I come in?"

"Dale, what a surprise," Clare said, opening the back door. Dale's jeans were muddy and his shirt was askew. He looked as if he might have been in a fight since Lillie Mae saw him at the church an hour earlier.

"Come in," Clare invited, her tone of voice unnatural. "Lillie Mae's here."

Dale's face turned scarlet. "Lillie Mae," he gulped. "It's so good to see you. I didn't know you and Clare were visiting. I can come back at another time. I just wanted to talk to Clare about the concert in Antioch next month."

"Billy's coming home soon, and I don't have time today," Clare said. "We can talk at choir rehearsal on Wednesday."

Dale backed out the door. "Good idea. I'll be going now. Give my best to Billy."

"Tell me what's going on Clare," Lillie Mae said after Dale left. "I don't believe that Roger had a nosebleed. I want you to tell me the truth."

"I'll tell you what happened, Lillie Mae, but you must promise not to pass judgment."

"I promise."

Clare told her story. "I had just finished running the vacuum cleaner in Billy's room when I heard a car door slam. I looked out the window and saw the yellow Hummer in the driveway. A jolt rushed through my body, since it was an odd time of day for Roger to come home and frankly, I didn't know what to expect.

"I heard the back door open and close, and Roger walking into the kitchen, his heavy boots plodding across the wooden floor. Shaking myself loose, I moved away from the window and into the hall. I waited for Roger to call out to me, but he didn't.

"When several minutes passed and I still heard no sounds or movements, my curiosity took over. I went down the steps quietly and entered the kitchen. Roger was at the sink scrubbing his hands and arms. He had rolled up the sleeves of his shirt and was using the bar of lye I use to clean the outdoor rags to get himself clean. I asked him if he was all right.

"Roger jumped as if startled and turned around to face me," Clare continued. "I can't tell you how shocked I was at his appearance. He looked as if he had been in a fight. There was blood on his shirt, his eyes were swollen, and his nose looked like it might have been broken. There was dried blood all over his face and his clothes were filthy.

"Not saying a word to me, Roger turned back to the sink and continued to scrub.

"I asked him what happened, forgetting that in our family you don't ask those sorts of questions. I stepped back in case he became angry."

Clare paused.

"What happened next?" Lillie Mae asked.

"He told me to leave him alone. Each word sounded as if it pained him to say it. I'll be gone, he told me, as soon as I clean myself up."

Clare looked Lillie Mae in the eyes, her own shining with unshed tears. "Although his words were gruff, he didn't seem to be angry with me, Lillie Mae."

Lillie Mae nodded.

"Billy's coming home today, I told him. 'He called me this morning after you left to tell me he'll be here in time for supper. I know you want to see him.' When he looked at me, Lillie Mae, I wanted to cry."

"Oh my," Lillie Mae said, finding Clare's words hard to imagine.

"Roger told me he had a job he had to do tonight and wouldn't be home for dinner. He said to tell Billy he'd talk to him in the morning."

"What did you say then?"

"I didn't say anything. I just stared at him. It was Roger who did the talking."

Clare caught her breath. "I wish things were different, he told me. I'd like to have dinner with you and Billy more than anything in the world, he said. But I can't and that's that. I don't want to talk about it anymore."

"This doesn't sound like the Roger I know," Lillie Mae said. "What happened next?"

"I asked Roger what was wrong and he told me to go upstairs and bring him down a clean work shirt and some pants. His voice was still gruff, but his eyes were soft.

"I've cleaned up the worst of the mess he told me when I got back with his clothes. Taking them from me he went into the downstairs bathroom to change. When he came out he looked directly at me, Lillie Mae, more miserable than I ever remember seeing him."

Clare paused again.

"And," Lillie Mae prodded.

"He told me he was sorry for the mess and if there was any way he could change things, he would."

"What did he mean by that?" Lillie Mae asked.

"I don't know," Clare said. "All I know is that something is terribly wrong."

"I see," said Lillie Mae.

"Roger was ready to leave, and I could tell he was still in a great deal of pain," Clare said, continuing the story. "Tell Billy I'm sorry I won't be here this evening, he said right before he left. He sounded so sad, Lillie Mae."

"Did he leave then?"

"Yes, but he told me to tell Billy he'd see him tomorrow."

"What are you going to do, Clare?"

"I don't know, Lillie Mae."

"Let me help you clean this mess up," Lillie Mae said. "You want the kitchen clean when Billy gets home."

"Thanks, Lillie Mae. I could use your help."

"Then you have to call Charlie Warren," Lillie Mae said.

"No," Clare said. "Not yet."

*   *   *

Lillie Mae was setting the table and Clare was shredding cabbage to make Billy's favorite coleslaw when they heard a car pull into the driveway. Wiping her hands, Clare went to the door.

"It's Billy," she said, rushing outside.

Lillie Mae followed her and stood on the back step, watching Clare and Billy greet each other.

"Billy, it's so good to have you home," Clare said, taking her son into her arms as soon as he stepped out of the truck and held him in a bear hug. Tall and broad like his father, he had her dark hair and coloring. His eyes were crystal blue.

"It's good to be home," Billy said. An impish grin on his lips, he asked. "What's for supper, Mom?"

Ruffling his hair, Clare laughed. "You never change, my boy. You always think of your stomach first." Taking his hand, she squeezed it. "You look wonderful, son. Is everything all right with you?"

"I'm doing great, Mom." He reached into the back of his truck and took his overnight bag plus a huge laundry bag out. "Better than you, I think. What's up with your face? It looks like you walked into a wall."

"That's just what I did," Clare laughed. "Enough about me. I want to hear all about you. How is school going? Any new girlfriends I should know about?"

"School's fine. Only four more weeks and twelve more exams and the term will be over. Yippee. And as far as girls go," he added, with a whimsical sneer, "there are far too many to talk about."

"You silly goose," Clare said, happier than Lillie Mae had seen her in many months. "Come on in, and I'll make you a sandwich to bide you over until dinner."

"Hi, Lillie Mae," Billy said as he passed her. "Good to see you."

"Your mother's talked of nothing else since hearing that you were coming home. It is so good to see you, too, young man," Lillie Mae said, patting him on the back as he passed by.

*   *   *

Clare was taking the first load of clothes out of the washer and putting them into the dryer, while Billy sat at the table eating a sandwich, chatting with Lillie Mae. They heard a car pull into the driveway.

"Maybe that's Dad," Billy said, getting up to look. Clare had mentioned that his father probably would not make it home for dinner that evening, but Billy hadn't believed her. Lillie Mae looked for the quickest exit in case it was Roger. But it wasn't.

"It looks like Patrick Goody's mother," Billy said.

Clare put the clothes she was folding on top of the dryer and went to the door.

"What can I do for you?"Clare asked when Mabel came up the back steps and stood at the back door.

"I'm looking for Roger," Mabel said. "Patrick's gone missing, and I need to see if Roger knows where he is."

"Roger's not here," Clare said, stepping outside. "I don't know where he is. Patrick called the other day looking for Roger, and I talked to him then. Why do you think he's with Roger?"

"I don't know that he is with Roger. Honestly, Clare, I'm at my wits end," Mabel said. "I guess I'll go up to Carl Lewis' place and see if Patrick might be there. I'm sorry to have bothered you. I can see Billy's home."

"I wish I could have helped you more." Clare followed Mabel down the steps and to her car. "How is your mother holding up through all this?"

"She is tired, and frustrated, and scared. Patrick gone missing has not helped either one of us."

"I'll visit her soon," Clare promised as she stood by Mabel's car door. "I've been thinking about her. But I thought the last thing she needed today was me around. Tell her to call me if she needs anything, though."

"Thanks, Clare," Mabel called. "Please call Mother if Patrick should show up here anytime this evening. My cell phone's dead, but I'll stop by Mother's house off and on to see if Patrick has shown his face. Honestly, Clare, I can't believe that boy has disappeared. Sid Firth pleaded with him to stay with Mother, but he paid no attention."

"If I see him, I'll tell him to go straight to his Grandmother's house."

"What was all that about?" Billy asked when his mother came back inside the house. "What's going on around here? Seems a bit crazy to me."

Clare told him what she knew about the events of the last couple of days, leaving out the part where she found Roger covered with blood. She watched Billy's expression change from one of puzzlement, to concern, and then to disbelief when she told him about Patrick's arrest.

Lillie Mae added what she knew.

"Patrick has issues, but he's never been into drugs," Billy said. "What's Dad's role in all this?"

"I don't know," Clare said, warning Lillie Mae with a glance to stay quiet. "He's been acting strange the last couple of days, son. It's so odd that he's not here to have dinner with you tonight. He really wanted to, you know."

"I might know where Patrick is." Billy stood up quickly and moved toward the door. "I'm going to take a walk before dinner and see if I can find him."

Clare objected at first, but then let Billy go.

"I promise, Mom, I will not do or say anything stupid, but Patrick's been a friend in the past. I don't want to see him get himself into any more trouble than he's already in. I'll take care."

"I need to get going, too," Lillie Mae said once Billy left. "Thanks for the dinner invite, Clare, but you and Billy need this time together."

Lillie Mae realized before she was out of the front yard that she was still wearing one of Clare's aprons. Taking it off, she headed back to the house to return it. As she rounded the corner to the backyard she heard Clare speaking on the phone.

"I'll meet you on the trail in five minutes," she said, her voice shaky.

Hiding around the corner, Lillie Mae watched Clare leave the house through the back door, her jacket in her hand, heading toward the hiking trail behind her house.

*　　*　　*

Lillie Mae walked back home, her mind lost in her afternoon at Clare's, when she met Joyce Castro carrying a basket covered with a checkered cloth and a red bow tied around the handle.

"What do you have there, girl?" Lillie Mae asked, eying the basket.

"It's dinner for Sam and Margaret. I'm taking it over to them. Want to walk with me?"

"Sure," Lillie Mae said, thinking she'd seen a bit too much of her neighbors that day.

"I asked Carlos to come along with me, but he hates to be around sick people, so I let him off the hook when he said he had to run a quick errand. Do you need anything from the store, Lillie Mae? I'll give him a ring on his mobile if you do."

"Thanks, but I'm good."

Joyce and Lillie Mae walked the short distance up the road to the Jenkins' house together. Listening to the sounds of the country—the chirping of the birds, a dog barking in the distance—Joyce looked around her at the signs of the new spring.

"The forsythia in your front yard is in full bloom," Joyce said, pointing at the flower bed in front of Lillie Mae's pretty yellow Arts and Crafts house. "How beautiful it is—and look at Hester's tulips. The new bulbs she planted last fall are up already."

"Your Bradford Pear tree is covered with lush white blossoms, too," Lillie Mae said, pointing toward Joyce's yard. "This is one of the prettiest springs I can remember. The old wives say a cold winter brings a hearty spring, and it looks like they're being proven right."

"I love our small village," Joyce said, smiling. "I'm so glad Carlos and I decided to give up our apartment in D.C., and come live here full time. I miss the restaurants and theatres at times, but for days like today, I would have given up all the restaurants in the world just to be here."

"The Jenkins' house looks dark," Lillie Mae said when they got closer. Walking up the steps to the back porch, Joyce peeked in a window, but the blinds were drawn, so she could not see inside.

Nobody answered when Joyce knocked on the back door. She waited a minute or two and then knocked a second time. Not wanting to disturb Margaret if Sam happened to be out for a late walk, or on an errand, she placed the covered dish by the door, and then walked around to the front of the house with Lillie Mae to see that all was in order. Seeing Sam's car in the driveway, she knew he had to be close by. An idea struck her.

"Maybe Sam's fallen asleep," Joyce said.

"That must be it," Lillie Mae said, remembering how tired he looked when she was helping him earlier. "Of course, the man's exhausted, and when Margaret fell asleep, he probably drifted off himself."

"I'll call Sam later to make sure he picked up the casserole," Joyce said. "I don't want to wake him now."

When the two women turned to go to their respective houses, a green Mini Cooper caught Lillie Mae's eye. "Isn't that Carlos' car?" she asked, pointing in the distance.

"It looks like it," Joyce said. "But, he's going the wrong way."

Joyce stopped and stared at the car. "Carlos was going to the store, not up the mountain," she said, apparently dumbfounded. "I can't think where he might be going."

"I'm sure he will have a good story when he gets home," Lillie Mae said, surprised by Joyce's reaction.

"You're probably right," Joyce said, still looking puzzled.

"I'm hiking in the morning. Any interest in coming along?" Lillie Mae said.

"Maybe," Joyce replied, still looking up toward the mountain.

"I leave early. Around six."

"That is early," Joyce said, her attention drawn back to Lillie Mae. "Let me think about it. I'll call you later."

"Okay," Lillie Mae said, with a wave as she headed home.

* * *

"I'm not going to go hiking with you in the morning, Lillie Mae," Joyce said when she called a couple of hours later. "Six is just too early."

"That's fine," Lillie Mae said, actually relieved. She liked walking solo on her morning hikes, and this was going to be her first long hike of the season.

"Sam called a little bit ago," Joyce added. "Thanked me for the casserole. Said he discovered it when he went out to get his mail. And as I suspected, he had dozed off."

"Did he say how Margaret was doing?" Lillie Mae asked.

"She's better and apparently enjoyed her dinner."

"Glad to hear the folks in our little village are snug tonight," Lillie Mae said. "Did Carlos make it home?"

Joyce rushed her next words. "Yes, Carlos is here. You have a good walk in the morning. Gotta go," she said and hung up.

That was weird, Lillie Mae thought hanging up the phone and returning to her book.

7

"Charlie, it's Lillie Mae Harris here!" Lillie Mae screeched when Charlie Warren answered the phone after three rings.

"What's going on?" he asked, his voice groggy.

"You've got to come help me!"

"Come where, Lillie Mae?" he asked. "It's six twenty-two in the morning, according to my clock. Is this a joke?"

"This is no joke, Charlie. I'm at High Mount."

"Explain yourself then."

"There's a body lying in the woods off the hiking trail not far from here!" Lillie Mae shouted into the phone. "I just found it."

"Okay, Lillie Mae. Stay calm," Charlie said, now fully awake. "Tell me what's going on."

"It's too long a story to explain over the phone. I'll tell you when you get here," Lillie Mae said. "Just come, now, please. I'll wait for you, but make it fast."

"I'll be there in fifteen minutes," Charlie said. "Find a safe place to wait. If you get spooked, call me on this phone."

Lillie Mae felt she was teetering on the brink and wondered how she'd get through the next fifteen minutes. A woman of action, she climbed up the rocks to the peak of the mount, and then sat on the huge boulder where the hang gliders took off during the summer months. The spacious valley view, now draped in the early morning sun would normally sooth her, but not today. Settling onto the rocks, she remembered the water bottle in her backpack. Taking the canvas bag off her back, she placed it on the rock in front of her. Finding the water bottle, she undid the cap and took a sip, then checked the bag for any hidden treasure.

"A Snickers bar!" she exclaimed a moment later. "Thank you, thank you, thank you." She tore the wrapper off and popped it in her mouth.

"Just what I needed," she said, when the treat was gone.

Looking down at her trousers leg, she saw the tear at the knee, and remembered falling as she climbed up the steep hill from the trail to the High Mount landing, more scared than she'd ever been in her life. She remembered the pain, but knew at the time it wasn't serious. Just a scrape. There was blood, or was it mud, on her pants. She tried to brush it off with her hand, but nothing happened, so she decided it must be blood. No big deal. The pants were old, but they were her favorite for hiking. She'd be sad to throw them away.

The first hike of the year is always the best one, she thought. She felt cheated of a special pleasure. The hike had started out so well, and then this.

She checked the time on her cell phone. It was six thirty-five, just ten minutes since she'd hung up with Charlie. Any minute now he'd be here, she hoped. One Mississippi, two Mississippi popped into her brain.

A twig snapped, and a shiver ran down her spine. Turning to look behind her, she glimpsed the tail end of a deer headed into the woods. She was still alone, thank goodness, as the image of the dead man flashed through her mind. He was probably an old hunter or a hiker who just died. Those things happened all the time, she guessed.

The phone rang, cutting the silence.

"Lillie Mae, Charlie here. Are you OK?"

"I'm still here on the rocks, if that's your question. Where are you?"

"I'm almost there. I called the station and alerted them to the possibility of a body on the trail, so they're sending a crew over. Don't panic if you hear sirens."

"I see car lights, Charlie!" Lillie Mae exclaimed, jumping up from the rock.

"Stay put, Lillie Mae—I'll park by the landing and be with you shortly," Charlie said, hanging up.

A few minutes later, she spotted Charlie walking toward her, cell phone at his ear, a coat over his arm. A tall, lean young man, Lillie Mae thought him a beautiful sight, almost angelic with the sun reflecting on his face. "Thank goodness you're here, Charlie," she yelled, waving her arms from the top of High Mount.

Snapping his phone shut, Charlie climbed up the boulder. "Here's a jacket," he said. "I thought you might be cold."

"Thanks," Lillie Mae said, taking the coat and throwing it over her shoulders. "I am shivering. Not sure if it's the cold or the fright."

"Probably both," he said. "Let's sit here until the crew arrives. How are you holding up?"

Charlie settled beside her on the rock.

"I'll live, but I wish you'd brought coffee," Lillie Mae, said snuggling into the jacket and rubbing her hands together.

Charlie smiled. "You're a trooper, Lillie Mae. The crew will bring a thermos. It'll just be a couple more minutes before they get here. Then all hell will break loose."

"What a morning," Lillie Mae said, shaking her red curls.

"Tell me about it," Charlie said. "And I haven't had the morning you've had. So how'd you find a body, my dear Ms. Harris?"

"It was horrible, Charlie, or at least when I found the body it was horrible," Lillie Mae said, repositioning herself on the rock. "Before that the hike was pretty great."

"Why did you go hiking this morning?" Charlie asked, more curious than anything else.

"I love walking early in the morning when most of the world is asleep. It cleanses my mind," Lillie Mae said. "The weather's been so nice the last couple of days, and, with all the to-do with Hester, I wanted to get out in the mountain air this morning while I could, just to feel free."

"So what happened?" Charlie asked.

"It was still dark when I left the house this morning, so I carried a small flashlight. I usually do, even in the summer. I took my usual route from the trail head at the Mount Penn Park south to High Mount."

Lillie Mae hugged herself with her arms, trying not to shiver. "About a half hour into the hike, it was light enough to put the flashlight away, so I stopped to trade it for my binoculars. Several types of sparrows migrate this time of year, and it was just light enough to try and spot one. But instead of a bird, I saw this blob on the ground some twenty yards off the trail. It was lying in a cleared area, so it was easy enough to spot. At first, I thought it might be an animal, a dead deer maybe, or even a bear. It's not unheard of in these parts for a hunter to make a hit and not realize it."

70

"Go on," Charlie said, nodding agreement.

"I wasn't exactly scared, no adrenalin pumping then, but I was cautious. I moved a little closer, just a yard or two off the trail, and looked through my binoculars again. It was then I knew it was no animal. It was definitely human, and it wasn't moving."

Lillie Mae shivered.

"I tried to stay calm, but I wanted to get out of there. At first, I walked slowly up the trail, glancing over my shoulder from time to time to see if I was being followed. Then I began running, slow at first, then faster and faster. I tripped climbing the steep hill from the trail up to the landing," she said, gesturing toward the area below the boulder. "I skinned my knee, but I made it to High Mount safely. That's when I called you."

"Are you sure the person you saw was dead, not just sleeping?"

"No, but if I were a betting woman, I'd bet my money that man was not alive."

"Did you see anybody else out this morning?" Charlie asked, looking over his shoulder, as if confirming no one was around them now.

"No," Lillie Mae said. "I rarely do on my morning hikes."

"Did you hear anything unusual?"

"Not really. Often I talk to myself or sing when I'm out in the morning, so there could have been noises I didn't notice. It was a fluke I saw the body at all. If I had stopped anywhere else, or started the hike earlier or later, the light would have been different, and I would have never noticed it."

"That's how it happens, Lillie Mae."

"I hope it never happens to me again," Lillie Mae said.

"Hear the sirens, Lillie Mae?" Charlie asked, looking back toward the High Mount road.

Lillie Mae nodded, a dire look lingering on her face.

"It's all going to start now," Charlie said, taking hold of Lillie Mae's arm. "Let's get off this rock."

* * *

The sun was now shining brightly high above the horizon. It was going to be another beautiful spring day. Too beautiful for all this, Lillie Mae thought.

Captain John Alton, Charlie's boss at the Antioch police station, a swarthy man of some forty years, leaned over the corpse, his

71

hands in gloves, and his body draped in a blue plastic coat. Charlie Warren was standing behind him, similarly clad. Lillie Mae was still there, but well out of the way of the action.

"Where is that coroner?" Captain Alton asked Charlie, checking his watch. The firemen and ambulance drivers had arrived on the scene, and with little else to do, were helping Sergeant Paul Lowman, a fellow police officer, to finish cordoning off the area.

"Go get those firemen out of here, Charlie, Alton ordered. "They're walking all over the crime scene. And that woman over there," he said, pointing to Lillie Mae. "Why is she here?"

"That's Lillie Mae Harris," Charlie said. "She found the body. I'll take her home when I'm done here."

Captain Alton nodded to Lillie Mae. "You can stay put, dear," he said in a loud voice. "But don't mess with the crime scene."

Lillie Mae stared at the ground, wishing she were anywhere else.

"Stand back," Charlie said to the other emergency workers strolling through the woods. "The police are busy here. Please stay out of the way."

"I don't know why I bother," John Alton grumbled, clearly frustrated. Originally from Baltimore, he had said often enough that he resented being assigned to what he considered a backwoods precinct. Unfortunately, for him, the promotion to captain came with what he described in his favorite bar as this God awful place.

"This crime scene is in shambles," he screamed at Charlie, shaking his head. "Whose idea was it to use those damn sirens this morning?"

"Please let me through," said a crusty little man carrying a satchel. "The police called me this morning to come up here and look at a body. I'm Dr. James Phillips."

Lillie Mae watched Paul Lowman check his credentials and let him pass.

"Over here, Dr. Phillips," Charlie called.

"Well, he looks dead to me," the doctor said in a monotone, a few minutes later, after a superficial examination. "Let me turn him over and see what else I can find."

Dr. Phillips turned the body over, and then studied it for a couple of seconds.

"Someone closed the victim's eyes and mouth," the doctor said, looking intently at the face. "I'd call it a sure sign he was brought to this site from somewhere else. Way too neat for my liking. Dried blood on his forehead indicates he was hit with something hard."

He dropped down on his knees to take a closer look.

"That blow there is what killed him," Dr. Phillips said, pointing at the bloody dent in his forehead. "By the look of the injury, he was probably hit with a rock or a club. The bruises on his face and knuckles indicate there might have been a struggle, but he looks peaceful enough, so the fight had to have happened at a different time than the murder."

Charlie cringed at the word murder.

"Anybody know who he is?" Captain Alton asked.

"I do," Charlie said, his first suspicion confirmed as soon as the doctor turned the body over. Darting a glance at Lillie Mae, who was still too far away to see the victim's face, he swiftly turned his head back to the body.

Captain Alton looked up and saw a small crowd hovering on the far edge of the trail. "Get those people out of here!"

Spotting some familiar Mount Penn faces, Charlie rushed toward them, his arms waving. "Get back," he yelled. "Or you'll be arrested. Go back to High Mount right now and wait in the parking lot. I'll be there in a few minutes with an announcement."

"Go after them, Charlie, and make certain they don't come back here," Captain Alton said. "Say your piece, and send them away— now. Then, take that woman home." He pointed at Lillie Mae. "Come back here as soon as you can. We need to talk."

Charlie climbed up the bank to High Mount a few minutes later, looking strained and very serious, Lillie Mae at his heals. "Go stand over there, out of the way," he said to her, pointing to a clump of trees just on the other side of the landing.

"Ladies and gentlemen," Charlie said, taking center stage, his voice loud and sure. A hush came over the group that included many familiar Mount Penn faces.

"I am going to ask you nicely, folks, to disperse now, and go back to your homes."

The crowd rustled, and then settled quickly.

"We have verified that the man found just off the trail this morning may have died under unusual circumstances. I cannot tell you much more than that at this time. We are not disclosing the victim's name until we confirm his identity and contact his next of kin. I can tell you that he is a local man."

"Is it foul play?" came a voice from the crowd. Lillie Mae stood on her tip toes to see who had asked the question. It was Tim Carroll, a reporter from the *Antioch News*.

"The circumstances are suspicious, but we do not know enough yet to make an announcement," Charlie continued, as if he hadn't been interrupted. "We are going to move the body, now. We need you all to leave, so that we can do this. We will make a formal announcement as soon as we have more information. Again, please go home now. Loiters will be arrested and taken to the Antioch jail."

Lillie Mae looked around the crowd, mentally noting who was there. And who was not.

"Also know, I may be stopping by some of your homes shortly to ask you and your family questions concerning this matter. Please make yourself available. Thank you all very much."

Lillie Mae thought that the last couple of words out of Charlie's mouth would get the folks of Mount Penn away from there, and into their homes, quicker than anything else he might have said.

Charlie turned to leave, without taking any more questions.

"I'm driving you home, Lillie Mae," he said, guiding her toward his truck once the last of the curiosity seekers had left. "You need to get some rest before I come back and question you proper."

"Are you going to tell me who the dead man is?" Lillie Mae asked, not sure she really wanted to know.

"No," Charlie said. "Not yet. But when word gets out, you'll be one of the first to know, I'm sure."

8

Typing up a storm on her on her new Apple laptop, lost in the world of her own tale, Lillie Mae was jarred back to reality by the chime of her doorbell. Peeking out the window by her desk, she saw Clare at the front door, fidgeting like a two-year-old boy who needs to pee.

"Coming," Lillie Mae called.

"Is it Roger?" Clare spurted when Lillie Mae opened the door.

"I don't know, Clare," Lillie Mae said, knowing exactly what Clare was asking. "I was never close enough to the body to see who it was, and when I asked Charlie, he wouldn't say. Come in and sit down."

Lillie Mae reached her hand out to Clare and guided her into the room. "Sit, dear," Lillie Mae said. "Let me get you some coffee."

"Don't leave me, please," Clare said, taking hold of Lillie Mae's arm and pulling her down beside her on the sofa. "I'm crazy with worry. Too much has happened the last couple of days, and now this."

Clare's eyes filled with tears. "Roger hasn't been home since yesterday, Lillie Mae. He hasn't talked to Billy at all. Not even a phone call. There is something terribly wrong."

"That doesn't mean that Roger's dead," Lillie Mae said. "Don't jump to conclusions."

"But it's the other things, too. The phone calls. Billy. Just everything."

Lillie Mae suspected by everything she was referring to Dale Beavers.

"What's going on Clare? Tell me."

"You were there when Mabel Goody stopped by the house yesterday looking for Roger."

Lillie Mae nodded. "I went home shortly after she left."

"Then Billy went out," Clare said. "He thought he knew where Patrick might have gone, so he went up the mountain to check."

"Did he find Patrick?"

"He said he didn't, and he had no reason to lie."

75

"Where did you go, Clare?"

"How do you know I went somewhere?"

"I saw you. I remembered I was wearing your apron and was bringing it back."

Clare stared at Lillie Mae as if deciding how much to tell her. "Where I went is incidental," she finally said. "It's what happened after I got back home that's more important."

"What was that?" Lillie Mae asked, her curiosity piqued.

"Billy was in the kitchen finishing up dinner. Believe it or not," Clare said a half smile on her lips, "the boy likes to cook. Anyway, he was stirring the gravy and asked me to mash the potatoes."

"You said he had gone looking for Patrick Goody but didn't find him."

"That's right," Clare said. "He went up to the old hangout close to High Mount, but nobody was there. It's an old shack half falling down. You've seen it."

Lillie Mae nodded.

"Billy was sure somebody had been there recently, though. Said there been a scuffle. Blood was everywhere."

"Roger?" Lillie Mae asked.

"I don't know, but I thought the same thing," Clare said. "Billy wanted to call Charlie Warren, but I told him no, saying it might look bad for Patrick."

"Makes sense," Lillie Mae said.

"Billy agreed. Said he guess he watched too much TV. He's such a good boy, Lillie Mae."

"Billy's a wonderful boy, Clare. You should be proud."

"We had a nice supper. Billy talked about school and then reminisced about his high school years. I guess his father not being at dinner brought up special memories from the past."

A frown furrowed Clare's forehead. "It was at the end of supper that the phone rang. I thought it might be Roger, so I rushed to answer it. But it wasn't."

"Who was it?" Lillie Mae asked.

"I don't know," Clare said. "But it wasn't Roger. The voice was weird, muffled. I'm not sure if it was a man or woman." Clare paled as if reliving the experience. "I saw you, the voice murmured. You're going to be sorry."

"What—what were they talking about?" Lillie Mae asked cautiously.

Clare dropped her head into her hands. "I don't know."

"You need to call Charlie Warren," Lillie Mae said. "Right away."

"I saw Charlie up at High Mount this morning," Clare said her blue eyes even bluer, through unshed tears. "I thought he'd be around to the house to talk to me by now."

"You were up there this morning? I didn't see you."

"The sirens were crazy loud," Clare said, a slight blush appearing on her cheeks. "Dale Beavers asked me to drive up to the mount with him to see what was going on."

"Yes," Lillie Mae said, drawing out the word.

"Charlie saw us together. The way he looked at me, Lillie Mae. Shocked like." Tears streamed from Clare's eyes. "What if the dead man is Roger? I feel so guilty."

"Go home, Clare. Call Charlie."

"There's something else," Clare said slowly. "It concerns Dale Beavers."

"Yes," Lillie Mae said, again drawing out the word.

"We're not having an affair," she said. "But we have become friends."

"Yes." Lillie Mae wasn't sure she wanted to hear more.

"Dale wants me to leave Roger."

"How do you feel about that?"

"Roger's my husband, Lillie Mae. There have been times in my life when I've been scared of him, and even times I've hated him, but he's Billy's father, and because of that, in my own way, I love him."

Lillie Mae stood up. "Let's go, Clare. I'll walk with you back home. You have to talk to Charlie Warren. Now!"

*   *   *

Clare and Lillie Mae were sitting in Clare's kitchen sipping coffee when they heard a car drive up. Billy had not returned from his morning outing, so Clare said it might be him. Lillie Mae hoped it was Charlie. She had called him and left a message for him to drop by Clare's house as soon as possible.

"I'll check who it is," Clare said, rising from the table and walking to the back door. A lightning stab went through her body when she saw Charlie Warren getting out of his truck.

"It's Charlie," Clare said.

"Stay strong girl," Lillie Mae said.

Clare watched Charlie scan the area, as if looking for something, before lowering his head and walking toward the house.

"Charlie, come in," she said, opening the door, her body noticeably shaking.

Charlie stepped quickly toward her. "Clare, are you all right?"

"Is it Roger?" Clare asked in a voice barely above a whisper.

Charlie's eyes darted to Lillie Mae sitting at the table, then returned to Clare.

"No, it's not Roger," he said, reaching out and touching Clare's arm. "Is that what you thought? No wonder you look so scared. Clare, I'm so sorry. I should have called and told you sooner. I didn't know you thought it might be."

Charlie looked at Lillie Mae again. "It was Carl Lewis' body you found this morning. We released his name an hour ago. I thought sure you would have heard by now."

"Carl Lewis?" Clare said, grabbing hold of Charlie's arm to steady herself.

"Carl Lewis," Lillie Mae said. "Was he murdered?"

"Looks that way," Charlie said.

Charlie put his hand on Clare's shoulder. "I do need to speak to Roger. When did you last hear from him?"

"Yesterday," Clare said, sitting at the kitchen table. "What makes you think Roger's involved in all this?"

"I don't know that he is involved. But, I don't know that he isn't. That's why we need to talk."

"I wish I knew where Roger was," Clare said. "He told me yesterday morning he had a job that might take all night, but I thought sure he'd be home this morning. It's not like him to stay away for two days, especially with Billy home."

"How did he seem to you when you last saw him?"

"What do you mean?" Clare skipped her eyes from Charlie to Lillie Mae.

"Did you notice anything unusual about Roger, Clare? It's not a hard question."

"I just can't think now," Clare said. "This has all been too much for me. I told you I don't know where Roger is, and I'm worried about him."

Clare turned around to face Charlie, her face scarlet. "You know Roger doesn't tell me what he's doing, so don't ask me any more questions right now, please. I'm at my wits end."

Charlie moved towards the door. "Okay, Clare. I'll go for now, but I'll check back here later. If you hear from Roger in the meantime, tell him to call me."

Just as he reached the door, Charlie turned back. "Don't try to handle this without me, Clare," he said. "I'm on your side."

Charlie motioned to Lillie Mae. "Come outside with me," he said. "There's something I want to ask you."

Perplexed, Lillie Mae followed him out the door.

*   *   *

Dale Beavers was locking up the front door of the Mount Penn Community Church when Charlie pulled up and parked not ten feet away. Smiling, he waved a greeting, but his smile faded when Lillie Mae stepped out of the car.

"Lillie Mae," Dale said. "I heard you had quite an adventure this morning."

"I did," Lillie Mae said, her eyes moving from Dale to Charlie.

"Do you have a minute to talk?" Charlie said, holding out his hand to Dale. "I'd like to ask you a couple of questions. Lillie Mae's riding with me to the police station but needed to stop by the church first. Mind if we talk while I wait for her."

"Sure," Dale said. "What's up?"

"I have to pick up an envelope from Reverend Caven's office," Lillie Mae said, walking toward the back of the church. "Don't mind me."

"Is this official?" Dale asked Charlie, a frozen smile on his face.

"I guess it is." Charlie looked uncomfortable. "I saw you up on the mountain this morning, so I know you know why we have to do this. It's in regards to the investigation of the Carl Lewis murder."

"Carl Lewis was murdered?"

79

Fear appeared on his face.

"It looks that way," Charlie said. "We're questioning a number of people in Mount Penn, hoping someone might be able to provide us with a clue, or at least something to go on. You were on my list, so I thought this as good a time as any. I just have a few questions for you."

"Should we go into the church?" Dale asked.

"That's probably a good idea," Charlie said.

When the two men had entered the small old-fashioned building and were seated on one of the wooden pews facing each other, Charlie had second thoughts. "This is a bit awkward," he confessed, glancing towards the front of the church where a picture of Jesus carrying a lamb served as the backdrop to the minister's podium. "It just doesn't seem like quite the right place to talk about murder."

The comment was an ice breaker. Both men smiled and instantly seemed more comfortable with each other.

"So what can you tell me, Dale?" Charlie said, hearing sounds of Lillie Mae rustling in the background.

"Not much." Dale lowered his head and shook it from side to side.

"Truth, now," Charlie said. "I saw you with Clare Ballard this morning. What's up with that?"

"Clare and I are friends." Dale tried to keep the emotion out of his voice. "Lately, we've been singing together, so we see each other more."

"Is your relationship with Clare any more than that?" Charlie asked reluctantly.

Dale's face turned red, and his voice became louder. "What does my relationship with Clare have to do with Carl Lewis' death?"

"Listen to me, Dale." Charlie said, losing patience. "Everything I ask is important. Please answer the question."

Dale clinched his jaw. "There is nothing between me and Clare Ballard. We're friends." Dale hesitated, and then added, "I'd like it to be more. Clare doesn't."

Charlie reached out to Dale. "Do you know where Roger Ballard is, Dale?"

There was a long silence. "I wish I did," Dale finally said, then added quickly, "for Clare's sake. She's frantic with worry."

"Have you seen Roger in the last couple of days?"

Dale hesitated again before answering. "Charlie, I don't know anything about the murder of Carl Lewis, and I have no idea where Roger Ballard is. That's all I have to say."

Standing, Charlie sobered even more. "I don't believe you are telling me the whole truth, Dale, but I'm certain what you've said is true. You'd be smart to trust me in the future. I'm here when you decide to tell me everything you know."

Dale dropped his head, but said nothing.

Charlie walked toward the door. "Lillie Mae," he called.

"Here," Lillie Mae said, a little quicker than Charlie anticipated. She walked into the sanctuary from the back door.

"Let's go," he said, opening the door. "Remember what I said Dale. I'm here for you if you want to talk."

As they walked out of the church, Lillie Mae heard Dale mumble, "Thanks."

* * *

"What did you think, Lillie Mae?" Charlie asked as they drove away from the church.

"The same thing you did. Dale told the truth, but not all the truth."

"He's innocent enough of the crime I'm investigating," Charlie said. "I doubt if he knew Carl Lewis, much less had a reason for killing him. It's his relationship with Roger Ballard that concerns me."

"Dale's in love with Clare. She probably loves him, too, but is stopping the feelings because of Roger. It's probably that simple. Not easy, but simple."

Charlie nodded. "You're probably right, Lillie Mae."

"Where are we going now?" Lillie Mae asked, enjoying the ride.

"Janet and Pete's," Charlie said. "We won't stay long, but they'd be horribly disappointed if I didn't talk to them. It's not official, but we won't tell them that."

Lillie Mae laughed.

Pete Hopkins was lying on the driveway, half of his small body hanging out from under the back of his new black truck, when Charlie and Lillie Mae drove up. Pete stuck his head out from under the truck when he heard the car drive up, so only the top of Pete's head, one arm, and his legs could be seen.

"Looks like someone left their toy doll outside on the driveway," Lillie Mae said, waving to Pete.

"Afternoon, Pete," Charlie said, with his usual friendly manner.

"Afternoon, Charlie. Afternoon, Lillie Mae."

Pete jumped up. "I guess I know why you're both here. Quite the morning, Lillie Mae. Aren't you something? Finding a body."

"Too much excitement if you ask me," Lillie Mae said, noticing that Pete was getting skinnier, then she remembered Janet's diet. Pete turned back to Charlie hardly able to contain himself.

"You want to talk to me and Janet about Carl Lewis' murder, don't you?"

"Yes, Pete. That's why we're here. Is this a good time?"

"Sure," Pete said. "Janet's watching her afternoon stories, but I'm betting she'll be pleased as punch to be interrupted."

Lillie Mae and Charlie followed Pete into the house.

"Janet, look who's here," Pete said, walking into the living room.

With a start, Janet jumped up awkwardly from the cranberry leather recliner she was lounging on, and a Snickers' wrapper fell to the floor. When she bent over to pick it up, Lillie Mae noticed the tell-tale signs of chocolate on one side of her mouth. Wearing bright orange peddle-pushers and a matching shirt with a large ostrich outlined in rhinestones, Lillie Mae immediately thought of Halloween.

"Charlie's here to ask us some questions about Carl Lewis' murder." Pete walked over and picked up the remote off the coffee table and turned off the TV.

"Oh yes," she said. Lillie Mae noticed Janet's eyes darting around her chair as if searching for other errant candy wrappers. "We were expecting you to stop by today."

"Sit down," Pete said. "Coffee or tea?"

Both visitors shook their heads.

"No thanks," Charlie said, taking a seat on the flowered sofa. "It has been quite a day," he admitted, as he looked first at Pete, and then at Janet. He saw a childlike expectancy on their faces. "But we need to get serious now."

Janet squirmed her way back into the lounger and Pete sat in a straight wooden chair he pulled into the room from the dining room. Lillie Mae and Charlie were cushioned on the deep-seated sofa.

"You heard it was Carl Lewis's body that Lillie Mae found this morning," Charlie said, settling his legs, which had suddenly appeared close to his chin.

"Oh, yes," Janet said, nodding her head. "It's been the main topic of gossip this afternoon."

"A terrible man," Pete mumbled. "No one should be murdered, but he's been a blight on Mount Penn for too many years."

"Any idea about who might be involved?" Charlie asked.

Pete and Janet looked at each other eyes wide. "Oh, no," said Janet. "We don't know."

"Well, there was that thing with Hester Franklin's grandson, Patrick Goody being up at Carl Lewis' place the other day," Pete said. "But you know all about that."

"I do," Charlie said. "What else do you know?"

"It was odd," Janet said, rolling her eyes to the ceiling as if in thought. "You know, Pete, when Harriet called looking for Hester and couldn't find her."

"When was this?" Charlie asked.

"Just before dinner time yesterday," Pete chimed in. "I remember because I was so hungry, you see. Me and Janet are on these diets, and I get hungry, Charlie."

Lillie Mae had to pinch herself not to laugh. Pete looked so sad. Charlie nodded.

"Janet was taking the broiled salmon out of the oven when the phone rang. I told Harriet that Janet would call her back after we had our dinner, but she insisted on talking to Janet right away."

Pete was frazzled just telling the story. "I told her all we had for lunch was a chicken leg and green beans, and supper was the salmon and a salad, but she didn't seem to think that was important."

Pete looked around the room, Lillie Mae suspected in search of help.

"Obviously, she's never been starved before," Pete added, his voice lowered.

"What did Harriet want?" Charlie asked.

"She was worried about Hester," Janet said. "She told me she had called to find out how Hester was doing after her morning at the courthouse, but nobody answered the phone. After trying again several times, she called me. Somebody should pick up, she complained. If Hester's resting, Mabel or Patrick should answer the phone."

"So Janet told Harriet we'd walk up to Hester's place and check on them," Pete said. "But I insisted it would be after our dinner."

"I said it would be good exercise," Janet said, equally proud.

"Did you go?" Lillie Mae asked.

"Oh, yes," Pete said. "We walked up the road right after dinner."

"And," Charlie prodded.

"Hester was home," Pete said.

"And," Charlie prodded again.

"Mabel and Patrick were with her," Janet said.

"And," Charlie said for the third time. "Stop beating around the bush, folks. Tell me what you found when you got to Hester's house."

"Mabel seemed surprised to hear that Hester had left the house," Janet said. "When she asked her mother where she'd been, Hester flushed and said it was nobody's business but her own. Said she was too worried and restless to stay in the house by herself, so she went out for a walk."

"And there was something else," Pete said.

"OK," Charlie said, losing patience.

"It was Patrick," Janet blurted out, the chocolate smear still on the side of her mouth. "He'd been in a fight. There was blood all over him."

9

"Hester's place, I'm assuming," Lillie Mae said as she crawled back into the passenger seat of Charlie's truck."

"Hester's place," Charlie confirmed.

Mabel answered the door when Charlie knocked. "Charlie, Lillie Mae," she said, obviously surprised to see Lillie Mae. "Come in."

Hester sat in a high back Queen Anne chair, as rigid as a queen. "Charlie, Lillie Mae," she nodded.

"How are you today, Hester?" Lillie Mae asked.

Hester's eyes moistened, but she checked herself. "It's all too much, Lillie Mae," she said. "What's happening to our little village? First drugs, now murder. I don't know how much more I can take."

"It'll get better," Mabel said, moving swiftly to her mother's side. "Tea or coffee."

"No, thank you," Charlie said. "Let's sit down, please. I want to ask you some questions. Lillie Mae's here to listen and for support, if you need her."

Mabel raised her eyebrows, but said nothing.

"Where's Patrick?" Charlie asked when everyone was settled.

"He's upstairs in his room," Mabel said. "Do you want to talk to him?"

"I will, later," Charlie said. "But I want to talk to you two first."

Lillie Mae could feel the tension in the room.

"When you and Patrick left the courthouse yesterday," Charlie said, his voice sterner than Lillie Mae remembered hearing before, "Sid told you to go straight home and get some rest. I know that, because he told me he had. He also told me that he warned you not to get into any further trouble. Do you remember?"

Mabel curled her lip, but said nothing. Hester sniffed and nodded.

"Did you listen?"

Hester turned on Lillie Mae. "You told him!"

"I didn't tell Charlie anything," Lillie Mae said. "Your reaction just now is what told him something wasn't right."

"I told you to keep your mouth shut, Mother!" Mabel said. "You're going to get us all into trouble."

"Listen ladies," Charlie said, holding up his hand. "Enough. I want you to tell me the truth. Then, I'll talk to Patrick. Do you understand that there's been a murder in Mount Penn, and your family is involved, whether you like it or not? You could be in more trouble than you ever dreamed. If you're innocent, you have nothing to fear from the truth. So, start talking."

Charlie eyes moved between the two women.

Hester moaned, and Mabel squirmed in her seat. "Okay, Charlie, we'll talk to you," Mabel said, casting a sidelong look at her mother.

"Good," Charlie said, pulling out a notebook. "Tell me what you've been up to."

Mabel took a deep breath and started talking. "When I got to Mother's house after Lillie Mae dropped me off at the Mountain View Inn, she told me that Patrick had gone out. I was scared he might get himself into trouble, so I went out to find him."

"I begged the boy not to leave," Hester said, looking to Lillie Mae for confirmation. "But he wouldn't listen to me."

"Where did you go before that?" Charlie asked, his eyes fixed on Mabel.

"What do you mean?" Mabel asked, her eyes wide.

"You didn't come straight here after Lillie Mae left you off," Charlie said. "Where did you go?"

Mabel looked relieved, as if Charlie had asked a question she could answer. "I had some errands I had to do, and I wanted to stop off at my house. My luggage was lost, and I was planning for Patrick and me to stay with Mother for a couple of days, so I needed to get some things. I guess, all told, it took me less than an hour to do what I had to do, and then drive here."

"So, where did you go when you left your mother's house?"

"To Clare's house," Mabel said. "I was looking for Roger, but he wasn't there, and Clare didn't know where he was. So, I drove up to Carl Lewis' place."

86

"Carl Lewis' place?" Charlie shouted, half rising out of his chair. "You went to Carl Lewis's place and this is the first time you're telling me?"

"I thought Patrick might have gone there. But, I could tell right away nobody was around. I only stayed a couple of minutes and didn't even get out of my car. To be frank, Charlie, I was scared, so when I saw that Patrick wasn't there, I left. It was no big deal. It didn't occur to me to tell you before now."

"Then where did you go?" Charlie asked.

"I just drove around," Mabel said. "I do that sometimes, to think. I wasn't gone much more than an hour. When I got back here, Patrick's motorcycle was in the driveway. I can't tell you how relieved I was."

Mabel paused for a moment, then added. "I didn't murder Carl Lewis, Charlie."

Charlie nodded. "Was your mother home when you got back?"

"Yes, of course," Mabel said, obviously surprised by the question.

Charlie turned his attention to Hester. "And where did you go yesterday afternoon, Hester?"

Hester's eyes grew large as she sank deeper into her chair. At the same time, she looked relieved to tell her story. "Patrick and I had a huge rift after Lillie Mae dropped us off here," she began. "I begged him not to leave, but he paid no attention to me. He told me I didn't understand. Then Mabel got back, and found out Patrick had gone, and she was angry with me. After she stormed out of the house, I was beside myself with worry. I tried to lie down like I was told to do, but I couldn't rest. So, I got up and went for a walk up by the church. It was such a beautiful day, I'm glad I did. I wasn't out much more than an hour. When I got home, I felt a little better, but was still tired. The air helped me settle though, so I went upstairs and took a nap."

"So you were asleep when Patrick got home?"

"Yes, I guess I was. Mabel and Patrick were both here when I came back downstairs."

"What were they doing?" Charlie asked.

"What do you mean?" Hester asked, surprised by the question. "They were in the kitchen. Why?"

87

"Call Patrick downstairs," Charlie said. "I want to talk to him now."

Moments later Patrick appeared in the doorway.

"You've got a lot explaining to do," Charlie said. "I'm going to ask you one time to tell me where you went yesterday afternoon, who you talked to, and how you got those bruises on your face."

Charlie moved within inches of Patrick's face.

"One time," he continued. "And, if I'm not satisfied with your answers, son, I'm taking you to the Antioch jail."

Patrick hung his head.

"Do you hear me, Patrick?" Charlie added, not waiting for an answer. "Start talking."

Patrick looked at his mother.

"Tell Charlie what happened, Patrick," she said. "And I mean everything."

Patrick walked over to the chair that Charlie had vacated, and sat down.

"I didn't murder anybody," Patrick said. "And I'm not sorry I went out yesterday. I did what I had to do."

"What was it you had to do?" Charlie asked.

"To meet Roger Ballard. I thought he had set me and Jerry Foster up for the drug bust, and I wanted to hear what he had to say."

"Did you find Roger?" Charlie asked, scrutinizing Patrick's face.

Patrick hesitated, looked at his mother, then his grandmother. "Yes, I met him up at the old hangout close to High Mount."

"How did you know where he was?" Charlie asked.

"He called me on my cell phone, shortly after I got out of jail. He asked me to meet him there. I had left him several messages before, but, frankly, I was surprised when I heard back from him. He swore to me then that he had nothing to do with the drugs in Jerry's truck and was as surprised by what happened as I was. I didn't believe him, and I was still angry, but I agreed to meet him and hear him out."

"What happened then?" Charlie asked

"I rode my motorcycle up to High Mount, and then walked the trail down to the old hideout. Roger was sitting on a rock when I got there. I was beside myself, angry, so I called him to come down. When he was in front of me, I took a punch at him. We scuffled. He was yelling the whole time to stop, that he wanted to talk, that he wanted to tell me what he knew, but I had to get the fight out of me. It didn't last long. Roger only fought back to defend himself."

Patrick touched his face. "He got a few good punches in, though."

"What happened when you two stopped fighting?" Charlie asked.

"We talked. He convinced me the job at Carl Lewis' was legitimate. His customer in West Virginia was real, and angry, because he didn't get his piping. Roger also told me Carl Lewis had called him when he was on his way up the mountain, and told him there was no need to come to his place that morning, because the shipment of pipes hadn't come in yet. Carl apparently told Roger that Jerry and me had arrived there early, and he had sent us on our way. Of course, that was a lie."

"So, why didn't Roger call you when all this happened?" Charlie asked. "I know you tried to get him."

"Roger is good to work for. He pays good, and right away. But he wasn't easy to get on the phone. According to Roger, though, he went onto his next job. Said he must have accidentally switched his phone off. My guess is, he thought it was settled, and he didn't want to be bothered."

"Did you believe him?" Charlie asked.

"Not at first, but the more he talked, the more I believed he was telling me the truth. He seemed upset at what happened to me and Jerry. Swore to me he knew nothing about the drugs. Besides, he said, we were friends of Billy's, and he'd never compromise a friend of Billy's. He told me he'd take care of it."

Charlie perked up.

"What do you mean, take care of it?"

"I don't know, Charlie," Patrick said, shaking his head. "Those were his words. Once he was finished talking, he asked me to leave it to him. Said he was meeting someone else, and he wanted me gone before they got there."

"Did he say who he was meeting?" Charlie asked.

"Nope," Patrick said. "I didn't ask, and he didn't tell."

"What happened then?" Charlie asked, jotting down some notes.

"I walked back up to High Mount, got on my motorcycle and rode home."

"Did you see anyone on your ride down the mountain?"

"There were plenty of cars on the Mount Penn road, but I didn't pay any attention to them. Nobody I recognized. And I suspect nobody recognized me either."

"Have you talked to Roger since yesterday?" Charlie asked, still making notes.

"No," Patrick said. "My cell phone battery is dead and I can't find the charger. I must have left it at home. Mom and Grandma won't let me out of the house, so I can't go home and get it. I've just been upstairs sleeping. I didn't even know about all the excitement on the mountain this morning until Mom told me, right before you came."

"Have you worked for Roger before?" Charlie asked.

"Yeah," Patrick said. "I've done lots of jobs for Roger. Mostly delivery stuff. I haul piping and other plumbing supplies for him. Jerry Foster and me do the jobs together since he has the truck. We pick up the stuff at one place, and deliver it to another. When Roger called and asked us to pick up some piping from Carl Lewis' place and deliver it to West Virginia, it was just a routine job to us."

Charlie turned his attention back to Hester.

"Did you get any phone calls while Patrick and Mabel were out?"

The question startled Hester.

"Let me think," she said. "There were two. One from Alice asking how I was doing, and one from Sam Jenkins."

"What did Sam want?" Charlie asked.

"He wanted to know how I was doing and if I needed anything."

Charlie stood up abruptly and beaconed to Lillie Mae.

"That's all the questions for now," he said, suddenly in a hurry to leave. "But I'm telling all three of you to stay out of trouble. And, I mean it. Trust me guys, you don't want me to come back here because I've heard you've gotten in some sort of mischief. If I do have to come back, friends or no friends, it'll be with handcuffs and a warrant."

"Where to now?" Lillie Mae asked, standing beside Charlie's truck, her hand on the door.

"Since we're here, let's go pay Sam and Margaret Jenkins a visit."

Lillie Mae nodded and followed Charlie across the street.

Charlie knocked, waited, and knocked again.

"I'm almost sure they're home," Charlie said. "Let's go around the back and check."

Just as they were turning to go, Lillie Mae heard rattling at the front door. "Wait."

A moment later the door opened.

"Lillie Mae, Charlie," Sam Jenkins said, looking at them through a half-opened door. "You should have come to the back door. It took me a minute to realize someone was knocking. We rarely open this door. Good to see you."

"We're here to ask you a couple of questions," Charlie said. "Is this a good time?"

"This is a fine time," Sam said, smiling. "I've heard from the neighbors that you two were out and about asking questions. Not certain if I can help you, but do come in, and I'll do my best."

Sam opened the door wide and ushered the pair into the house. "Margaret's napping," he said.

"How is she today?" Lillie Mae asked.

"Quite good," Sam said. "But she tires easily."

"Tell her I asked about her," Lillie Mae said.

"I will," he said, more flustered than before. "Come into the living room, please," Sam said, leading the way. "Can I get you some coffee?"

"None for me," Lillie Mae said.

Although she'd been in Sam's and Margaret's house often enough, she'd rarely been in this room. White struck her as the theme. The walls were white, the crown molding white, the furniture white, mixed with chrome and glass. The oak floors offered the only warm color in the room. It was stark, but quite pretty, Lillie Mae thought.

"None for me either," Charlie said, looking around the room apparently as interested as Lillie Mae in the décor.

Sam offered Lillie Mae and Charlie seats on the white leather sofa that took up most of the far wall. Lillie Mae noticed that the room was immaculately clean. Sam was the only thing that didn't fit into the room. He was too comfortable looking for this stark white room. The room was much more Margaret, who, despite her illness, was always immaculately dressed with every hair in place.

"Thank you again, Lillie Mae, for your help yesterday," Sam said. "I won't forget your kindness. It feels so nice to have everything back in order."

"Alice and I were over here in the afternoon, helping with the dishes," Lillie Mae explained. "It was the least we could do for Sam and Margaret after their day at the hospital."

"Can I ask Margaret a couple of questions?" Charlie asked, his notebook out again.

"Oh, dear, no, Charlie," Sam said. Still standing, he walked to the door as if barring anyone's exit from the room. "Margaret knows nothing about these terrible happenings in Mount Penn, and I don't want her to know. She's much too fragile to deal with a possible murder in our own backyard. Besides, as I mentioned before, she's napping."

"Very well, Sam," Charlie said. "But I still need to ask you a couple of questions.

"Ask away," Sam said, stepping back into the room and sitting down in a white leather lounger opposite Charlie.

"Who told you about the murder, Sam?" Charlie asked.

"Hester Franklin was the first to break the news," Sam said quickly. "I called her earlier today to find out about all the sirens. Joyce Castro called later, checking up on Margaret, and she basically repeated what Hester had said."

"Did Margaret ask you about the sirens?" Charlie asked.

"She did," he smiled, showing a less than perfect smile. "And I fibbed a bit. I told her it was probably some test. She wasn't much interested, so I didn't have to elaborate." Sam paused a moment as if thinking. "Actually I didn't know what the sirens were either until Hester told me about the murder. When I found out, I was glad I had made up my little story."

"Did you know Carl Lewis?" Charlie asked.

"I knew of him, of course." Sam's eyes darted from Lillie Mae to Charlie. "But I didn't really know him. We don't travel in the same circles."

"You walk up his way all the time," Charlie said. "Did you ever run into him?"

"I may have seen him once or twice out in his yard, and even threw my hand up to him on occasion, but I don't remember ever talking to him. I knew what he was known for, and I didn't approve."

Charlie paused before asking the next question. "Carl Lewis stopped by your house when you were away, Sam. Do you have any idea why he might have done that?"

"Lillie Mae told me yesterday when she and Alice were here helping to clean up the kitchen, that Carl Lewis stopped by my house while Margaret and I were at the hospital," Sam said. "As I told her then, I have no idea why he would have come here."

"Roger Ballard also was seen at your house yesterday."

Charlie watched Sam closely.

"Lillie Mae told me that, too? I know Roger, of course, but not well. I often pass his house on my walks, and we both raise our hands in greeting when we see each other. But, I don't think I've said more than ten words to the man in my life."

"Why do you think he'd come to your house?" Charlie asked.

"I have no idea," Sam said, looking puzzled. "Maybe it had to do with that new water system the county is putting in up here on the mountain. Probably wanted to sign me up or something. He must have known I'd taken Margaret to the hospital. News spreads so fast in this village whenever she has one of her episodes."

"Where do you go on your walks, Sam?" Charlie asked.

A big grin spread across Sam's face. "Usually I walk up toward High Mount. I hike the full two miles each way, when I can, but that's not often. I don't like to leave Margaret alone too long, you see. I go out when she's napping."

"Do you often meet people on your walks?"

Sam looked confused by the question. "Sometimes," he said. "Mostly neighbors, but occasionally I'll meet a stranger. Why do you ask?"

"When was the last time you took a walk?" Charlie said, ignoring Sam's question.

Sam appeared to think. "Yesterday afternoon, I guess while Margaret was resting. I didn't go far, but it was such a nice day, I took advantage of a quiet half hour in the woods."

"Did you meet anyone when you were out yesterday?"

"No, and I was surprised," Sam said. "On such a pretty day, I'd expect to meet someone. I often do."

Margaret's faint voice came from the bedroom. "Sam, are you there?"

"Margaret is waking up," Sam said, becoming noticeably edgy. He stood up, placing his feet slightly apart as if ready to run. "I'm sorry, but you'll have to leave now."

Charlie and Lillie Mae stood and Sam ushered them quickly to the door. "I don't want Margaret to know you're here, you see," he said, lowering his voice. "She's still weak, and the news would be too much for her just now. Please go."

"I may need to come back," Charlie said, as he stepped out the door, Lillie Mae on his heels.

"Do come back anytime," Sam said, holding the door open. "You'll want to talk to Margaret when she's feeling a little better."

"Sam," Margaret called again, louder this time.

"Just a minute, sweetheart—I'll be right there," he called back, then turned to face Charlie and Lillie Mae again. "I'm sorry, but I have to go right away," he said, ushering them outside and closing the door behind them.

*　*　*

"Charlie, Lillie Mae," someone called when they stepped off Sam's front porch. Turning around, they saw Alice walking their way.

"Janet called earlier and told me you two were all over the village, chatting up the neighbors, as Joyce would say. Come to the house, and let me give you some tea and cookies. You must be exhausted."

"That would be welcomed," Charlie said, his face transformed by the warm smile on his lips as he and Lillie Mae followed Alice across the street and into her house.

"Down, Alfred—sit Alfred, and hush," Alice said to the Jack Russell terrier who quickly obeyed, his tail beating the floor.

Charlie reached down to pet the small dog, who gazed up at him with approval. "Looks like Alfred's becoming a good guard dog."

"He's still in training," Alice said, beaming at her small friend. "Some days are better than others. Now you two go with Alfred into the living room while I get the tea and cookies."

"I love this house," Charlie said. "Especially after being at the Jenkins' place. Those white leather couches were nice, but it's all too modern for my taste."

"Me, too," Lillie Mae said. "Alice's house is just like her. Warm and comfortable."

"And old," Alice called from the kitchen, giggling.

Charlie was down on the floor petting Alfred, and Lillie Mae was curled in a chair resting her eyes, when Alice entered the room a few minutes later, a tray in hand. Setting it down on the coffee table, she offered Charlie a glass of iced tea.

"Sugar?" she asked.

He shook his head.

Lillie Mae opened her eyes and smiled.

"Sugar?" Alice asked again, handing Lillie Mae a glass.

"No, thanks," Lillie Mae said. "This is the best treat I've had today."

Alice passed the plate of raisin oatmeal cookies to Charlie.

"These cookies have soothed many a weary soul," Charlie said.

"Mmmm," Lillie Mae said when it was her turn for a cookie. "I use your recipe, Alice, but my oatmeal raisin cookies never taste as good as yours."

"You two," Alice said, blushing. She sipped from her glass of tea and nibbled a cookie with her guests.

"The news is quite horrible."

Alice set her glass down and scooped Alfred into her arms and hugged him. "I can't believe there has been a murder in Mount Penn."

"Did you know Carl Lewis?" Charlie asked Alice.

"I knew who he was, of course," she said. "But I didn't know him personally. We all knew Carl Lewis sold drugs out of his trailer and has done so for years. But, he stayed to himself, mostly, and I rarely saw him."

"When did you last see him?" Charlie asked.

"Funny you should ask," Alice said. "I was out in the yard tossing a ball to Alfred, and I noticed Carl Lewis driving up and down Mountain Avenue in that old black truck of his yesterday morning after I got back home from Thursday morning breakfast. I watched him drive slowly up the street, then back again. I suspect he turned around at the church. Then, he was gone. Lillie Mae saw him, too. She said she called and told you about it."

"She did," Charlie said. "Seen anything of Roger Ballard by any chance?"

"It's hard to miss Roger when he's out and about," Alice said. "And, I do see him off and on. He's always driving around in that big yellow Hummer of his."

"Did you see him today?" Charlie asked.

Alice scrunched her eyes as if in thought. "You know, I haven't seen him at all today, now that you mention it. I saw him yesterday, though, and I almost called you. He races that big monster of a car down these country streets, and if a child, or dog, ran out suddenly, there could be a terrible accident."

"I wish you had called me," Charlie said. "I need to talk to Roger."

"Do the police have an idea who killed Carl Lewis?" Alice was shocked by her own question.

"I couldn't tell you if I did know, but frankly, Alice, we have no idea. Carl Lewis had dealings with all kinds of people. Finding his murderer is not going to be easy. Right now, I'm asking the questions, and Lillie Mae is doing the listening."

Lillie Mae beamed.

"Frankly Alice, I can use your help, too. You talk to a lot of people. Keep your ears and eyes open. Let me know if you hear something you think is unusual or interesting. I've something to confess, ladies," Charlie said, looking embarrassed.

"What's that?" Lillie Mae asked.

"This is my first murder investigation."

"Well, I never," Alice said, "but then there hasn't been a murder in Mount Penn in fifty years. Not since the old railroad resort days back in Henry Ford's time."

"So, I need your help ladies. People in small villages know things about their neighbors and will often offer up the best information."

Charlie paused, looking first at Alice, and then Lillie Mae.

"Lillie Mae, Alice, I have your first assignment."

"Yes," Lillie Mae said, excited.

Alice only stared at Charlie.

"Go talk to Joyce and Carlos. I think you'll find out more from them than I can."

"I'm not sure," Alice said. "I don't want to spy on my neighbors and friends."

"Tell them what you're doing, then," Charlie suggested. "Get their support. I'm not sure it'll work, but let's give it a try."

10

"This is our first time at being detectives," Lillie Mae said to Alice on their walk over to Joyce and Carlos Castro's house. "Our goal will be to get information from our neighbors and friends, things they might not be willing to tell Charlie, but Charlie needs to know, without harming them or compromising our friendships."

"It's a tall order, but Charlie gave us plenty of leverage," Alice said. "I'm not fooling myself that this is going to be easy," she added. "It's not. We're going to be tested."

"That's true," Lillie Mae said. "Joyce and Carlos should be an easy first interview, though, since they're not remotely connected to the murder of Carl Lewis."

"So, let's have some fun with it," Alice said.

"Should we tell Joyce what we're doing?" Lillie Mae asked. "I didn't say anything when I called to let her know we were coming."

"Not just yet," Alice said. "Once we know for sure what we're doing, we'll tell all the ladies of the Thursday morning breakfast club."

"Agreed," Lillie Mae said.

Joyce opened the door almost immediately after Lillie Mae knocked. "Alice, Lillie Mae," she said. "I'm glad you called, and asked to stop by. Come on into the living room, and we'll visit. Carlos is in his studio working, so we have the house to ourselves."

Minutes later the ladies were all gathered in Joyce's surprisingly comfy living room, Lillie Mae and Alice curled up on the antique French sofa, Joyce on the antique Victorian carved back chair, all with coffee cups in their hands.

"So, what do you think about all this Carl Lewis business?" Lillie Mae asked Joyce.

"Crazy. Who would have believed there would ever be a murder in Mount Penn? Wait," she said. "That sounds like a good title for a mystery novel to me—Murder in Mount Penn. You should write it, Lillie Mae."

The women chuckled.

"Seriously," Joyce added, in her most proper English accent. "This is not funny. Carl Lewis, sleaze that he was, is dead, and somebody murdered him. That somebody is probably part of a drug community that we know nothing about. But, his murder still affects us. Our house is the closest to the crime scene, if you think about it."

"You're right. All the land between here and High Mount is national park. Does it frighten you?" Alice asked.

"No, of course not," Joyce answered quickly. "Carlos and I are perfectly safe here. Murder, or no murder. None of this has anything to do with us."

"Remember last evening when we were walking home from delivering the casserole to Sam and Margaret, and I saw Carlos driving up the mountain instead of into town," Lillie Mae asked, as casually as possible. "Did he ever tell you where he was going?"

Joyce sipped her coffee, looking over the rim of the cup at Lillie Mae, as if stalling. "He didn't," she finally said.

"Oh," Lillie Mae said, raising her left brow.

"But he did tell me about his trip to town to buy wine," Joyce added, and then smiled. "I thought it was quite funny, although Carlos was not amused at all."

"What happened?" Alice asked, accepting the offered diversion.

"He was gone for hours, so naturally, I worried. I tried calling his cell phone, but nobody answered, which worried me even more. So, when he got home, he got the stare, a warmed up dinner in the microwave, and the questions."

"Of course," Alice said.

"Seems he drove to Antioch to buy several bottles of Alamos wine, his favorite Argentine brand, and an avalanche of disasters befell him."

Joyce's eyes glistened with pleasure as they moved from Alice to Lillie Mae.

She continued her story. "First, Carlos discovered the battery in the Mini Cooper was dead when he went to leave the liquor store. Of course, the car wouldn't start. Just that horrid grinding noise over and over. I can hear the language he must have used, and it's not pretty."

"I've had that happen to me before," Lillie Mae said. "The car starts fine one minute, then refuses to budge the next. You don't want to hear the language I used either."

"Carlos called Triple A to come help, but according to him, they were as slow as molasses getting there. That's when he discovered he'd forgotten to charge his cell phone. He said he was lucky to get the one call through before the phone went dead."

"Oh, dear," Alice interjected.

"I was the winner out of it all, though," Joyce said with a smile. "Carlos felt so bad about being away as long as he was, and not calling me, that he went back into the liquor store and bought me a box of Godiva chocolates—want a piece ?"

"Sure," Lillie Mae said, as Joyce jumped up to leave the room to get the box. Then to Alice she asked, "What do you think?"

"Strange, but believable," Alice answered. "Triple A would have paperwork."

When Joyce returned with the box of candy, Lillie Mae opted for a chocolate strawberry, and Alice picked a truffle.

"Mmm," was the collective sound of appreciation.

The phone rang.

Joyce popped up again.

"Be right back," she told the ladies, and moments later added, phone in hand, "It's Harriet. She wants to talk to you, Lillie Mae."

Surprised, Lillie Mae took the receiver.

"What the hell is going on over there?" Harriet's loud voice stormed through the receiver. "Drugs, murder, mayhem. Ever since Kevin and I moved away from the mountain, there's been one insane event after another."

"Calm down, Harriet," Lillie Mae said, rolling her eyes.

"Janet said the police think Roger Ballard murdered Carl Lewis."

"Roger Ballard?" Lillie Mae said. "I've been with Charlie Warren most of the day, and this is the first I'm hearing about that rumor. Roger's missing, and Charlie's been asking for him, but nothing's been said about Roger being the murderer. I have no idea where Janet came up with that tale."

"Kevin and I are coming over to your house, and we'll all go down to Clare's together. We need to talk to that girl."

"Whoa, Harriet," Lillie Mae said, aghast. "That's not a good idea."

"We'll be at your house at six o'clock."

The phone went dead.

Lillie Mae handed the phone back to Joyce who had been hanging on every word, then sank back into the sofa. "Harriet's dragging Kevin over to my house this evening and wants us to go to Clare's. She said Janet told her the police suspect Roger of murdering Carl Lewis."

"What next?" Alice said. "I suppose I should come, too. What time are they getting to your house?"

"Six," Lillie Mae said. "This is not a good idea."

"Carlos and I will come, too," Joyce said, looking a bit too pleased. "If this is true, Clare will need all our support."

"I doubt if Clare needs the entire community of Mount Penn on her doorstep for support, but this scheme seems to have grown into an avalanche that can't be stopped." Lillie Mae stood up. "I won't be surprised if Pete and Janet don't show up, too."

"I'll call them," Joyce said. "And Hester and Mabel. They'll want to come, too."

"This is not a game," Lillie Mae said. "I'm not comfortable with everyone going to Clare's this evening. We're just asking for trouble."

Alice stood up, looking as anxious as Lillie Mae. They thanked Joyce again for the chocolates and said good-bye.

Once outside, she asked, "Should we call Charlie?"

"Yes," Lillie Mae said, fearing there was disaster ahead. "We have to call Charlie."

* * *

"Janet's not too far off, although I have no idea where she got her information," Charlie said when Lillie Mae called to tell him about the plan to storm Clare's house later that evening. "Roger has lots of questions to answer. I want to find him before somebody else does."

"What do you mean?" Lillie Mae asked, more worried about Roger Ballard then she thought she ever could be.

"That man's hiding from somebody. Either it's us, the police, because he murdered Carl Lewis, or from the people he knows killed Carl Lewis. Either way, we want to find him as soon as we can."

"What do you think about us going to Clare's this evening?" Lillie Mae asked.

"Actually I'm okay with it," Charlie said. "Let's stir things up a bit. Maybe the ruckus will bring Roger out of hiding. I'll be close by, Lillie Mae, so don't worry. I'll check with Captain Alton to make certain he agrees, but I suspect he'll want to come along."

"I'm not sure about this," Lillie Mae said. "So much can go wrong. Clare's fragile, and fragile things break."

"There's a murderer loose in Mount Penn, Lillie Mae. We need to find him and quick. While this may not be the best plan, it is a plan. Nothing's going to stop Harriet Peterson from going to Clare's this evening, so we might as well go, too. You can be the checkpoint from your end, and I'll be the checkpoint from mine."

"I guess you're right, Charlie," Lillie said, accepting the inevitable. "Let's just hope nothing goes too terribly wrong."

*   *   *

"Kevin wants me to take him everywhere, then he sits on his side of the car griping about my driving the entire trip," Harriet complained, walking through Lillie Mae's back door at six o'clock.

Kevin followed reluctantly.

"Stop driving so fast, he says, when I'm barely going thirty-five miles per hour. He is such an old fuddy-duddy. Are you ready to go?" Harriet asked, eying Lillie Mae.

"I'm almost ready," Lillie Mae said. "Let me get my purse." "Alice is going to help Joyce round up the other Thursday morning ladies and any husbands that want to come along, and then they'll all come down together to Clare's later."

"I said six," Harriet said, looking at her watch. "It's time to go, Lillie Mae."

"I'm coming," Lillie Mae said, following Kevin and Harriet out the door.

"Hurry up and get in the car, girl," Harriet commanded. "Let's get this show on the road."

Lillie Mae did as she was told.

The sun, just beginning to drop in the west, threw a splendid orange and pink glow over Clare's house when Harriet pulled into her driveway a few minutes later.

Although Roger's Hummer was nowhere to be seen, there were several other cars parked there.

"Looks like Billy's home," Harriet said, noticing the small black truck in the driveway.

"And Dale Beavers is here, too," Lillie Mae noted.

His red Eddie Bauer Bronco sat haphazardly beside Billy's truck, as if he'd parked in a hurry.

"Maybe we shouldn't bother them, if they have guests." Kevin said, flinching in his seat.

"Nonsense," Harriet interrupted, opening the car door and jumping out. "Besides, it'll be fun to join their party."

"Fun?" Kevin scowled. "You must be insane, woman."

Despite his objection, he took her arm, and they walked toward the house. Lillie Mae stayed just behind them. When they reached the back step, they saw that the door to the kitchen was standing open, and people were scurrying about.

An ear-piercing scream cut through the air.

"That sounds like Clare!" Harriet yelled. She burst into the kitchen, Kevin and Lillie Mae at her heels.

The trio stopped in their tracks, their mouths hanging open in shock, when they took in the scene in front of them. Billy, Clare, and Dale huddled in the center of the room, like a football team discussing their next play. Billy's shirt, spotted with blood, was torn at the sleeve. Dry, crusty blood caked his nose, and his left eye, half-closed from swelling, was a purplish blue color. Clare, her eyes wide with terror, stared up at them. Her lovely black hair, usually in a ponytail, hung loose, damp and matted to her head, as if she had been doing heavy exercise. Blood dotted her shirt, and her jeans. Her knuckles, clinched loosely in a fist, had the same purple hue as Billy's nose. Only Dale Beavers appeared neat and tidy, though certainly not calm.

They turned and looked in horror at the new arrivals. Clare sank to the floor.

"Oh, my God," she sobbed.

Dale dropped to his knees beside her.

"What the hell are you doing here?" Billy gasped.

103

Clare, scrunched on the floor, sobbed. Dale, on his knees beside her, wrapped his arms around her shoulders, ignoring everyone else in the room.

"Get the hell out of here!" Billy yelled, his face so red Lillie Mae was afraid he might pop.

"Billy, stop that talk right now," Clare said through her tears. "You know you don't speak to your elders like that. I don't know why you're here." Looking as confused as she was in disarray, she stared up at Lillie Mae, her face swollen and distorted. "But, now that you are here, you should be the first to know."

"The first to know what?" Lillie Mae asked, grabbing Harriet's hand.

Tears streamed down Clare's face. "My husband is lying dead in our back yard."

"Roger, dead?" Lillie Mae uttered, dropping Harriet's hand, and moving closer to Clare.

Clare looked up at Lillie Mae again, a wry smirk on her face. "Won't the Thursday morning breakfast ladies celebrate that?" she said. "You've all wanted him dead for years."

Dale pulled Clare to him. His eyes darted first to Lillie Mae, then to Harriet, pleading with them to stay in check. Billy was bent over the sink, his head hanging. Lillie Mae thought he must be crying.

"Dead," Harriet whispered, grabbing Kevin's arm to steady herself.

"Where, how, when?" Lillie Mae stuttered, not sure she wanted to know the answers.

"As Clare just said, Roger is lying in the backyard," Dale said. "We found him just a few minutes ago."

Dale darted a look at Clare, then continued. "We were just going to phone the police when you arrived. As you can see, Clare and Billy are very upset. I was trying to calm them down before we made the call." He didn't explain how he came to be there.

Dale looked at Lillie Mae. "If you come and hold Clare's hand, I'll call them now."

"No!" Clare shrieked. "Not yet."

Dale's eyes met Clare's. "We have to call Charlie Warren, Clare. You agreed."

"Why did you come?" she said, glancing up at Lillie Mae though tear-soaked eyes. "We were going to take care of everything. Now it's too late."

"Too late," Harriet echoed.

Kevin squeezed his wife's arm, leaned over and whispered in her ear loud enough for Lillie Mae to hear. "Shut up, Harry. Don't say anything. Pretend you're not here."

Harriet turned her head towards her husband, and then shook his hand off her arm.

Sirens, at first barely audible in the distance, soon blared loudly. Standing close enough to the back door to see out, Lillie Mae watched as three police cars drove into the driveway.

"The police are here," Lillie Mae said.

"Oh no," Clare wailed. "Can it get any worse?"

Kevin and Harriet moved to the far corner of the room, as if trying to disappear into the wall. Lillie Mae walked back from the door and dropped on the floor beside Clare. The room went silent, as the terror in the air took over. Car doors slammed. Clare sank further into the floor, held up only by Lillie Mae's arm. Billy stood as still as a statue by the sink. Only Dale moved. He walked reluctantly, yet steadily, toward the door and opened it.

"Come on in," Dale invited as if hosting the party Harriet had envisioned earlier.

Captain Alton and Sergeant Paul Lowman, a long legged young police officer Lillie Mae had met before, walked into the kitchen. Charlie followed them.

"We were just about to call you," Dale said, his eyes darting to Clare.

"You were going to call us?" Captain Alton said. He walked farther into the kitchen.

The scene that greeted them could not have been more unexpected. Lillie Mae and Clare sat on the floor, staring up at them, like two little girls caught playing hooky from school. Their faces, sullen; their eyes filled with fear. Billy Ballard stood at the sink. When he turned to look at the men, a strange sneer twisted his usually angelic face. Kevin Peterson was standing in the far corner of the room, looking very uncomfortable, and very out of place. Harriet waited at his side, looking like a rabbit ready to jump. Dale Beavers stood in the center of the room, as if he were the master of ceremonies at this bizarre circus.

"What's going on here?" Captain Alton asked.

The room fell silent for what seemed like an eternity. Clare finally answered, her voice surprisingly calm. "My husband is dead. His body is lying in the back yard."

"Roger is dead?" Charlie asked, looking stunned.

"We found Roger's body in the back yard just a few minutes ago," Dale explained. "As I just told Lillie Mae, we were getting ready to call the police when these people showed up."

All three policemen looked at Lillie Mae, Kevin, and Harriet, as if noticing them for the first time.

"Dale was just picking up the phone to call you when we heard the sirens," Clare said.

Clare stopped talking as suddenly as she had started. "Why are you here?" she finally asked. "You couldn't possibly have known about Roger."

It was Captain Alton who answered her question. "We wanted to talk to you, Clare, and we wanted Roger to know we were coming to do that. We thought the sirens might bring him out of hiding. We were putting a show on for Roger's benefit."

Clare let out a horrible sound—a wail or a strange laugh. "What a waste of a perfectly good show," she said through her tears. "Roger's not talking to anybody now, is he?"

Covering her face with her hands, Clare continued to sob. Lillie Mae reached down to comfort her, but Clare pushed her hand away. Harriet moved closer, but remained quiet.

The men in the room just stared.

*　*　*

Clare led the police officers through the kitchen door and into the back yard. Dale followed the small group, staying close to Clare. Billy trailed Dale. Lillie Mae looked at Harriet, then at Kevin. Silently, they agreed to follow everyone else out the door. The uninvited trio stayed far enough back to be out of the way, but close enough to hear what was going on.

Clare walked toward the hiking trail at the far end of the yard. A bundle lay at the edge of the fence, but it was hard to see more than the form. When Clare got to within fifteen feet of the dark mass, she froze as if she could no longer move her feet.

"He's over there," she pointed.

The officers moved in the direction of the body. Dale moved toward Clare. She slumped into his arms and covered her face with her hands. She gently sobbed.

Billy walked ahead and joined the officers. He took hold of Charlie's arm as he looked down at his dead father's body. Harriet and Kevin stayed some twenty feet away watching the scene in front of them as if it was part of a play, and they were the audience. Lillie Mae walked up closer to the body, standing behind Billy.

"It's Roger Ballard—that's for sure," Charlie said. He had moved ahead of the group and was leaning over the body. "I'd recognize that jacket of his anywhere."

Captain Alton stooped to get a better look. He picked up Roger's hand to confirm that he was dead, although the required confirmation was only routine.

Roger was lying face down on the ground in almost the exact position as Carl Lewis had been found earlier that morning. But, it was the back of his head that had been bashed in, not the front as in Carl's case. It was obvious that he had died on the spot, not moved there from somewhere else. Even in the twilight, the officers could see the blood.

Billy turned away, his expression pained but stoic, as he walked toward his mother. When he touched her arm, Clare looked up at him, her face streaked with tears. Dale, who had been hovering over Clare, walked away.

Captain Alton took out his cell phone and made a call to the Antioch police station. Charlie guided Lillie Mae toward Clare and Billy. Harriet and Kevin moved farther into the shadows. Dale had stayed back with Sergeant Lowman.

Captain Alton told the dispatcher to tell whoever came to the crime scene not to use any more sirens. Unfortunately, it was probably too late, since the locals had already been alerted.

"Shall I cordon off this area?" Sergeant Lowman asked Captain Alton.

Captain Alton nodded. "But, don't touch the body," he said, his loud voice uncompromising. "I just got off the phone with the coroner, and he's promised to be here in a few minutes. I also called for backup police officers. Charlie, you take Clare and the others back into the house. I'll be there shortly."

He pointed at Lillie Mae, who was still standing close to Charlie. "And you, my dear, can make them all some coffee."

*   *   *

Charlie ushered Billy and Clare back into the house. Harriet and Kevin followed, maintaining a comfortable distance.

Lillie Mae was following them into the house to make coffee as Captain Alton had demanded, when her cell phone buzzed. Taking it out of her pocket, she distanced herself from the group and whispered, "Lillie Mae here."

"Lillie Mae, it's me, Alice," Alice said, rushing her words. "We heard the sirens and we're on our way to Clare's. Joyce and I have assembled Pete and Janet, Hester and Mabel, and of course, Carlos. We'll be there shortly."

"No!" Lillie Mae said in as loud a voice as her whisper would allow. "Don't come."

But, it was too late. Alice had already hung up the phone. When Lillie Mae tried to call her back, she got an out-of area-message, something that happened too often in Mount Penn. "Not now," Lillie Mae said, slamming her phone into her pants pocket.

When she came through the door, Lillie Mae saw Clare and Billy sitting at the kitchen table with Charlie. She moved to the other side of the big room, to make the coffee. Fortunately, Clare's coffee marker was all ready to go, so she turned it on. Harriet busied herself making a refreshment tray. Lillie Mae took down cups and plates from the kitchen cabinet and carried them to the table. Kevin moved a chair to the far corner of the room, near the entrance to the hallway, where it was dark, and sat down.

"It will take a few minutes to get things in order outside," Charlie said.

Clare looked at Billy, then nodded.

"Is there anything I can get you to make you more comfortable while we wait?" Charlie asked.

Clare shook her head.

Billy, looking at the floor, ignored Charlie's question.

The room fell silent. Only the dripping of the coffee, and the rustle of Lillie Mae and Harriet fixing the refreshments, could be heard.

"Is this really happening?" Clare said a few minutes later, her sweet voice quivering, her eyes glazed over in a stare, as she looked at Charlie. "Please, tell me it's a bad dream."

"I'm afraid it's all too real, Clare," Charlie said. "I am so sorry. Try to settle yourself. I know it's not easy, but you're going to need all the strength you can muster to get through this."

Captain Alton entered the room a few minutes later, Dale at his heels. A bull in a candy shop entered Lillie Mae's mind as Alton's presence took over the room. The coffee finally ready, Lillie Mae carried the pot to the table. Harriet, who had set a tray of muffins and cakes on the table earlier, placed a bowl of fresh strawberries in front of Clare. The room, startling quiet a few minutes earlier, seemed to come back to life.

Charlie stood up and stepped back from the table.

"Dale, please take a seat," he offered, his hand outstretched.

Dale moved the chair close to Clare, but then moved it back when he caught Billy's eye. Billy shifted his gaze to his mother, shook his head, and then dropped it into his hands. Clare continued to stare straight ahead, rigid, as if she were looking at a ghost. Nobody spoke.

"I know this is a terrible time for all for you." Captain Alton began, breaking the silence. "But there are a few things you need to know."

Clare and Billy shifted their glassy stares to the officer. Dale reached out for Clare's hand, but she pulled it back.

"We've confirmed that Roger was murdered, and we're going to need your cooperation to find out who did this terrible thing. That means we have to ask you some questions. The more you help us now, the quicker we can find out who did this."

A wrenching sound interrupted the officer. All eyes turned to Clare, who had slumped over in her chair. Dale moved quickly to catch her arm to keep her from falling on the floor. Billy jumped up, and rushed to his mother. Dale pushed him away.

"Haven't you done enough already?" Dale said, under his breath as his arm encircled Clare's waist, and he lifted her. "She's fainted. I'm going to move her to the sofa in the living room."

Dale carried Clare into the living room and lowered her to the sofa. Billy and Charlie followed Dale into the room, Lillie Mae behind them. Harriet moved to a corner once she was in the room.

Captain Alton stood in the doorway between the living room and the hallway. Kevin stood beside him.

Clare came around a few moments later. She stared up at Billy, ignoring Dale. Her eyes were glazed over and her lips trembling. She looked around the room as if trying to remember where she was and what was going on. Her gaze moved again, and finally rested on Charlie.

"I have to tell you what I've done," she said, trying to sit up. Before she could say anything else, she fell back on the sofa.

*　*　*

Clare, revived from her faint, sipped on the glass of water that Kevin had fetched from the kitchen and handed it to Lillie Mae to give to her. Lillie Mae placed a pillow behind Clare's back, and helped her to sit up, so that she could take the liquid.

Clare handed the glass back to Lillie Mae. "I'm feeling much better now. I'd like to talk."

"Don't say a word, Clare!" Dale urged.

"No!" Billy gasped, staring at his mother with horror. Captain Alton, having kept a cautious eye on the boy since coming into the room, moved closer to him, but did not restrain him in any way.

"Go on," Charlie pressed. "What is it you want to tell us, Clare?"

Clare took hold of Lillie Mae's hand, and settled into the sofa. Avoiding everyone else, she looked straight into Charlie eyes. "It was me," she said, her voice crisp and clear. "I'm responsible for Roger's death."

"No!" Billy said, trying to rush to his mother.

Captain Alton grabbed his arm this time, keeping him from moving.

Too shocked to do anything else, Lillie Mae could only stare at her friend for what seemed like a full minute. Finally, she said in a very low voice that only Clare could hear. "That's impossible, Clare. You couldn't kill anyone."

"I killed Roger Ballard," Clare said, this time in a very low voice, looking directly at Lillie Mae.

A loud knock at the kitchen door caused everyone in the room to turn and stare, including Lillie Mae, who suddenly remembered what was going to happen next.

"Find out who's there, and get rid of them!" Captain Alton said.

Before Charlie could take action, a mob of people rushed into the room. Pete and Janet led the way, Joyce and Carlos were behind them, Alice was holding on to Hester's arm, and Mabel trailed. Sergeant Lowman, a frantic expression on his face, brought up the rear.

Janet spotted Harriet, and waved. "I was hoping you'd be here," she said loudly. I've been worried sick since we heard the sirens. We came as quickly as possible."

"Get these people out of here!" Captain Alton said forcefully.

Charlie seemed at a loss to know how to comply. He opted for the last person in, and grabbed Mabel's arm. The two had never seen eye to eye, and today was no exception.

Mabel shook her arm out of Charlie's grasp, but he grabbed her wrist. "We're not leaving until we find out what's going on here. Regardless of what you think, we still have some rights in this country—one of those being the right to assemble. Now, unhand me, Charlie Warren."

Charlie dropped her wrist, and stepped back. He turned, and glared at Lillie Mae. Lillie Mae glared back, thinking this was as much his fault as hers.

"Clare has confessed to murdering Roger," Lillie Mae said, staring at the newcomers, her mouth gaping.

"That's ridiculous," Alice said.

"Nonsense," Janet said.

"Oh, my God, no," Hester said.

"Not Clare," Joyce said. "Impossible."

"Now listen here, ladies," Captain Alton said, then paused, "and gentlemen. This is a very serious situation. I'm going to take Clare to the Antioch police station with me, now, and I don't want any of you to do anything to stop me. If you won't leave here immediately, and go back to your homes, like I've asked, you must stay out of my way, and let me do my job."

"The crew is here," Charlie said, looking at a text message on his cell phone from Sergeant Lowman, who had gone back outside once he saw he could do nothing to help inside. "Paul wants to know what to do."

"Tell him to take care of them," Captain Alton said. "Clare has confessed to the murder of her husband, Roger, and I need to take

111

her with me to Antioch," he explained again, as if talking to a group of children. "Charlie will stay with you until we leave."

Captain Alton turned to Charlie, who nodded that he understood. "I hold you responsible for keeping these people out of my way."

Charlie nodded again.

"Clare, are you ready to leave?" Captain Alton asked, his voice kinder than Lillie Mae expected.

Still holding on to Lillie Mae's hand, Clare slowly stood up. Lillie Mae passed her hand to Captain Alton, just as a father passes his daughter to her future husband at a wedding. Clare looked around the room and seemed confused to see so many people there.

"I'm sorry," she said, as if she was being a bad hostess. "But, I have to go with the police officer, now."

Everybody talked at once. Only fragments of words could be understood. "No, Clare," seemed to be the most frequent phrase.

"I'm ready to go," Clare said, holding Captain Alton's arm and moving with him toward the entrance to the hallway.

Dale tried to follow, but Charlie held him back.

"We'll call Sid Firth and have him meet you at headquarters," Hester called after Clare.

"Thanks," Clare called as she passed into the hallway. "Please do that."

When Clare was out of the room, Billy dropped to the sofa and slumped into a ball. Dale walked over to him and put his hand on his back, but Billy brushed it away.

"What are we going to do?" Joyce asked, as the door shut on their friend.

The Thursday morning ladies made a circle in the middle of the room, their arms linked. The men stood back from them, as if attempting to protect them from the next disaster.

"That's easy," Lillie Mae answered, ignoring Clare's confession. "We're going to find out who really killed Roger Ballard."

11

"Are all the Thursday morning ladies coming today?" Lillie Mae asked, leaning down to pet Alfred who had greeted her with a great deal of enthusiasm when Alice opened the door at nine the next morning.

"Everybody but Margaret," Alice said. "She actually answered the phone when I called earlier to let her know we were meeting today. She said she'd had a bad night and wasn't up to all the excitement, but did want to participate if she could. I thought Hester might want to stop over later, and fill her in on what we're doing."

"Good idea," Lillie Mae said. "Maybe I'll go with her. I'd like to get to know Margaret better."

A tap on the door and a yelp from Alfred announced more arrivals. Before long, Alice's living room was bursting with activity. Joyce, Janet, Harriet, Hester, and Mabel drank coffee and munched on cake. With so much chatting going on, the room sounded like the Mount Penn Community Church on a Sunday morning before the services began.

Lillie Mae took control. "You all know why we're here," she said in a booming voice that silenced the other conversations. "We're going to get Clare out of this mess she seems to have gotten herself into."

Heads bobbed. Alfred yelped. "Hush," Alice said to the errant pup, her index finger at her lip.

"What can we really do?" Mabel asked.

"Good question, Mabel. There's a lot we can do." Lillie Mae glanced around at the eager faces staring up at her. "But we need a plan. Let's brainstorm. Come up with some ideas. Then we'll make assignments, and get busy."

"It's worth a try," Mabel said.

"Ok," Lillie Mae said. "Let's go around the room. Everyone has to come up with an idea. Mabel you write them down. Alice, you go first."

"Let me think a minute." Alice said. "Wait! I've got one. Why don't we interview each other?"

Hester's jaw dropped.

"Do you think one of us murdered Roger Ballard or Carl Lewis?"

"No, of course not," Alice answered quickly. "But we may know something we don't know we know. Charlie Warren tells us that all the time. Talking it out might lead to a clue hidden deep down in the recesses of our minds."

Alice allowed that thought to make the rounds, then she said with a small grin, "And besides, we shouldn't eliminate any suspects yet."

"It is a good idea." Lillie Mae nodded to Mabel who was already writing the suggestion down. "Now you, Hester."

"Oh, dear," Hester said. "I can't think of a thing."

"I have an idea, Mother," Mabel said. "You and I can talk to Jerry Foster's family. Ask them questions. We should anyway because of everything that's going on with Jerry and Patrick."

Hester nodded, and Mabel added the idea to the list.

Ideas spewed out at a rapid pace from that point. Interviewing Dale Beavers and Billy Ballard were at the top of the list. Talking to Charlie Warren and Sid Firth came in second and third. Only Lillie Mae was interested in going to the jail to talk to Clare.

"We must keep copious notes," Alice said, her bright blue eyes aglow.

"Let's make a sample set of questions so we have somewhere to start," Joyce suggested. "I'd be willing to take a stab at it."

"I want to help, too," Janet blurted.

"Everybody gets to help," Lillie Mae said.

Janet looked pleased.

"The list is a good idea," Lillie Mae continued in a more formal voice. "But don't be limited by it. Each interview is personal."

Everyone nodded agreement.

"Any more suggestions?" Lillie Mae asked, scanning the paper that Mabel handed to her.

The room was quiet.

"Then we all know what we need to do, right!" Lillie Mae asked in her best cheerleader voice.

"Yes!" the ladies shouted in unison.

Waking with a start, Alfred joined in the cheer with a yelp. Alice held him a little tighter as the pep session continued.

"We all have what we need to do it, right?" Lillie Mae cheered.

"Yes!" the women answered, this time a little louder.

"We all know why we're doing this and believe in the cause?" Harriet said.

"Yes, yes, yes!" the ladies chanted.

Alfred yelped again, his tail wagging rapidly, brushing against Alice's chest.

"Then let's get started," Lillie Mae said, taking hold of Hester's hand and pulling her up.

The rest of the ladies stood, grabbed hands, and formed a circle.

"Yes, yes, yes!" they cheered.

*   *   *

"Hester, Lillie Mae, come in," Sam said, swinging the door open almost as soon as the ladies stepped onto the back porch. "Margaret's waiting for you in the living room."

Sam took the plate of muffins from Hester and set them on the kitchen counter.

"Thursday morning breakfast club detectives," he chuckled.

"How is Margaret today?" Hester asked, casting a disapproving glance towards Lillie Mae who suspected she was none too pleased by Sam's reaction to their project.

"This little adventure has done her a world of good, let me tell you," Sam said, gesturing them into the living room. "Come see for yourself."

"It's good of you to come," Margaret said, looking surprisingly strong and hearty from her seat on the sofa. It was hard to tell whether she had lost any more weight from her recent ordeal, but Lillie Mae didn't think so. Her porcelain skin glowed this morning.

"So much excitement," Margaret bubbled. "Thanks for the casseroles and sweets you've brought. They have been delicious."

A huge grin spread across Sam's face. "Hester brought us a lovely plate of muffins this morning, dear," he said, stepping toward the kitchen. "I'll bring them in with some coffee in just a minute."

"You are all so kind to us," Margaret said, her eyes watering. "We do love living here in Mount Penn."

"How are you feeling, dear?" Lillie Mae asked, genuinely interested.

"I have my good days and bad," Margaret said, motioning to Hester to join her on the sofa. "But the doctor told me I'm making excellent progress. He wants me to get out more. Be part of the community. And you're giving me that chance. Tell me what I can do to help Clare."

Hester sat down beside Margaret on the white leather sofa. Lillie Mae chose the chair opposite, so she could observe. Thinking Margaret a little too eager, she quickly excused her, realizing none of what had happened was real to her. She had not seen Clare's confession.

"Sam's told you about all the excitement we've had here on the mountain the last couple of days?" Hester asked, taking a notepad and pen out of her purse.

"Oh, my goodness, yes." Margaret rolled her eyes and gave a slight cough. "I just can't believe such terrible things have happened here in Mount Penn. Two men murdered and Clare Ballard in jail. Unbelievable."

"But, you gals are going to prove her innocent," Sam said from the kitchen.

"We are," Hester said.

"Hester's asking all the questions today," Lillie Mae said. "I'm just here to observe."

"You know I never liked that Roger Ballard," Margaret said. "And Sam didn't like him either. There was something suspicious about him."

Sam came back into the room carrying a tray with three cups of coffee smiling in his absentminded way. "Milk, sugar?" he asked, putting the tray down on the coffee table.

"Did you know Roger Ballard well?" Hester asked, surprised at Margaret's admission.

"Oh no," Margaret said. "I didn't know him at all. It was just a feeling I had."

"I knew who Roger was," Sam said, bustling around the coffee table ordering the cups. "I never liked him. Too full of himself for me."

"I didn't know the other man who was murdered at all," Margaret said. "Carl Lewis, you said his name was. Did you know him, Hester?"

"I knew who he was, of course." Hester said, smiling a thank you to Sam and picking up a sugar spoon. "He was not a good man, though. But even so, he didn't deserve to die the way he did."

"No one deserves to be murdered," Margaret said. "But I guess it's better that a bad man dies than a good one."

Margaret caught Sam's eye. "The muffins," she said.

"Of course," Sam said, hurrying out of the room.

"What can I do to help Clare?" Margaret asked, turning her attention back to Hester. "I won't be able to leave the house, you know. Not for a couple of days."

"Actually, there's lots you can do," Hester said. "We've come up with a plan, you see, to gather information by talking to our friends and neighbors. It should be easy for us, since we all love to talk."

"Did you hear that Sam?" Margaret giggled as Sam walked back into the room carrying the plate of muffins. "Hester says I'm to be a Thursday morning detective."

"Wonderful news," Sam said, still smiling. "Can I help too?"

"Maybe," Hester hesitated; then she checked with Lillie Mae who raised an eyebrow. The ladies had not talked about excluding the men in their scheme, but no one had suggested they be included either.

"When we ask you questions over the next couple of days, talk to us," Hester said to Sam. "Telling us what you remember will be the best help."

Lillie Mae was proud of how quickly Hester thought on her feet. Quite the good little detective.

"Of course, I'll cooperate," Sam said. "But, you know Margaret and I were gone when most of the excitement happened."

"I can't wait to get started," Margaret interrupted, her cheeks flushed. "Tell me what to do, Hester."

Hester spent the next several minutes sharing the plan with Margaret while Sam poured more coffee, than tidied up the table. When Hester had pulled the page with the interview matrix Alice and Harriet had drawn out of her notebook, and handed it to Margaret, Sam sat down beside her to look over her shoulder."

"According to this matrix, I need to talk to Lillie Mae, Alice, and you from the breakfast club," Margaret said, glancing up at Hester.

"And Pete and Carlos, if you get the chance."

"She can ask me questions, too," Sam said, winking at Hester.

"You can cross me and Lillie Mae off your list just by asking us some of the sample questions I have right here with me. What do you think?"

"When do I begin?" Margaret asked, her eyes twinkling.

Hester reviewed with Margaret the set of starter questions. "You have to keep detailed notes," Hester said, her voice firm.

"Get me a writing tablet," Margaret said to Sam. "I have some questions to ask these two ladies."

*   *   *

Lillie Mae was walking back to her house when she heard her name called. Turning around, she saw Dale Beavers coming toward her dressed in an old pair of jeans and a wrinkled tee shirt.

That boy had a bad night, she thought.

"I have to talk to you," Dale said, running to catch up to her. "It's about Billy."

"Billy?" Lillie Mae said, stopping to wait for Dale. "Is he all right?"

"No, Lillie Mae, he's not all right. He's devastated. His father's dead, and his mother's in jail. But he didn't do himself any harm, if that's what you're asking."

"Are you worried about that?"

"Not really, but anything's possible. So I stopped by his house this morning to check on him. I wasn't sure he'd let me in, since he's so angry with me, but he did."

"Why is he angry with you?" Lillie Mae asked.

"He blames me for his father's death, " Dale said, his voice hard. "He thinks his mother killed his father because she and I are having an affair."

"That's ridiculous," Lillie Mae said. "Isn't it?"

"I told him he was wrong about everything," Dale said, close to tears. "His mother and I are just friends, and we are not having an affair. Besides, as far as I knew, his father didn't even know we were friends. He was much too busy with his own life to give much attention to what Clare was doing."

118

"Did Billy believe you?"

"I doubt it. Billy is not in any state to change his mind. What's worse is Billy refuses to talk to his mother."

"We have to do something about that," Lillie Mae said. "Clare needs that boy right now more than anything."

"That's what I told him, too. But he believes his mother killed his father."

"How could he possibly believe that?" Lillie Mae was genuinely astonished.

"Because she confessed to doing it," Dale said, as if the answer was obvious. "My Mom doesn't lie, is what he told me."

"What did you say to that?" Lillie Mae asked.

"I told him the truth. That Clare lied for the one and only reason she would lie. To protect him."

"And?"

"He went berserk. Said he'd done nothing wrong and didn't need protection."

"What did you say to that?"

"That the last time his mother had seen him, he was covered with blood. That was right before we found Roger's body. What do you expect her to think, I asked him."

Lillie Mae nodded but kept walking. "Billy has to be going crazy with worry."

"I asked him where the blood came from," Dale said.

"That's a big question," Lillie Mae said, "What was his answer?"

"He said it was none of my damn business what he had been doing, then quickly turned the tables on me. Asked if it wasn't me his mother was protecting. His fist was clinched so tight, I was sure he was going to take a punch at me, but he didn't. Instead, he broke down," Dale said, his own eyes filling with tears. "I'm not sure which was worse, Lillie Mae."

"Did he calm down?" Lillie Mae said.

"He turned away from me and just stood there silent for a few moments. Then, in a very low voice, he said he didn't know what to think or do anymore. My dad is dead, he said, in a way that broke my heart."

"What do you mean in a way that broke your heart?" she asked, her feelings clumped in her stomach.

119

"Like he loved him," Dale said.

"Of course, Billy loves his father. His loves his mother, too, and she's the one that's still alive."

"I asked him again to go see his mother," Dale said. "He finally agreed, but he doesn't want to go alone. I'd go with him but he wants none of that. Will you go with him, Lillie Mae?"

"Of course, I'll go with him. Should I call him now?"

"Yes, and there's one other thing."

"What's that?" Lillie Mae asked, raising her eyebrows.

"It's what Billy said just as I was about to leave."

'Yes," Lillie Mae said, not sure she wanted to know.

"What if she did kill my father," he said. Dale's eyes filled with fear. "What if Clare did kill Roger, Lillie Mae? What are we going to do?"

*　　*　　*

"Sid, it's Lillie Mae Harris here."

"I was just going to call you," Sid said.

"Me?" Lillie Mae asked. "Why were you going to call me?"

"You go first, dear, since you made the call."

"It's Billy," Lillie Mae said. "He's agreed to come and see Clare. Can you get him and me a pass? He's uncomfortable going alone, and I've agreed to go with him. I've just gotten off the telephone with him."

"This is good news. Clare refuses to tell me what happened last night. That's why I was going to call you. Thought if anyone could talk sense into her, it would be you. Let's hope Billy can convince her to speak to me. When do you want to come and see her?"

"This afternoon?" Lillie Mae asked.

"Make it tomorrow morning," Sid said. "I can get a pass for Billy easy enough. It's a pass for you that I'm going to have to work on. But I'll get you one, don't worry."

"Call me when you have the passes, and I'll let Billy know," Lillie Mae said. "Anything new going on with Clare? If I'm going to be there when Billy talks to her, I should know."

"Nothing new that I know. As I said before, she won't talk to me. Watching that beautiful young woman sitting across from me in that drab visitor's room at the Antioch jail, tears in her eyes, hands clasped on her lap, refusing to tell me what happened—it's ripping me apart."

120

"This is all so awful," Lillie Mae said. "We've got to do something to help her."

"She keeps saying she killed Roger." Sid paused to swallow. "I don't believe it, of course, and I've said that to her, but she shakes her head like it's me who doesn't understand. Honestly, Lillie Mae, I don't know what to do next. Maybe Billy can talk some sense into her."

"I can't imagine what's going through that woman's mind," Lillie Mae said.

"I asked her if she murdered Carl Lewis, too?"

"What did she say to that?"

"She was surprised by the question. Said she thought the police believed that Roger had killed Carl Lewis. Roger killed Carl, and I killed Roger, was how she put it."

"She has an answer for everything," Lillie Mae said.

"I told her the police want to solve these crimes in record time. Since you've confessed to killing Roger, you might as well be Carl's murderer, too. It would make it all very simple for them. I thought that would upset her but she said it didn't matter. If she had to go to jail, it might as well be for two murders as one."

Lillie Mae shook her head. "I can't believe this."

"Since rational talk wasn't doing any good, I tried to scare her. I was really mad at this point, you see. So I screamed at her. 'You've spent one night in jail,' I said. 'Do you want to spend the rest of your life behind bars? And believe me, lady, it won't be a place like this. This is like the fucking Waldorf Astoria compared to where you'll be going.' Do you know what her answer was, Lillie Mae?"

"What?" Lillie Mae asked, surprised at Sid's choice of words. "Please don't use foul language around me. I don't deserve that." After taking a deep breath, her voice softened and she continued, "You did what you had to do, Sid."

"I pleaded with her. I asked why she was being so stubborn, refusing to let me help her at all. Please, Clare, I begged."

"Did that work?"

"No," Sid said, sighing. "She said she'd been in a jail her entire life and saw no reason why the rest of her life should be any different."

"That girl sounds depressed to me."

121

"Of course, she is depressed, Lillie Mae. Wouldn't you be under the circumstances?"

"I guess so."

"So, I tried a different tactic. I asked her who she thought killed Roger. She refused to answer. So I asked her what happens if she is wrong about who she thinks did it. What if Billy or whoever she's protecting had nothing to do with the murder? What if someone else committed the crime? What if Roger had nothing to do with Carl Lewis' murder and that whoever murdered Carl also murdered Roger? What then? Do you want a murderer to go free because of you?"

"That sounds good to me," Lillie Mae said. "What did she say to that?"

"She said she killed Roger. Said she'd killed him in many little ways for many years, and should be punished."

"Get those passes, Sid. Billy and I need to talk to that woman as soon as we can."

12

"Now who's that," Lillie Mae said to herself, hearing the knock at the door just as she sat down at her computer to work on an article for the *Antioch Gazette* on spring flower arrangements. She was still waiting for Sid to call back about the passes for her and Billy to visit Clare. Checking out the front curtain, she saw Janet standing on the porch, her head turned back toward the street.

"Come in and have a cup of coffee, Janet," Lillie Mae said, glancing at her watch. It was just after ten o'clock in the morning, and it already felt like she had been through a full day. "But, I only have a half hour."

"I'd love a cup of coffee, Lillie Mae," Janet said, nodding as if agreeing to the time restriction. "I'm here to interview you. Ask you questions about discovering Carl Lewis' body and all. Oh, Lillie Mae—you're my first interview, and I'm so excited."

"Yes, of course you are."

Janet never failed to brighten her spirits. Dressed in a bright coral pants suit, she waddled into the house, her breath labored as she moved to the kitchen and sat down at the breakfast table. Rummaging through her huge coral purse, she brought out a pencil and pad. Lillie Mae placed a cup of coffee and a muffin in front of her and then sat down.

"I can't eat the muffin," Janet said, adding a third teaspoon of sugar to her coffee. "Do you have any cream?"

Lillie Mae took a carton of half-and-half out of the refrigerator.

"I'm on a diet you know," Janet reminded Lillie Mae. "I'm not losing as much weight as I thought I would, but I do think I'm a little slimmer."

Lillie Mae handed the carton to Janet and sat down again, thinking that she really looked no different than she had before the diet.

"Okay, fire away," Lillie Mae said, when Janet finished stirring her coffee and had taken a leisurely sip. "Ask me whatever you'd like."

Janet took her reading specs out of her purse and put them on. Black frames with small red and blue hearts around the rim, her eyes now enlarged by the lens, it took all Lillie Mae's resolve not to laugh.

"We all know that you discovered Carl Lewis' body," Janet read from the pad of paper she had brought. "Can you tell me if there were any unusual circumstances around that event?" Looking up at Lillie Mae, she had a proud smile on her lips.

"Everything was unusual that morning." Lillie Mae burst into laughter. "I found a dead body, for goodness sake."

"Oh, yes, of course." Janet said. "That would be unusual now wouldn't it?" She repositioned herself in the seat and looked at the muffin. "But think, Lillie Mae. Was there anything else that was unusual? You know," she added, looking very serious. "not the way it should have been."

Lillie Mae sat back in her chair to consider the perfectly good question.

"Not really. I did hear some rustling in the trees, but I assumed it was a deer or some other animal. And besides that's not really unusual. I hear noises all the time when I'm walking early in the morning. With no one else around the sounds can be amplified, you know, and occasionally I get a little jumpy. But it was a normal morning. I can't think of anything out of the ordinary."

Janet unconsciously picked up the muffin and took a bite. "How did you discover the body?"

"I heard a bird call, and I wanted to check it out since I didn't recognize the sound. I had brought my binoculars with me, as I usually do on my walks, and I was taking them out of their case when I saw something lying on the ground about twenty yards away from where I was standing. I thought at first it might be a hiker sleeping or maybe a dead animal, but to tell you the truth it upset me. When I looked at it again through the binoculars, I could see it was definitely human.

"When it still didn't move after a couple of minutes, I got spooked. That's when I started to run. As I was making my way up the trail, I fell down and scraped my leg, but I was so scared at that point, I don't think I felt a thing. You know the rest."

"Who do you think killed Carl Lewis?" Janet asked.

Lillie Mae sat very still for a few moments. "I don't have a clue," she finally answered. "Everything points to Roger Ballard, but since Roger's been murdered, we certainly can't be sure. Why? Why do you ask?"

"Pete thinks it has something to do with drugs."

Lillie Mae looked down at Janet's plate and noticed that the muffin was gone. "He could be right—would you like another cup of coffee and muffin?"

"Oh, yes." Janet said, her diet apparently forgotten. Lillie Mae filled her friend's cup and then poured herself a second cup of coffee, set a plate of muffins on the table, and settled in her chair again to continue the interview.

*   *   *

"We're here to see my mother, Clare Ballard," Billy told the woman sitting behind the desk in the gated area of the Antioch police station. The middle-aged lady looked up at Billy, a bored expression on her face.

Lillie Mae stepped up behind Billy and showed the woman the pass Sid had given her that morning.

"Fill out these forms," she said. "Bring them back when you're done."

Billy and Lillie Mae carried the papers over to the table on the far side of the room.

"This is all too much, Lillie Mae. Mother in a place like this."

"Calm down, Billy," Lillie Mae said, seeing his hand shake. "Try to get yourself under control. Take things step by step. Let's get these forms done first."

When they finished the paperwork, they carried the forms back to the woman at the desk and watched as she scanned the pages and put them into a wire basket.

"I need your picture IDs," she said.

Billy took his drivers license out of his pocket and handed it to her. She glanced at the picture and then at Billy, handed the license back, and told him to go take a seat in the front area where someone would call him. She repeated the process with Lillie Mae.

Billy took a seat as far away as he could from the two other people sitting in the room and stared ahead at the gray wall. Lillie Mae sat beside him. Time crept by at a snail's pace as they

125

watched the tall, thin, attendant come into the room, call a name, and then lead someone out of the room. Finally, it was their turn.

"Billy Ballard," the man called. "You're here to visit Mrs. Clare Ballard?"

"Yes. She's my mother."

"Lillie Mae Harris," the man called. "You're also here to visit Mrs. Clare Ballard?"

"I am," she said.

"Follow me," he said.

Lillie Mae looked around the drab room where the attendant led them and spotted Clare sitting at a small table.

Lillie Mae thought she had never seen Clare looking so forlorn or so old. As she approached, she saw some light come into Clare's eyes and a small, wan smile appear on her lips when she looked at her son.

"Billy, you came—thank you," Clare said, her eyes brightening even more. "Lillie Mae," she nodded.

Billy took a seat across from his Mother. Lillie Mae sat down beside him, feeling uncomfortable but knowing Billy wouldn't be here if she hadn't agreed to come along. But, this was their time and she knew to respect that.

"How could you, Mother? How could you do this to yourself?"

"I'm so sorry about so many things, Billy. If I could make it different, I would. You must be going through hell."

"Dad's in the morgue," he said. "They won't let me see him, and they won't release his body. I don't know what to do."

"Sid Firth will help."

"Why did you confess to killing Dad?" He sounded like a small boy. "I know you didn't do it. I know you couldn't have done it."

"I had to." Clare's voice was surprisingly calm.

"Talk to Sid," Billy pleaded. "Tell him everything you know. Tell him exactly what happened. He wants to help you, but he can't if you won't talk to him."

Clare kept looking at her son as if she were exploring every inch of his face. She had the same wan smile on her lips. But she didn't speak.

Billy leaned across the table, reaching his hands out toward her.

"You know the ladies of Mount Penn are all pretending to be detectives," he said, sneaking a look at Lillie Mae. "They're trying

126

to find Dad's and Carl Lewis' murderer. You're lucky to have so many friends who believe you're innocent. Please Mother, help them to help you."

"I'm doing what's best." Clare said, her eyes meeting Billy's.

"No, you're not!" Billy said, raising his voice. "You're being selfish."

"Selfish?" Clare looked as if she'd been slapped.

Lillie Mae bit her tongue to stay quiet.

"Yes, selfish. Someone murdered Dad and Carl Lewis, and that person is still on the loose in Mount Penn. You're hampering the investigation, Mother, by refusing to talk. How would you feel if someone else got murdered?"

Clare looked up at her son, horror in her eyes. "But I did kill your father, Billy. I am the murderer."

*   *   *

Lillie Mae waited outside the Mount Penn Community Church for Dale Beavers to come out. She heard him playing the organ, and didn't want to interrupt him with her news. She didn't have long to wait. Ten minutes later, the music stopped, and Dale came out the door.

"I'm sorry to bother you, Dale, but this is urgent," Lillie Mae said, taking his arm and moving with him toward her car. "Billy and I were just at the jail visiting Clare. There are things you need to know."

"Is she all right?" He turned to face Lillie Mae. "I want to visit her, but I'm not family, so I can't get in."

"I'm almost sure Sid Firth will get you a pass if he thinks you'll cooperate," Lillie Mae said.

"What do you want me to do?" Dale asked. "I'll do anything to help."

"Talk to Clare. See if she'll tell you who she's protecting," Lillie Mae said, looking him straight in the eye. "It's not you she's protecting, is it?"

"I did not murder Roger Ballard, if that's what you came to find out," Dale said, sounding more sad than angry. "There's been many a time I wished he was dead. But, I didn't murder him, Lillie Mae. And Clare knows I didn't murder him. It's not me she's protecting."

"Is it Billy?" Lillie Mae asked.

127

"I honestly don't know," Dale said. "When I stopped by Clare's place yesterday evening to see if she was all right, I found Billy and Clare arguing in the kitchen. Billy looked like he'd been in a fight. His nose was covered with blood, and his eye was swollen. Clare didn't look much better. Her knuckles were bruised and she had spots of blood on her shirt."

"What did you do?" Lillie Mae asked, understanding Dale's certain shock.

"I asked Clare to tell me what was going on, but she and Billy just looked at each other. The next thing I knew, she was screaming. I tried to calm her, but she pushed me away. Sobbing, she said she and Roger had been fighting in the back yard, and she hit him with a stick. Scared that he would come after her, she dropped the stick and ran up to the house. But he didn't follow her, and she was worried she had hit him harder than she thought. She asked me to go outside with her to check on him. I agreed. Billy, who had not uttered a word since I had arrived, followed us. That's when we found Roger lying in the back yard, dead."

Lillie Mae stared, too shocked to speak.

Dale's hands trembled. Taking a deep breath, he continued. "Clare became hysterical. She fell on Roger's body and kept yelling, no. It took awhile, but I finally got her back into the house. Billy helped. We were going to call the police. Really we were. We had only been in the house a couple of minutes when you showed up with Harriet and Kevin. You know the rest."

"Do you believe Clare murdered Roger?" Lillie Mae asked.

Dale stared at her, but his eyes were blank.

"I don't think Clare is capable of murder, certainly not under normal circumstance," he said. "But, I don't know if what happened that night was normal or whether something inexplicable happened, and Clare flipped. Or she might have been defending herself. I wish I did know. She's told me no more than she's told you." Dale dropped his head, and Lillie Mae felt him catch a sob. "I'm being haunted night and day by the thought that Clare is all alone in a jail cell. If she's convicted of murder, her future will be even worse. She's a good woman, Lillie Mae. She doesn't deserve any of this."

"You need to keep the faith, Dale. I still believe Clare is innocent, and I'm going to do what I can to prove it." Lillie Mae put her arm around Dale's shoulder. "But you need to do what you can do, too. Please talk to her. Convince her that she has to talk to Sid. He's got to know what happened that night, before the police find out."

"Get me a pass, and I'll go and see her. We are friends, and she knows how much I care about her, but I don't know if she'll talk to me."

Dale used the back of his hand to wipe the tears away.

"Do you want me to drive you home?" Lillie Mae asked.

"No, thank you," Dale said. "I'll walk. I need time to think."

"I'll let you know when I get the pass," Lillie Mae said, her heart going out to the young man. "If you can't get Clare to talk to Sid, you're going to have to tell him what you just told me."

Lillie Mae got into her car and closed the door. When she looked over her shoulder at Dale, he was already walking away.

13

"You're up and about early this morning," Hester said, when she opened the door to Lillie Mae.

"Couldn't sleep," Lillie Mae said, handing Hester a plate of biscuits. "So I baked. Care to give me a cup of coffee and a chat?"

"Sure," Hester said. "You look as if you need a pick-me-up." Hester glanced at the clock on the kitchen wall. "I have plenty since church was canceled today. Sit down for a spell."

"I'm crazy with worry," Lillie Mae said. "What are we going to do, Hester? Clare is digging herself into a deeper and deeper hole. One she may not be able to get out of. I want to help, but I can't do it all. Clare has got to come to her senses."

"You have to let Sid and Charlie do their jobs, Lillie Mae. You're taking on too much responsibility in all this. Stop interfering."

Lillie Mae looked at her friend sideways and wondered if she was about to interfere again. "There's been something nagging at me, Hester."

"What's that, dear?"

"Where did you go the evening Carl Lewis was killed?"

Hester poured Lillie Mae a cup of coffee. "It's not where I went that I didn't want to talk about," Hester said, carrying the full cup of coffee back to the table and setting it front of Lillie Mae. "It was what I saw when I got there that I chose to keep to myself."

Lillie Mae braced herself for the worst.

"I walked up to the church. It was so lovely outside. Crisp and cool just how I like it. I had been through so much that day, you see, I just wanted some quiet time to myself in a place where I felt safe." She rolled her eyes up as if to the heavens. "But comfort was the last thing I got, let me tell you."

"Why, what happened?"

"It's not what, it's who," Hester said. "Clare Ballard and Dale Beavers, that's who."

"Clare and Dale?"

"They were snuggling each other is what they were doing," Hester said. "In church, yet."

"Maybe he was just comforting her," Lillie Mae said, remembering she had seen them at the same place earlier that day.

"Seriously, Lillie Mae, I don't know what to think. But, whatever those two were doing they shouldn't have been doing it in church. That's all I want to say about the matter."

The sound of a car door slamming interrupted the ladies.

"Goodness me, it's Mabel," Hester said, after walking over to the back door window to check. "I wonder what she wants this morning."

"She's not still staying with you?" Lillie Mae asked.

"No, she and Patrick went back to their own house yesterday."

Mabel came through the door a moment later. "Lillie Mae," Mabel said, looking surprised. "You're up and out early."

Mabel, normally seen in business attire or pressed jeans, was wearing a sweat suit and sneakers with no makeup, her curly hair flying in several directions.

"You OK?" Lillie Mae asked. "You look as worse for wear as I do."

"I haven't slept much since getting back to Mount Penn. None at all when I was here with Mother. I've taken time off from work, but the extra free time isn't helping any. I feel like I'm losing my mind."

"Do you want to talk to your mother alone?" Lillie Mae asked. "I can leave."

"Stay," she said. "You're going to find out soon enough what I'm going to tell Mother. It's probably best you hear it from me rather than someone else."

"What is it, Mabel?" Hester asked, her hand resting on her daughter's arm. "I knew something was wrong, but I didn't feel comfortable asking you what it was."

"Of course, something's wrong, Mother," Mabel lashed out, tears forming in her eyes. "Patrick's been arraigned for transporting drugs, and Roger Ballard's been murdered."

"Why are you so upset about Roger Ballard?" Hester looked genuinely surprised. "If Clare wasn't in so much trouble, I'd say goodbye to bad rubbish."

131

"There's something you need to know about me and Roger," Mabel said, casting a brief glance at Lillie Mae. "Roger and I were friends."

"Friends," Hester echoed. "Since when has Roger Ballard been a friend of yours?"

"You know we were in school together. Clare, Roger, and I were pals, even though he was a senior when Clare and I were freshmen. Clare was Roger's girlfriend, but Roger and I were friends, too. We used to talk, you see, and, we never really stopped."

"Even when you were married?" Hester asked.

Mabel turned to Lillie Mae and shook her head, as if warning her to stay quiet.

"Yes." Mabel lowered her head. "Roger helped me through many a bad time."

"Roger Ballard?" Hester's mouth hung open. "I can't believe Roger ever helped anybody through anything."

"Roger wasn't as bad as his reputation." A hint of a smile formed through Mabel's tears. "He was just a nice guy to me."

"Did you have an affair with him?" Hester's hands were folded in front of her as if praying the answer was no.

Mabel looked squarely at her mother. "Roger was there when I went through the divorce. You know how bad it was for me at the time. He and Clare were having problems then, too, and we comforted each other. It was never more than that, and it was short-lived. Our friendship meant more to us than a love affair."

"I can't believe this." Hester's face had gone white, and her hands shook. "My own daughter and Roger Ballard. If you hadn't told me with your own lips, I never would have believed it."

"There's more," Mabel said.

"More?" Hester asked.

"The night before he was murdered, I called Roger. He agreed to meet me."

"You called Roger Ballard?" Hester's eyes were as wide as saucers.

"You know I was out looking for Patrick, Mother. I even drove up to Carl Lewis' place. When I couldn't find him, I called Roger, and he actually answered his phone. He was surprised to hear from me but agreed to meet at the old hideout close to High Mount."

"He must have just murdered Carl Lewis," Hester wailed.

"Roger did not murder Carl Lewis. And he did not set up Patrick either. Patrick had just left, right before I got there. I'm lucky we didn't run into each other. Roger was a mess, anxious and on edge, but not angry with Patrick, or me, or anybody. He convinced me he had nothing to do with the drugs or with setting up Patrick and Jerry. I believed him."

"How do you know he was telling the truth?" Hester asked.

"Because Roger was scared, Mother—really scared." Mabel stood up and began pacing. "He was the one who found Carl Lewis dead earlier. Way before he talked to Patrick. It was Roger who moved Carl's body from the hideout at High Mount to the trail."

"Roger moved Carl Lewis' body?" Lillie Mae said, pacing the floor with Mabel. "Why did he do that?"

"He was protecting Patrick. It's well known that the hideout was one of Patrick's favorite places to hang out," Mabel said, turning to Lillie Mae. "Roger thought Patrick was being set up again. He begged me that if something happened to him to tell Clare and Billy he was innocent of killing Carl Lewis."

"But you said nothing to the police," Lillie Mae said.

Mabel hung her head. "I know," she said. "I didn't want the police to know my role in all this. We'd been warned by Charlie Warren what would happen if we didn't listen to him and stay out of trouble."

"Did Roger know who murdered Carl Lewis?" Lillie Mae asked.

"Not for sure," Mabel said. "But, he had an idea."

"Who did he say the murderer might be?" Hester blurted.

Mabel stared at her mother for a long moment. "He didn't tell me," she said, then lowered her voice. "I wish he had."

"I can't believe any of this is happening," Hester said.

Mabel stopped pacing and put her arm around her mother's shoulder. "I'm so sorry to drag you into all of this, Mother," she said."

"You have to call Charlie Warren right away," Lillie Mae said, reaching for Hester's phone. "Or I will."

Mabel nodded.

Lillie Mae punched in the number and handed her the phone.

*　　*　　*

133

Lillie Mae had walked outside to look at her garden and was taking in a deep breath of the fresh mountain air when she noticed Alice walking her way.

"Where are you off to this afternoon?" Lillie Mae asked, stooping to pull a lone weed out of the garden.

"I'm going to see Joyce and Carlos," Alice said. "Want to come along?"

"Why not," Lillie Mae said. "I'm not getting anything else done today."

"Are you sure this is a good time for a visit," Alice asked Joyce when she opened the door to the two ladies a couple of minutes later.

"Absolutely," Joyce said. "Carlos and I are looking forward to a chat with our two favorite lady friends."

From behind his wife, Carlos moved forward to give Alice, then Lillie Mae, a welcome hug.

"So good to see you," he said, stepping back. "It's been too long."

Alice snickered. "It's not been that long, but it's good to see you, too, Carlos."

Joyce led them into the living room. "I have some coffee ready. Please come and sit for awhile."

Joyce pointed Alice and Lillie Mae to a large vintage French sofa. Carlos sat opposite the women, an antique marble coffee table separating them.

"I just love this room." Alice said. "It is so inviting, and you have a wonderful view of the valley from this window. Your view is second only to Lillie Mae's in Mount Penn."

Lillie Mae accepted a cup of espresso from Joyce who had carried an Art Deco tray into the room with four elegant porcelain cups and a plate of biscotti. Lillie Mae suspected the furnishings and accessories were real and mentally tallied the tag. Impressive, she thought.

"Are you enjoying living here in Mount Penn full time?" Alice asked, sipping the bitter coffee and turning up her nose.

Carlos, who had also taken a cup of espresso from Joyce, held his cup in a surprisingly dainty way, his right pinky in the air.

"Joyce and I love it here and have no remorse about selling our D.C. apartment," he said. "We'd grown tired of living in the city, you see."

"I sometimes think I might like to live somewhere besides Mount Penn," Alice said. "All I know is the mountain."

"So, what do you make of all this excitement?" Carlos said.

Lillie Mae, huddled in the corner of the plush but comfortable antique sofa, listened to Carlos' accent, and Javier Bardem popped into her brain.

"I want these horrible crimes solved and our peaceful little village back to the way it was. We've always been busy bodies, but now we look suspiciously at each other and question everybody's behavior and motives. It's killing our community."

Alice smiled unconsciously. "I guess that didn't come out right."

"But, you're right, Alice," Carlos said, glancing at his wife. "Crime, especially a terrible crime like murder, doesn't just kill the victim. So many other people suffer, too. Innocent people."

"You're talking about Clare," Joyce said.

"Of course, I'm worried about Clare," Carlos said. "But I'm worried about Billy, as well. And Hester and Patrick. What do you make of it all, Alice?"

Alice picked up a biscotti and began to nibble on it. "It's all very odd," she said, her eyes darting to Lillie Mae, then back. "But, I agree with you. There are a lot of people to worry about."

"I know this is crazy," Joyce said. "I'm beginning to think Clare really believes she killed Roger."

"Clare's in shock and the shock has confused her," Lillie Mae said. "That's why it is important for us to do what we're doing to help her. Ask questions. Be available. Clare can no longer do that for herself. Too much has happened to her, and her thinking is skewed. She needs our help."

"We have to find the real murderer before something else awful happens," Alice said.

"I believe whoever killed Carl Lewis killed Roger Ballard," Carlos said.

"Why do you say that?" Lillie Mae asked.

135

"I just feel it. I know it's silly, but nothing else seems quite right. I think you ladies should focus your attention on Carl's murder, not Roger's."

"Interesting," Lillie Mae said. "Maybe you're right."

"There's something in the back of my mind that I feel is important, but I can't for the life of me recall what it is," Alice said. "That's why I want to talk to as many people as I can. Something someone says may spark my memory."

Joyce glanced at Carlos, then back to Alice. "Be careful where you say that, Alice. You don't want to upset someone."

"I don't even know if it is important. It's so silly getting old. It's so easy to forget things, and they just nag at you all the time. It'll come to me, I know. But, you're right. I'll be careful what I say from now on. How I hate this."

"What's that?" Joyce asked.

"I hate being afraid in my own village. Things can't get back to normal too soon for me."

"For all of us" Carlos said, nodding his head.

"I talked to Margaret this morning," Joyce said, deliberately changing the subject. "She called me."

"That's unusual," Lillie Mae said. "Margaret rarely calls anyone. She must have been working on her list of people to interview."

"Exactly," Joyce said. "She was in better spirits than I've heard her in a long time. She started the conversation by calling me sweetie. She's never done that before."

"She never called me sweetie," Lillie Mae said.

"What did she want?" Alice asked.

"She asked to meet with me later today. I agreed."

"Are you going over to her house?" Carlos asked, apparently hearing the news for the first time. "If you do, I have a magazine for Sam that I've been saving. Will you take it with you?"

"Yes," Joyce said. "Margaret told me her new medicine is working wonders, and she's feeling so much better, but she's still doesn't want to venture out of her house yet."

"You'll have a nice visit," Alice said, distracted.

"We need to go," Lillie Mae said, rising and nodding to Alice who rose as well.

The women quickly made their way to the door, Joyce and Carlos behind.

"Take care of yourselves, ladies. And call me, if you need anything," Joyce said, watching Alice and Lillie Mae walk up her driveway and back onto the street.

Turning back, Lillie Mae noticed a frown spread across Joyce's face.

14

"Lillie Mae, it's Pete here," a man's anxious voice announced when Lillie Mae answered the phone after being awakened in the middle of the night by its sharp ringing. "You've got to go see if Alice is all right."

Glancing at the clock she saw it was just past three in the morning.

"Alice?" Lillie Mae said, her mind clearing. "What's up Pete?"

"Janet and me heard this dog barking but didn't pay any attention at first. Then the barks got more frantic, and knowing Alfred is the only dog in the neighborhood, we suddenly realized Alice must be in some kind of trouble. You have to go over to her place right away. You're her closest neighbor and can get there the fastest. Me and Janet will meet you there just as quickly as we can."

Lillie Mae threw on an old pair of jeans and a plaid flannel shirt and was out of the house in less than two minutes. Hearing Alfred's loud yelps as soon as she was outside, she cursed herself for the ear plugs she wore to bed. Running at full speed, she was in Alice's backyard in just over a minute. Spotting Alfred at the far end of the yard, she saw that he was covered with a net that kept him from moving. Although he was struggling to get out, Lillie Mae thought he wasn't hurt.

Casting a look around, she saw what looked like a body lying close to the fence in Alice's back yard, not far from where Alfred was trapped. Leaving Alfred, she rushed toward it. Alice, dressed in her night gear, was lying face down in the yard. Her heart pounding so hard she could feel it in her throat, Lillie Mae looked down at her friend. She was sure she saw Alice move, but was too afraid to check. Alfred continued to yelp from his prison.

"Lillie Mae!" Pete shouted.

"Over here!" Lillie Mae yelled back. "It's Alice. I'm sure she's alive, but she needs help!" Kneeling down, she picked up Alice's wrist to feel her pulse.

"She is alive," she said, feeling a huge rush of relief. "Thank God for that. But, I have no idea how badly she's hurt."

"Is she going to be all right?" Janet asked, breathing heavily from the trip up the road.

"Not if we don't take some action. Go inside the house and call an ambulance, and then call the police," Lillie Mae ordered. "Hurry!"

Janet, wearing an orange bathrobe and a pair of black rubber boots, turned and walked as fast as she could up the stairs and into Alice's house.

*   *   *

Lillie Mae dressed in record time the next morning and was out of her house and on her way to the hospital within a half hour of getting Janet's call telling her Alice was doing better, sitting up in bed, and asking for her. According to Janet, the doctor had said that Alice's concussion was mild, and she would be back to herself in a day or two.

One of those people who regard speed limits as suggestions rather than law, Lillie Mae made her way along the country roads into Antioch in record time.

Swerving her little blue Toyota into one of the few spaces left in the hospital parking lot, Lillie Mae jumped out of the car, and ran toward the entrance to the hospital. When she reached the information desk, she had to pinch herself to stop from yelling at the elderly lady who asked her three times who she wanted to visit.

"Now settle down, dearie," the older women said to Lillie Mae. "What was your friend's name, again?"

Lillie Mae picked up the pen that was lying on the desk and wrote out Alice's name for the attendant to read.

"Oh, yes." The lady looked down through the spectacles that were falling off her nose. "Your friend is in room two forty-six. Just go down the corridor to the elevators. It's on your right when you get off the elevator."

Lillie Mae thanked the lady and left.

Alice, lying quietly in her bed, appeared to be asleep when Lillie Mae entered the room. Tears trickled down her cheeks as she looked at her friend, with her head bandaged and an IV in her arm, looking so vulnerable in the sterile hospital room. Walking over to the far side of the bed, Lillie Mae lifted Alice's hand and was relieved to feel it warm and alive in her own.

Alice turned and opened her eyes. "Good morning, Lillie Mae," she said. "Seems like I've become quite the nuisance of late, haven't I?"

Lillie Mae couldn't resist leaning down and planting a kiss on Alice's cheek. "What's a nice lady like you doing roaming the streets of Mount Penn in the middle of the night? Out looking for a good time?"

Even the small chuckle that escaped Alice's throat caused her to wince. "Ouch!" she exclaimed. "My head does hurt. This experience will teach me not to go out after midnight. If it was a good time I was looking for, I missed it."

"Do you feel like telling me what happened?" Lillie Mae asked.

"I'll tell you what I can remember," she said. "Maybe you can make some sense out of it."

"I'll try," Lillie Mae said.

"It was two-fifteen in the morning when Alfred woke me up to go outside," Alice said, speaking in a soft monotone. "I know because I checked the clock."

"Does he do that often?" Lillie Mae asked, more curious than concerned.

"No, never," Alice said quickly. "But the little rascal was insistent, prancing back and forth between the door and the bed, yelping to get me to move. When I finally got out of bed and put on my bathrobe to take him out, he jumped up and down like a puppy."

"Goodness," Lillie Mae said.

"When I opened the door, Alfred flew out into the yard barking and growling like nobody's business, running as fast as he could to the back fence. I thought it might be a wild dog or a deer in the yard, so I followed him, but I was cautious. I hadn't gone more than twenty feet when Alfred let out this loud yelp. Panicked, I ran toward him and I saw him lying on the ground whimpering. It was when I reached out to him that I felt the pain in the back of my head. I remember nothing else until I woke up here in the hospital."

Lillie Mae picked up Alice's hand and squeezed it. "I am so sorry this happened to you."

"Janet was here with me all night," Alice said. "The silly lady was wearing her pajamas and robe and a pair of black rubber boots. Can you imagine? I thought at first I was hallucinating."

Lillie Mae smiled, remembering the same sight from the night before.

"She told me she was in a hurry to get out of the house and Pete wouldn't let her wear her fluffy slippers, so she grabbed the boots because they were close at hand," Alice said. "It was so Janet."

"Janet can be resourceful with fashion," Lillie Mae said.

"I didn't care what she looked like," Alice said. "She told me Alfred had not been hurt, that you and Pete had gotten him loose from the net, and that he was staying with Joyce and Carlos until I got back home."

Lillie Mae nodded. "All that's true, dear. I checked on Alfred this morning. Joyce says he's mopping a bit, but other than missing you, seems just fine."

"Joyce called the nurse earlier with the good news," Alice said, her hand smoothing out the light blanket on her hospital bed. "Everyone's been very kind."

"Thank goodness you're going to be fine, too, dear," Lillie Mae said, thinking Alice's attack could have been so much worse.

"I've had better days," Alice said. "But I'll mend fast enough."

"Any idea who hit you?" Lillie Mae asked, not certain it was the right time to ask.

"The police asked me the same question. I honestly have no earthly idea why anyone would want to harm me."

"You're the last person anyone would want to hurt," Lillie Mae said

"Thank you for coming to my rescue, Lillie Mae. Janet told me it was you who got to the house first last night."

"I did. But it was Pete who called me and told me something was wrong, so you need to thank him, too."

"And Janet who rode with me in the ambulance, then stayed here until I woke up. That girl's a trooper. Pete came and got her this morning. I thanked him then."

"Yes, I know. Janet called me when she got home to tell me that you were awake and asking for me. She sounded exhausted, poor dear. I hope she's able to rest some today."

141

"Janet was wonderful to me," Alice repeated, a tear in her eye. "And I'm going to be fine," she added, as if trying to convince herself. "I bet I'm sore for a couple of days, though. The doctor was in earlier and said I could go home this afternoon. Would you mind coming back later to help me with the paperwork and then drive me home?"

"Of course, I'll come and help you this afternoon. It'll be my pleasure. I want you to stay with me a couple of days until you're back on your feet. Alfred's invited too."

"I appreciate your offer, Lillie Mae, but I'm not frightened to go home, honest," she said. "I'm happiest when I'm in my own bed, and I have Alfred to warn me of any danger. I just need to heed him better next time. I truly believe that the person who attacked me didn't mean me any serious harm. They wanted to scare me, that's all."

Lillie Mae looked at her friend and shook her head not at all sure she was right.

*　*　*

Lillie Mae hadn't been home ten minutes when she heard a rap at her back door. Hurrying into the kitchen she saw Joyce Castro standing there. "Come in, Joyce" she said, opening the door.

Alfred greeted her with a yelp.

"Alfred and I are out for a walk, and I saw your car in your driveway. Do you mind if we stop in for a visit? There's something I need to talk to you about," Joyce said, as she walked into Lillie Mae's kitchen holding onto Alfred's leash. Alfred, as if born to a lead, followed along contently.

"Come on into the living room," Lillie Mae said, eyeing her kitchen to see if it was neat enough for visitors. "I just got home from the hospital."

"How is Alice?" Joyce said. "I called the hospital earlier, and the nurse on duty said she was checking out this afternoon. She was busy with some tests, so the nurse wouldn't call her to the phone. She did say she'd let Alice know Alfred was settled."

"Alice is always Alice," Lillie Mae said. "She seems to have come through her latest adventure with minimum damage, thank goodness. I'm delivering her to her home later this afternoon. I asked her to stay with me for a couple of days, just until things settled down here in Mount Penn, but she refused. Said she liked being in her own bed."

"We need to keep a closer eye on her," Joyce said. "And that means you too, young man."

"Do you want some coffee?" Lillie Mae asked.

"No, thank you, but you get some for yourself," Joyce said, sitting down. Alfred plopped down on the floor by her feet.

"You said you wanted to talk about something?" Lillie Mae said.

"Yes," Joyce said, cautiously. "But I don't really know how to begin."

"Start at the beginning," Lillie Mae said.

"Remember when we saw Carlos driving up the mountain instead of toward town a couple of evenings ago?"

"I remember," Lillie Mae said.

Joyce looked down at her lap. "I finally got up the nerve to ask him where he was going that night," she said, raising her eyes slightly as if she wanted to gauge Lillie Mae's reaction.

"Where did he go?" Lillie Mae asked.

"I'll tell you that in a minute, but first, I'll tell you why I asked him."

"OK. I'm curious. Why did you ask him?"

Joyce looked around the room and took a deep breath. "Because he was out again last night."

"Last night?" Lillie Mae said. "When Alice was attacked?"

"Yes," Joyce said, glancing down at Alfred who had settled by her feet, his head resting on his paws.

"I asked him this morning where he'd been last night. At first, he beat around the bush, saying he couldn't sleep, and it was such a clear night, and he wanted to see the stars."Joyce hesitated. "I didn't believe him."

"What time did he go out?" Lillie Mae asked, her heart suddenly pounding.

"It was after one, maybe close to two, in the morning," Joyce said, her round eyes watering.

"But that's about the time Alice was attacked," Lillie Mae said. "Surely if he was outside, he must have heard Alfred barking."

"That's what I thought," Joyce said softly. "I insisted he tell me the truth, but he still wouldn't come clean. When I practically

143

accused him of attacking Alice, he finally told me what he'd been doing with his nights."

"So what did he say for himself?" Lillie Mae asked.

Joyce took a deep breath. "It all goes back to the evening we saw Carlos driving up the mountain. Do you remember, Lillie Mae?"

"Of course, I remember."

"Carlos was going to see Carl Lewis?"

"Carl Lewis!" Lillie Mae blurted.

"Not to murder him, dear. To buy marijuana from him."

"Marijuana," Lillie Mae said, astonished. "Well I never."

"I knew Carlos liked a little pot in his younger days, but I had no idea he still indulged on occasion. According to Carlos, it wasn't like that at all. He said it was because he'd been working so hard on these new projects of his, and the stress caused his neck to bother him something awful. His doctor said it's the start of rheumatoid arthritis, but he doesn't want to believe that. Instead of taking pain pills, he thought he'd see if smoking marijuana would help. Lots of states have passed medical marijuana laws, so what's good for the goose is good for the gander, he told me. All the traffic up to Carl Lewis' place that morning gave him the idea to go there and buy a bit of junk himself."

"Carlos was on the scene of the crime, then, "Lillie Mae said, incredulous. "Did he talk to Carl Lewis that night?"

"No, of course not," Joyce said, sounding impatient. "If he had, he would have let the police know. Carlos said nobody was at Carl's place when he got there. After a couple of minutes waiting, he turned his car around and headed to Antioch where he had planned to go in the first place. He knew of a man who sold the stuff there, so he went looking for him, found him, and bought some pot. Can you believe it, Lillie Mae?"

"It's quite the story," Lillie Mae said. "But I guess it's easy enough to prove."

Joyce went on. "Then, to make matters worse, he told me he'd smoked some pot the last couple of nights. The good news is that it has helped with his pain, but the bad news is he's been out and about when all this stuff has been happening around Mount Penn. So that's what he was doing last night. He walked up the High Mount road, found a comfy spot, and smoked his pot. He said if he

144

did hear Alfred barking, he was too stoned to pay much attention. By the time Pete brought Alfred over to our house in the wee hours of the morning, the drug had worn off."

"Didn't you smell it on him? Marijuana has a distinctive odor that's hard to miss," Lillie Mae said. "I've never used a drug in my life, and I know that."

"I have no sense of smell," Joyce said. "Never have. Carlos knows that."

"So, why didn't he tell you what he was doing before?" Lillie Mae asked, cautiously.

"Don't worry Lillie Mae, I asked him the same question. He said he felt stupid and juvenile, but the pot was doing him some good. His plan was to tell me what he was up to before buying any more."

"Did he say if he saw anybody else when he was on these nightly journeys?" Lillie Mae asked.

"I didn't ask him that."

"Do you think he was telling you the truth?" Lillie Mae asked.

"I hope so," Joyce said, her voice low.

*　　*　　*

Lillie Mae met Mabel and Patrick Goody in front of the Antioch police station. "This is it," she said, her posture straight and her manner no nonsense. "Are you two ready?"

"We're ready," Mabel said, her eyes meeting Patrick's. "Thanks for coming with us, Lillie Mae.

"Thanks, Lillie Mae." Patrick said reluctantly.

"I'm only here to support you," Lillie Mae said. "You're doing the talking when Charlie gets here. I'm just listening."

Mabel nodded.

Charlie Warren came to get them just five minutes after they checked in with the woman at the main office. "I've booked an interview room where we can talk," he said, shaking hands with Mabel, then Patrick, and nodding at Lillie Mae.

"Follow me," he said and led them down a drab gray hallway to a small windowless room that was furnished with only one small table and four chairs. A pitcher of water and four glasses sat in the center. Waving his hand he ushered them into the room, and shut the door behind Lillie Mae, the last person through.

"Please sit down," he said. He took the seat closest to the door and dropped a yellow pad on the table, as if claiming the space.

"You have something to tell me?" he said.

Mabel met his gaze. "We do," she said, picking up the pitcher of water. "Do you mind?"

"No, please help yourself," Charlie said.

"We wanted to meet with you today, Charlie, to tell you that Patrick and I both know that Roger Ballard did not murder Carl Lewis," Mabel said, taking a sip of water.

"How can you be so sure?" he asked.

"For a couple of reasons," Mabel said. "For one thing, he told us rather convincingly that he hadn't murdered him."

"When did you talk to him?" Charlie asked, jotting down some notes.

"The evening before Lillie Mae found Carl Lewis' body."

"You've already told me this," Charlie said.

"No," Mabel said quickly. "We told you that Patrick met with Roger, but we didn't tell you I met with him, too."

"So, what did Roger say that convinced you he had not murdered Carl Lewis?"

"Several things, really," Patrick said. "Roger was rattled and nervous when I got to the hideout, that old shed close to High Mount, but I didn't see it at first. I was mad, and I wanted him to pay for what I thought he'd done to me and Jerry. I told you all that."

Mabel reached out her hand to Patrick to calm him. "Take it easy, son," she said, as if in warning.

Patrick brushed her hand away, but he didn't seem upset.

"Tell me what you haven't told me, yet," Charlie said.

"It's about Carl Lewis."

"What about Carl Lewis?"

Patrick looked at his mother, and then at Lillie Mae, before turning back to Charlie. "Roger told me he had discovered Carl Lewis' body earlier that day. It was Roger who moved it from the hideout to where Lillie Mae found it on the trail the next morning."

"Roger moved Carl Lewis' body!" Charlie said, incredulous. "You knew Carl Lewis was dead before Lillie Mae discovered his body?"

"I guess so," Patrick said.

146

"Why didn't you come to the police?"

"Roger asked me not to, and I was already in enough trouble. I told Roger I wouldn't say anything, and I didn't. I hadn't seen Carl Lewis' body, nor did I know for sure Roger was telling me the truth."

"But you just said you thought Roger was telling the truth."

Patrick paused for a moment before speaking.

"Yes," he finally said. "I did think Roger was telling the truth. The next day when I heard Lillie Mae had found Carl Lewis' body, I knew it."

"How do you know Roger didn't kill Car Lewis?"

"Roger told me he hadn't killed him, and he had no reason to lie. He told me he had gone up to Carl Lewis' place to talk to him, but like with me and Mom, nobody was there when he got there. Then he went to the hideout because he thought Carl might be there. I guess Carl did some of his drug deals in the mountains, and used the hideout as a base, and Roger knew that. Carl was there, but, according to Roger, he was already dead."

"So, why did Roger move him?" Charlie asked, writing on the pad he had brought into the interview room.

"He didn't tell me, but I think it had to do with me and Jerry. It's well known the hideout is a meeting place for kids, as well as drug dealers, and Roger didn't want us to be involved any more than we were, I'm guessing."

"So, what other reason do you have for believing Roger is innocent of murder?" Charlie asked.

"He was scared," Patrick said. "I mean really scared. I've never seen Roger so edgy or nervous. He only sat with me for a few minutes. After that he was up pacing, looking over his shoulder as if expecting someone to come, and generally looking miserable."

Charlie turned to Mabel. "It was you Roger was expecting, isn't that true?"

Mabel cast an eye at Patrick, then turned back to Charlie. "Yes," she said, taking another sip of water.

"Did he tell you he had found Carl Lewis' body?" Charlie asked.

"No," Mabel said. "Patrick told me that much later. That's why we're here today."

"So what did you and Roger talk about?"

"I asked Roger pretty much the same questions Patrick had asked him earlier, and he gave me pretty much the same answers. Like Patrick, I was so mad at him when we first met that I took a swing at him. But, he grabbed my arm, and begged me to get a hold of myself. Then we sat down and talked. He convinced me in short order he knew nothing about the drugs and was as surprised as the rest of us at what had happened. The job he wanted Patrick and Jerry to do was real, he said. He told me he had worked with Carl Lewis lots of times in the past and that nothing about this job was unusual, until the drugs were found in Jerry's truck, and the boys were arrested."

"Did he have any idea who had put the drugs there?" Charlie asked.

"I didn't ask him that question, but I believe he suspected Carl Lewis. I also think he believed that Carl was only some bigger guy's pawn. As Patrick said, Roger was nervous and scared the whole time we were talking. He rushed me away. Said he didn't want anybody to see me with him. He didn't tell me who he was waiting to meet, but I certainly got the impression, he was expecting someone."

"Any idea who that might have been?" Charlie asked.

Mabel shook her head. "No."

"Can you think of anything Roger said during either one of your talks with him that would give you a clue as to who or what he was frightened of?"

"It could have been as much for me, as for himself," Mabel said, nodding as if just realizing this might be true. "And, I agree with Patrick, that he probably didn't know exactly who he was afraid of. I'm not sure it had anything to do with Carl Lewis, though. Roger was into all sorts of things, as you know. I think he believed that someone thought he knew too much. But what that might be, I have no idea. Roger didn't tell me."

"Do you think Clare Ballard killed her husband?" Charlie suddenly asked Mabel. "You knew Roger pretty well, from what you've just told me. Did Roger have a reason to think Clare would murder him?"

"Clare put up with Roger's shit for over twenty years, and if she didn't kill him during that time, I doubt if she would have killed him now," Mabel said. "Unless it had something to do with Billy."

148

"Billy?" Charlie said.

"But, Roger was as crazy about Billy as Clare, so I can't see him harming him," she added, as if dismissing the idea. "I wish I could help more," Mabel added, shaking her head. "I just don't know."

Charlie stood, marking the interview over. "I'll need you to work with one of the recorders here to make and sign a statement. I know we said this interview would be off the record, but neither one of you said anything that could incriminate you, and your information is important to the case. Will you give your statements?"

Mabel and Patrick looked relieved. They both agreed.

"Lillie Mae," Charlie said. "Please come with me."

Lillie Mae stood up and followed Charlie out of the room.

* * *

Lillie Mae walked into the visitor's room at the Antioch jail, having first dealt with the necessary paperwork. Scanning the room for Clare, her eyes finally rested on an aged version of the woman she knew, sitting alone at a table on the far side of the room wearing a loose fitting gray prison dress, her once beautiful hair now drab and lifeless, held back in a ponytail.

Lillie Mae was sure Clare had seen her enter the room, but made no acknowledgement of her, as she continued to stare at the plain-green wall. It was as if Clare had given up on life, Lillie Mae thought as she made her way across the stark, depressing room. In jail less than a week and Clare already looked pale and sick. Her shoulders sagged and her arms hung limp.

"Hi, Clare," Lillie Mae said, as she neared the table.

Clare looked up and offered a wan smile, but said nothing. The women could not touch because it was against jail policy, but at least there were no barriers between them.

Lillie Mae sat down opposite Clare at the small plain table. Neither woman spoke for a few moments. Lillie Mae hoped Clare would say something first, but she didn't. She didn't appear uncomfortable either. She sat perfectly still in her limpid pose.

"How are you doing, Clare?" Lillie Mae asked. She immediately felt terrible at asking such an inane question. But, she couldn't think of any other way to get the conversation started.

Clare didn't seem to notice.

"I'm fine."

Her face, stoic, she continued to stare straight ahead, refusing to meet Lillie Mae's eyes.

Lillie Mae, not able to stand the tension another minute, blurted out the words Charlie had told her to say. "Clare, you have to talk to Charlie Warren. Whatever you did, or whatever you think someone else did, it's time for you to talk. Did you know Alice Portman was attacked last night?"

Clare looked straight at Lillie Mae for the first time. Her eyes flew wide open. "No!" she cried out. "Is she all right?"

Lillie Mae told Clare what she knew about the attack, reassuring her that Alice was going to be all right, just as Charlie had instructed her to do.

"But, you can see that this mess in Mount Penn is not over just because you confessed to killing Roger. You have to tell someone what you know before more people are hurt. Clare, it doesn't matter whether you killed Roger or not, any more. This is not about you. This is about the people of Mount Penn. You have a responsibility to help the police discover what is happening, if your neighbors are going to feel safe in their homes again. The people of Mount Penn support you. They are praying for you and the breakfast ladies are out detecting for you, but you have to do your share, too. You have to tell the police what happened the night Roger was killed. You have to tell them everything you know."

Clare turned to look at Lillie Mae. Finally, she spoke. "I'll talk to Charlie. But I want Billy with me, and Sid Firth."

Lillie Mae offered Clare a small grateful smile. "Thank you, Clare. You are doing the right thing."

"I hope so."

Clare's eyes filled with tears.

* * *

Lillie Mae helped Alice out of the car, holding her arm as she went up the steps to her house. Joyce Castro was on the porch to greet the ladies, Alfred in her arms twitching and yelping, excited to see his mistress.

"You naughty dog," Alice said, greeting her canine friend. "Have you been making a nuisance of yourself for Joyce and Carlos?" She moved closer to him and petted his head.

150

"He was a perfect guest," Joyce answered. "Carlos enjoyed him so much he's talking about us getting a dog. But, when I asked him what kind, he said he really only wanted Alfred."

The ladies chuckled.

Joyce looked surprised to see how spry Alice looked. Her head was bandaged, but there seemed to be no other evidence of her mishap from the night before.

'You look wonderful," Joyce said.

"I'm better than expected," Alice giggled. "I just want to get into my house and settle down with Alfred again. I do hate hospitals, you know."

"As I told you before, Joyce, I invited Alice to stay with me." Lillie Mae had led her into the house and Joyce had followed, Alfred still in her arms. "But, she insisted on coming back here. I plan to stay with her this evening, though. She is a marvel, isn't she? I'd be petrified to come back to my home alone, but Alice is not frightened at all."

"Well, maybe a wee bit. But, I'm sure whoever hit me wanted to scare me, not kill me. I doubt if they will come back again."

"There's a shepherd's pie in the frig," Joyce said. "And a quiche for breakfast."

"Thank you, dear," Alice said, taking Alfred from Joyce. "You shouldn't have gone to so much trouble."

"I made the shepherd's pie, but Mabel brought the quiche over," Joyce continued. "Janet tossed up a big salad for you, and Hester dropped off a chocolate pie. Sam called and said he'd make dinner for you tomorrow. Everybody in town has been so worried. We're just glad you're home and will soon be back to normal."

"Whatever normal is," Alice said, with a smile so big it consumed her face. "It will take me most of tomorrow to thank everyone for their kindnesses. But well worth the time."

"You rest, for now, and let Lillie Mae pamper you," Joyce said. "And if you need anything, Lillie Mae, give me a call. I'm just a hop, skip, and jump away."

When Joyce left, Lillie Mae made a cup of tea for Alice, who had curled up on her sofa, Alfred at her feet. "You need to drink this tea, and then rest," Lillie Mae ordered, bringing a tray filled with all sorts of goodies into the room.

"That does sound like a good idea," Alice said. "I am a bit tired, my dear."

"We're going to find whoever did this to you, Alice," Lillie Mae said, looking fondly at her friend. "It's one thing to murder Carl Lewis and Roger Ballard, but when someone messes with Alice Portman, they're going to pay."

"Let's hope the murderer is behind bars before too much longer," Alice said. "I want my lovely little Mount Penn back to the way it was before all this mess started."

15

Lillie Mae was up and out early the next morning, arriving at Alice's house in time to fix her breakfast. The night before she had made certain Alice was safely tucked in her bed, all doors locked and windows secure, then went on home, as Alice had requested.

"How are you doing, sunshine?" Lillie Mae called up the stairs after using the key that Alice had given her to let herself in through the front door.

"You can come up, Lillie Mae. I'm almost dressed. Just feeling a bit stiff this morning," Alice called back, after shushing Alfred who had barked his warning once he realized a newcomer had arrived.

"I'll start breakfast," Lillie Mae said from the bottom on the stairs. "You take your time getting ready, dear. When you get downstairs, the coffee and quiche will be waiting for you."

"Now, doesn't that sound divine," Alice said. "You are spoiling me, Lillie Mae."

Lillie Mae decorated the breakfast plates with the fresh strawberries she found in Alice's refrigerator. Proud of the pretty breakfast she had put together, she sat down at the table to wait for her friend, sipping from a cup of strongly brewed coffee, thoughts of the day before whirling through her brain. Thank heavens it all turned out as well as it did, she thought. Alice's mishap could have been so much worse.

"How lovely," Alice said when she walked into the kitchen a few moments later. Alfred was at her heels.

Lillie Mae jumped up and rushed to her friend, welcoming her with a hug. "Aren't you smart this morning." Alice was dressed in a pair of jeans and long sleeve striped tee, a teal sweater thrown over her shoulders.

"Alfred needs to go outside," Alice said, opening the back door to let him out in the yard. "I'll take him for his walk a little later."

"You'll do no such thing. I'll take Alfred for his walk today," Lillie Mae said firmly. "It'll be a treat for me. Come and sit down, now, and eat your breakfast."

"If nothing else, Lillie Mae, this terrible incident has made it very clear how much I have to be thankful for."

"Thankful?" Lillie Mae asked, confused.

"For all the good people of Mount Penn. How wonderful you've all been to me."

Lillie Mae blushed. "It's you, Alice. We all care about you. Enough of the praise. Eat your breakfast."

Alice looked down at her plate, picked up her fork, and ate.

"You've outdone yourself," Alice said a few minutes later. "Breakfast was delicious. So much better than hospital food."

"Now you're overdoing the praise," Lillie Mae said. "All I did was assemble the food. Mabel made the quiche. I just heated it up. And the fruit was in your refrigerator."

"Well, you assembled very well," Alice said.

Alfred barked and scratched at the door. "I'll let him in," Lillie Mae said, jumping up and heading to the door.

"I'm feeling a bit like a queen this morning, Lillie Mae," Alice said, chuckling. "And, Alfred is being treated like a king. Let's hope he doesn't get too used to all this attention."

"Remember when you were telling Joyce and Carlos the other day that there was something you were trying to recall that didn't seem right, but it wouldn't come to you."

"I do," Alice said.

"Any idea yet what it might be you were trying to remember?" Lillie Mae asked.

"It's a feeling, Lillie Mae, more than a thing, I think," Alice said. "It's something that haunts me, but I haven't been able to put my finger on it yet. All this excitement hasn't helped."

"Maybe that's why you were attacked," Lillie Mae said, realizing that she might be speaking the truth. "Carlos warned you not to talk to people about it. Did you say anything to anybody?"

"I didn't, Lillie Mae," Alice said quickly. "Once Carlos told me to keep still, I didn't speak to anyone about my strange feeling. I heeded his warning."

"Did you tell anybody before you talked to Carlos and Joyce?"

Alice looked up as if trying to pluck an answer off the ceiling. "I honestly don't remember," she said a moment later. "My mind is so muddled."

"Maybe you should talk to Charlie again," Lillie Mae suggested, taking a sip of coffee.

"That's a good idea," Alice said. "Charlie wasn't with the police who interviewed me at the hospital. Call him for me, please, and let him know I want to talk to him."

"I'll call him this morning," Lillie Mae said, going to the back door where Alfred's leash was hanging on the knob. Alfred jumped up as soon as he heard her move. "Right now, I'm taking this little fellow for a walk."

When Lillie Mae returned with Alfred prancing behind her, refreshed, Alice was still sitting at the breakfast table, coffee in hand.

"You're back already," she said when Alfred came bouncing in the house. "I was just going to get up and take care of the kitchen."

"You'll do no such thing," Lillie Mae said, briskly. "You go into the living room, get comfortable on the sofa, and read last night's *Antioch News*. See if you can pick out the article I wrote."

Alice stood up slowly, stretched her arms out in front of her, then walked over to the counter.

"Did you get a byline this time?" she asked, picking up the paper and glancing at the front page.

"Nope," Lillie Mae said. "That's why you have to search."

Lillie Mae cleaned up the breakfast dishes in the kitchen while Alice looked through the newspaper.

Suddenly, Alfred stirred.

"Lillie Mae, there's someone rattling the front door," Alice called from the living room. "Who's there?"

Harriet Peterson gently kicked open the door a moment later, a casserole in her hands.

"How could you leave your front door unlocked?" Harriet scolded, coming through the door. "Anybody could walk right in."

"Looks like anybody did just that," Alice chuckled. "But it would be hard to get by Alfred's warnings."

"I could have been a murderer."

Harriet waved Alfred away with her free hand.

"I do hope not," Alice said. "We have far too many of those in Mount Penn at the moment. Be still, Alfred," Alice commanded.

Alfred quieted immediately, turned to chase his tail for a brief moment, before plopping his small body onto the floor by Alice's feet.

Lillie Mae walked into the room. "Did you say you were a murderer, Harriet? Who'd you murder? Kevin?"

She took the offered casserole from Harriet.

"Quit your joking, you two—this is serious," Harriet said in the same stern voice she had used earlier but, her expression softened when she looked at Alice. "I was shocked when Janet called and told me you were attacked in your own back yard, lured out by some maniac. You know I don't like to be shocked, I can tell you, but there's been enough happening here in Mount Penn since our last Thursday morning breakfast to shock us all for a lifetime."

"Do you want a cup of coffee?" Lillie Mae offered on her way into the kitchen with the casserole in hand. "There's a fresh pot brewing."

"Make it tea, and you've got a deal," Harriet said.

"I would have come to the hospital to visit you yesterday, but you were in and out so fast," Harriet was saying when Lillie Mae came back into the room. She sat beside Alice, leaned over and absently petted Alfred with her right hand. "That bandage around your head—do you need it, or is it for show?"

"A little of both," Alice admitted with a chuckle. "I'm feeling much better than I thought I would today. Thank goodness for that. I'm a tougher old broad than I would have guessed. My head hurts a bit, but I've been taking aspirins for that, and I'll take a nap later. My legs are stiff, probably from the fall, but other than that I'm as good as new. But, I am glad you've come to visit me. Makes all this seem worthwhile."

Alfred had moved and was now by Harriet's feet, his head on his paws, as if he knew his mistress was safe, and he wasn't needed at just this moment.

"What do you know of Clare, Lillie Mae?" Harriet asked. "I've been having the worst dreams about her lately. Hangmen are coming after her, and she's yelling in a voice that sounds nothing like hers, 'I murdered my husband!' She's covered with blood and walking like a zombie. Twice I woke up screaming and scared Kevin half to death. I'm so worried about her, there in that terrible jail, day after day."

156

"I went to see her yesterday," Lillie Mae said. "She's not doing very well, I'm afraid. The good news is she's finally agreed to talk to Sid Firth and Charlie. Once she tells them everything that happened the night Roger was killed, it won't be long before the bad guys are caught."

"Barbara and I were doing our grocery shopping in Antioch yesterday, and we ran into Rose Maynard," Harriet said, taking a sip of the brew.

"Has she moved into her house yet?" Alice asked, perking up.

"No, but she said the renovations are coming along. She and Barbara hit it off right away and exchanged phone numbers. I hope those two become friends once Rose is settled on the mountain."

"Do you think you'll make it to breakfast club on Thursday," Harriet asked Alice.

"No reason why I won't," Alice said, "if Lillie Mae will drive me."

"Of course, I'll drive you," Lillie Mae said.

The ladies chatted comfortably for the next half hour. No one mentioned the word murder or referred to any of the events over the last several days. It was Harriet who returned the conversation to the real world.

"I made Margaret a casserole, too," Harriet said, looking at her watch. "She's on my list of Mount Penn people to interview, and I must get on with it if I'm to be the best Thursday morning detective I can be. Do you want to come with me, Lillie Mae?"

"No, I'll stay here with Alice," Lillie Mae said.

"You go with Harriet," Alice chirped in. "Me and Alfred will take a wee bit of a nap while you're out. I know I've only been up a short time, but I'm already feeling a bit knackered."

"Do come," Harriet said. "Margaret's not the easiest person in the world to talk to, and you always have something to say. Besides, you can carry the casserole I brought for them."

"Okay," Lillie Mae agreed, standing up. "But only because Alice looks tired, and I don't think she'll rest if I stay here."

Harriet rose from her chair. Alfred, roused from a nap, jumped up and barked.

"Settle, Alfred," she said, petting his head again when she picked up her purse.

"Ready, Lillie Mae?" Harriet asked.

157

"Let's go while the sun's still shining," Lillie Mae said, following Harriet to the door.

"Thanks for everything, you two," Alice said. "I'll lock the door once you're out, Harriet. I don't want you to worry about me, dear."

"I'll be back later to check up on you," Lillie Mae said as Alice shut the door behind them and turned the lock.

*　　*　　*

"I've been gone from Mount Penn for less than six months, and the whole place falls apart," Harriet said to Lillie Mae on their walk to Margaret and Sam's house. "Two murders and an attack on Alice in just a couple of days. This place has gone super crazy. Something has to be done. Look around you, girl. You live in one of the most beautiful villages in the world, and all these bad things happen. This nonsense has to stop right away."

Harriet and Lillie Mae waited outside Sam and Margaret's front door for several minutes. Harriet had knocked twice, but there had been no response. Sam's truck was in the driveway, along with the new Chrysler sedan they had recently bought, so Lillie Mae was sure they were home. Just as Harriet raised her hand to knock a third time, someone on the other side rattled the door. A moment later it opened and Sam peeked around the side.

"Oh, Harriet, it's you," he said, in a surprised voice. "And Lillie Mae. Did we know you were coming for a visit this morning?"

"I'm sorry, Sam." Harriet said. "I didn't call. I drove over to Mount Penn to visit Alice and wanted to stop by and see you and Margaret while I was here. I brought a casserole."

Lillie Mae pushed the dish toward Sam.

"Do come in," Sam said, opening the door wider. "We're always delighted to see you Harriet, and Lillie Mae has become quite the fixture around here lately. Please ignore the mess. We weren't expecting company this morning."

"Look who's here," Sam announced as he lead Harriet and Lillie Mae into the living room where Margaret was lounging on the sofa. "Harriet brought us a lovely casserole for our dinner."

Looking around, Lillie Mae could see no mess. Everything was just as it had been during her last visit.

"Harriet, my dear. Thank you so much. You are always so thoughtful—and Lillie Mae, good to see you again," Margaret said,

158

holding out her hand in greeting. "Do come in for a few minutes and let's talk. Have you been to see Alice?"

"I stopped by her house before coming over here. She seems well enough considering all she's been through. The good news is she plans to be at breakfast on Thursday morning if she's up to it. What do you think, Lillie Mae?"

"Alice is doing remarkably well," Lillie Mae agreed.

"What a dreadful thing to have happen to one of us," Margaret said. "We must catch these villains before we're all murdered in our beds."

"There's not much danger of that," Lillie Mae mumbled.

"Will you and Sam be at breakfast this week?" Harriet asked, casting a sharp look at Lillie Mae.

"We're planning on it," Margaret said, "if I'm well enough. I enjoy the drive down the mountain almost as much as I enjoy breakfast. The view over the valley as you go around the bend on the Old Mount Penn road thrills me every time I see it."

"I'm going out for a walk," Sam announced, popping his head around the corner from the kitchen. "Do you mind, Margaret?"

"No, go," Margaret said. "Harriet and Lillie Mae will keep me company for awhile. Will you bring some coffee in before you leave?"

"It's all ready," he said, appearing as if by magic with a tray.

"You are a dear," Margaret said.

"I won't be gone long," he said. "But, I do want to get out in the fresh air while I still have a chance." Turning to look at the ladies, his usual grin planted on his face, he added. "Margaret will tell you about the little adventure we have planned."

"What did Sam mean by a little adventure?" Harriet asked, when the back door closed.

"Sam and I are leaving in just a couple of days for California. We're going to see Michael, my brother. He and I are so close, you see, and he's been worried about me. It's been almost two years since we've been together."

"Are you well enough for such a long trip?" Harriet asked.

"Everybody asks me that," Margaret chuckled. "I've checked with the doctor, and he says a change of scenery and a visit with my brother may be the best thing for me right now. Being house bound is exhausting, especially with all this terrible excitement here in Mount Penn. I'm just glad I'm feeling well enough to travel."

"Good for you, Margaret. Sounds like this trip will do you a world of good. Hopefully, everything here will be resolved before you leave. The murderers will have been caught, Clare will be out of jail and back in her own home, and you and Sam can fly away knowing all is well at home."

"Oh, I do hope so," Margaret said.

"Let's get down to the interview questions," Harriet said, taking her pad out of her purse.

Lillie Mae sat back on the leather chair and listened to the two ladies talk, but learned nothing new or interesting.

* * *

Lillie Mae, working at her desk, looked out the window and saw Sid Firth park his Mercedes in front of her house. She watched him get out of the car and walk up her front path. She stood and was at the door when he stepped onto her porch.

"Sid," she said in welcome. "What brings you here?"

"Good news for a change," he said. "Clare has agreed to talk to the police. Charlie said you had something to do with that, and I wanted to stop by and thank you."

"Come on in, and tell me what's going on," Lillie Mae invited. "Can I get you a cup of coffee?"

"None for me," Sid said, taking a seat on the sofa. "But, you help yourself."

"I'm floating from all the coffee I've had today," Lillie Mae said. "Tell me about Clare."

"She looked so much more alive when I met with her this time," Sid said. "I'm not sure what you said to her, but it must have worked. She'd washed her hair, and although it was held back in a ponytail, it looked shiny and healthy again. She even put on a touch of lipstick."

"Sounds like she's made it over the hump," Lillie Mae said.

"Once she made up her mind to talk, she wants to do it right away. So, I've set up a meeting with Charlie and Billy and Clare for tomorrow morning."

"Excellent news."

"And there's one other thing," Sid said, catching Lillie Mae's eye.

160

"What's that?"

"She wants you to be there."

"Me?" Lillie Mae was astonished. "Why me?"

"Because she trusts you and she believes you trust her. Anyway, will you do it? Will you come to the meeting in the morning?"

"Of course, I'll be there," Lillie Mae said.

"There's something else you need to know," Sid said.

"What now?" Lillie Mae said, uncertain if she wanted more information.

"Clare still believes she's responsible for Roger death."

"Is that what you believe?" Lillie Mae asked.

"To be honest, Lillie Mae, I'm not certain what I believe anymore. At worst, Clare was somehow involved, but, surely, whatever happened was an accident. We'll find out more tomorrow. Do you want me to pick you up in the morning?"

"No, I'll meet you at the jail—what time do you want me to be there?"

"Be there at nine. If all goes well, you should be finished by noon."

"Let's hope there are no new surprises," Lillie Mae said, following Sid to the door. "We've had far too many lately."

"You're right there, girl," Sid said, throwing his hand in the air as he walked back down the path to his car.

16

Charlie and Clare were in the interview room, when Sid Firth ushered Billy and Lillie Mae in and invited them to sit down. Clare watched in silence, her hands clasping and unclasping in her lap. She smiled when Billy entered the room, but instantly changed her expression when he turned toward her. He had aged ten years in a couple of days. His clothes were rumpled, and his beard unattended. He refused to look at his mother, looking first at Sid, and then at the floor. When he took his seat at the table, he shot her a quick glance, and then looked away again. Clare slumped lower on her chair, her expression mimicking that of her son's.

"How would you like this to proceed?" Sid asked, turning to Charlie.

"Since we're all here to listen to Clare's story, let's dispense with the preliminaries, and just let her get started? Is that OK with you, Clare?"

Clare took a deep breath, and then looked around the table again, as if to get her bearings straight. "Yes, I'm ready," she finally said, her voice soft, but clear.

She looked at Charlie as if for a signal to begin.

He nodded.

"Roger and I have always had what you might call a tempestuous relationship," Clare said, looking at Charlie, as if he were her audience. "But, over the years we have learned to live with each other. I can't say I loved Roger, but I learned to accept him and our marriage. Billy held us together."

Clare's eyes shifted for a moment to Billy, but returned to Charlie. "Roger and I both love Billy more than anything in our lives. We've always had that in common. So, I knew something was terribly wrong when Roger would not take the time to see him, even though he had called him at school and asked him to come home."

Tears formed in Clare's eyes. She turned her head to cough.

162

"Would you like some water before going on?" Charlie asked, picking up the water pitcher that was sitting in the middle of the table, along with four glasses, and a box of tissues.

"Thank you." Clare accepted the glass from him and took a sip. "I'll continue now," she said, checking with Charlie.

Charlie nodded encouragingly.

"Although Roger had been acting odd the last several weeks, I became really concerned when he didn't come home. Roger often stayed out late, and sometimes very late, but rarely, if ever, all night. It was mid-afternoon the following day that Roger finally showed up."

"I was upstairs getting Billy's room ready for his homecoming, when I heard Roger's truck pull into the driveway. The back door slammed shut, so I knew he had come into the house, but he didn't call for me, like he usually does as soon as he gets home. After about ten minutes, I got curious, and went downstairs to see what he was up to."

Clare dabbed her nose with a tissue. "What I saw when I got downstairs shocked me. Roger was standing at the kitchen sink, scrubbing his hands and arms. All I could see was blood, which was everywhere. He must have heard me come into the room, because he turned around. That's when I noticed his face was bruised and scratched."

Clare paused again and looked up to the ceiling, as if bringing her thoughts together. "I asked Roger what had happened to him, but he ignored me. Or, maybe he just didn't hear me."

She shook her head as if the idea had just come to her.

"When he turned and looked at me a few moments later, I could see he was in pain. His eyes were bigger and rounder than usual, and his mouth was contorted into an odd grimace. I stepped toward him, an offer to help, but he shook his head as if to bar me from coming closer. He asked me to go upstairs and get him fresh clothes."

"Why didn't you tell me this, Mother?" Billy said.

"Later," Charlie said, reaching his hand out to Billy. "Go on, Clare."

"When I came back downstairs, Roger told me he had to leave as soon as he changed his clothes. When I reminded him that Billy was coming home that afternoon, I could see real anguish in his

163

eyes when he said he couldn't make it home for dinner. He said he had a job or something to do that he couldn't get out of. I forget his excuse."

Clare coughed again, picked up the water glass, and took a sip. "Roger was a very different man that day," she continued. "Not only was he kind to me, but he had this gentleness about him that I hadn't seen before. Right before he left, he asked me to forgive him."

"Forgive him for what?" Charlie asked.

"He didn't say," Clare said, and then continued her story as if Charlie's question wasn't important. "Billy arrived home from school in the late afternoon, and everything seemed better. We talked and kidded with each other, and Billy suggested we get started fixing supper. I hoped Roger might still make it home that evening, so I peeled plenty of potatoes.

"Then Mabel Goody stopped by looking for her son, Patrick, and I think she asked for Roger, too. I couldn't help her. When she left, Billy told me that he had an idea where Patrick might be. He asked if I minded if he checked it out, and told him that was fine. When Billy left, I called Roger."

Clare paused again. This time Billy looked directly at her.

"I called Roger's cell phone number, and this time he answered, which surprised me since I had called him at least a dozen times already that day, and he hadn't picked up. I asked him if he would meet me at the trailhead in the Mount Penn Park. I told him it was important and he agreed to be there in ten minutes.

"When I got to the park, Roger was already there. He was nervous, jumpy like, and told me he could stay only a minute. I asked him what was going on, but he said he couldn't tell me. It was a windy afternoon, and the rustling of the leaves seemed to make him even more edgy. Then his cell phone rang, and after he took the call, he told me he had to leave. 'Tell Billy I love him,' he said, and then he was gone. He never asked me why I wanted to meet with him."

"Go on," Sid said when Clare paused again.

"I stayed in the park for a few minutes, just looking out over the valley, thinking. Then I walked up to the church. Dale Beavers was there, practicing the organ. He stopped playing when he saw me come through the front door. I sat down on a pew, and he came and joined me. I told him about my meeting with Roger. He could tell I was upset, so he reached over and hugged me. It was not a romantic hug. He was only trying to comfort me, but Hester Franklin came into the church just then, and she saw us. I'm sure she got the wrong idea, since she left in a hurry."

Clare hesitated again.

"When I got back home, Billy was in the kitchen putting the finishing touches on dinner. He was as happy as he'd been earlier. He told me he hadn't found Patrick, but he didn't seem concerned. I didn't tell him that I had met with his father."

"Why didn't you tell me you saw Dad?" Billy interrupted. "It might have made a difference."

"Enough," Charlie said, looking at Billy again. "You'll get your turn to talk to your mother later. Let her finish her story."

"Billy and I had a fun time finishing up supper and eating," Clare continued. "He told me about school, his classes and friends, and I told him about the singing competition that Dale and I were going to compete in."

Clare stopped suddenly and took another deep breath.

"Just as we finished dinner, the phone rang. I rushed to answer it, thinking it might be Roger, but instead this eerie voice started shouting at me. 'You were seen! someone said. I know what you did!'"

Clare eyes wandered toward Lillie Mae. "The voice was muffled, so I can't be sure if it was male or female, but I assumed it was a man. He scared me, and I dropped the phone. Billy picked it up off the floor and hung it up. I still have no idea who the caller was or what he wanted, but that strange eerie voice still haunts me."

Clare squirmed in her chair.

"Are you OK?" Charlie asked.

"This seat is uncomfortable," Clare said, "but I'll be fine."

Charlie nodded.

"The next morning, the sirens woke me," Clare said. "Although we rarely get that kind of racket in Mount Penn, I didn't pay much attention at first. I took a shower and dressed. When I got downstairs, Billy was already up and about, fixing breakfast. We were just talking about what to do that day when Dale Beavers called and asked if I wanted to ride up the mountain to see what was going on. I agreed to go. Billy stayed home.

"It was when we got to the top of the mountain that I first learned Lillie Mae had found a body just off the trail. It wasn't until later that it struck me that the dead man might be Roger. I became obsessed. Dale rejected the idea, but it made sense to me."

Clare looked directly at Charlie. "When you stopped by later that day and told me that the dead man was not Roger, but Carl Lewis, I thought that Roger had to have killed him. I saw him covered in blood. I saw him shaking with fear. I also knew that he felt some responsibility for the mess Patrick Goody and Jerry Foster were in. It all added up."

"When did you change your mind?" Charlie asked.

"I don't know that I did change my mind. Certainly not then. I was frantic with worry all day. Billy was gone most of the time, so I spent as much of the day as I could in the garden. In the late afternoon, when Billy got home, I asked him to sit down at the kitchen table so we could talk."

"What did you talk about?" Charlie asked.

"His Dad," Clare said. "I told him how much Roger loved him, but that he hadn't always been kind to me. I told him that I was thinking about changing my life."

"Change your life?" Charlie asked. "How?"

"That's not important," Clare said, losing her patience. "It has nothing to do with what I'm telling you now."

"What did Billy say then?" Charlie asked.

"He didn't have a chance to say anything because the phone rang. I rushed to answer it. It was Roger. He wanted to speak to Billy. Billy had come up behind me, so I handed him the phone."

"Roger?" Charlie asked, surprised.

"Yes. Billy agreed to meet him at the trailhead in the Mount Penn Park, where Roger and I had met the day before. He left immediately."

Clare's eyes automatically went to Billy, then back to Charlie. "At first, I thought the meeting was a good idea," she said, "then I had second thoughts. Billy was angry with Roger, and Roger was capable of anything in his current mood. Frightened for Billy, I went after him."

Clare stopped to take a deep breath.

"When I got to the park, I heard loud voices. Roger and Billy were screaming at each other. I ran the rest of the way to the trailhead, but when I got there, they were already in a fist fight. Billy was doing most of the hitting. Roger hit Billy once in the nose, but from where I was standing, I'd say Roger was just trying to defend himself. Roger was shouting, 'You don't understand, Billy! Please let me explain!'

"When I got close enough for them to see me, I screamed for them to stop. Roger glanced my way, letting his guard down, and Billy landed him a punch that felled him. When Billy saw what he had done, he took one look at me and ran away. I suspect he ran back to the house since he was there when I got home."

"What happened next?" Charlie asked.

"I was angry, but then, so was Roger. He accused me of telling Billy lies about him. Screamed it was my fault that Billy was so mad at him that he wanted to fight. Next, he yelled obscenities at me. He screamed that he knew I was having an affair with Dale Beavers and called me a whore. I lost it, I guess. There was a big stick lying right by my feet. I picked it up and hit Roger with it. Then, I ran."

Clare stopped again, and took a tissue out of the box on the table to wipe a tear that was making it's way down her cheek.

"Go on," Charlie said.

"I could hear Roger running after me. I stayed ahead of him until I got to our back yard. That's when he grabbed my left arm. I still had the stick in my right hand, so I turned and hit him with it. Hard. I know I made contact at least twice. I'm sure I hit his arm the first time, because when he turned away from me to grab it, I hit him again. I could have hit him in the back of the head. I don't know for sure, but Roger fell. I was so traumatized by this time, everything was a blur. I dropped the stick and ran into the house without looking back."

"What happened next?" Charlie asked, putting his hand on Clare's arm to help calm her.

"Billy was waiting for me when I came into the house. We had words. He wanted to know why I followed him to the park, and I wanted to know what he and his father had been fighting about. It wasn't long, maybe five minutes at most, that we argued.Then Dale arrived. I was hysterical by then. Dale tried to comfort me, but I was out of it by then. I begged him to go back outside with me to check on Roger. He agreed. That's when we discovered Roger was dead."

Clare hung her head.

"Did you think Roger was dead when you ran up to the house?" Charlie asked, casting a look at Lillie Mae.

"Of course not," Clare said, her eyes full of tears. "I never would have left him lying out there if I thought he was seriously injured. I thought I had stunned him, that's all. I was surprised when he didn't show up at the back door, but I figured he left when he saw all the lights were on at the house."

"Why did you and Dale go out into the back yard, if you thought Roger had left?" Charlie asked.

Clare looked at Charlie for a few moments before answering his question. "I was surprised he hadn't come up to the house, that's all. I guess I was scared he might be waiting outside for Dale to leave. That's why I wanted to check. To make sure he had gone."

"So you were surprised when you found him dead in your back yard?"

"Of course, I was surprised. I was shocked."

Clare broke into tears. When her sobs subsided, Charlie continued. "When you got to where you found Roger lying, do you remember if the stick you hit him with was still there?"

Clare thought for a couple of seconds, and then took another tissue to blow her nose. "I don't know," she said after a moment. "I wasn't thinking about the stick."

"When you found Roger, was he lying in the same position as when you left him?"

"I don't know that either. It all happened so fast, Charlie. I was scared and I just wanted to get away from him."

Lillie Mae could tell that Clare was losing her patience.

"Then what happened?" Charlie asked.

"Dale led me back into the house where Billy was waiting for us in the kitchen. I told Billy that his father was outside, dead. We were all upset and confused. We talked about calling the police. Dale was the one who insisted on us doing so. Just as we decided to make the call, Lillie Mae, Harriet, and Kevin showed up on the doorstep. A few minutes later, you and the other police officers arrived. You know the rest."

Charlie nodded his head. "Tell me about your confession, Clare."

Clare suddenly stopped. "You were there for my confession, Charlie. Sid knows I confessed, too, so I don't think I need to go through it all again for him. You heard me say I killed Roger, as did half the residents of Mount Penn. I'm tired. Do I have to go through it all again right now?"

"No, I guess not," Charlie said, looking at Sid for confirmation. "We'll talk more about that later. You've done a good job today, Clare. You've been brave."

"I have some questions," Billy said, looking at his mother.

"And you'll get a chance to ask them," Charlie said. "But first, Sid and I need to talk to your mother without you or Lillie Mae being here. But, I don't want either one of you to leave, yet. I need to talk to you both for just a few minutes once I finish with Clare. After that, Billy, you can spend some time with your mother."

Reluctantly, Billy rose, and he and Lillie Mae walked out the door.

*   *   *

"There's good news, Lillie Mae," Charlie said, after leaving Billy with his mother, and coming into the small interview room where she sat, closing the door behind him. "Roger Ballard was not killed with the stick that Clare hit him with."

Charlie sat down opposite her.

"Captain Alton received the forensics report several days ago, but kept the information private, until now," Charlie continued. "He wanted me to hear Clare's story before he told me the news. Roger Ballard was hit all right, but it was with a different stick .We found the stick Clare used to hit Roger, and there was no blood on it."

"So, how did Roger die?" Lillie Mae asked.

"According to the report, Roger had a number of bruises on his body. He had been through a couple of violent days, and the stories we're hearing validate that. Clare hit him twice with a large stick. We've confirmed that. There was a bruise on his arm that was probably from one of those blows. She also hit him on the back of his head. That blow certainly stunned him, and may have left him temporarily unconscious, but neither one of those blows killed him. It was the final blow that did the trick."

"So, you still think Clare killed Roger," Lillie Mae said.

"No, it wasn't Clare who delivered that fatal blow," Charlie said. "It was someone else."

"How do you know?" Lillie Mae asked.

"Because the blood that was on Clare was not Roger's blood, it was Billy's. Most likely Clare got blood on her when she tended to Billy's bloody nose. But Clare believed she had killed Roger. Her story proves that to be true."

"So, who did murder, Roger?" Lillie Mae asked, now on the edge of her seat.

"That's the million dollar question," Charlie said. "We know that whoever killed Roger, killed Carl Lewis, too. And, that same person is most likely responsible for the attack on Alice Portman. Our killer is ruthless, and knows what he's doing."

"Why do you say that?" Lillie Mae asked.

"The killer was watching Roger's house, waiting for him to return. Just like the police, the killer thought Billy was the drawing card. So when Billy rushed out of the house that night, he followed him, and watched everything that happened. He was lucky, because Billy and Clare played right into his hands. When Clare hit Roger on the head and left him in his own back yard, the killer was there. He used whatever weapon he had brought with him to strike the fatal blow. Roger was dead just minutes after Clare went inside the house."

"Oh, my goodness!" Lillie Mae exclaimed.

"And that's not the worst of it," Charlie said.

"What do you mean?" Lillie Mae said, her eyes big and round.

"He's not done."

"Why do you say that?" Lillie Mae asked, alarmed. "Surely, no one else will be harmed."

"Not only do I think it's possible that someone else will be harmed, I think it's probable. But, it would be a certainty, if we let Clare go free now. The man who did these terrible things is afraid of what someone knows. That may be Clare, or it may be someone else, so for now we must continue to hold Clare in prison. It's for her own safety. I've talked to Sid Firth, and he agrees. We're not telling Clare that we know she's innocent, and I want you to promise you'll not discuss what happened here today with anybody."

"Why are you telling me all this?" Lillie Mae asked, not sure she wanted to know what the police were thinking.

"Because I need your eyes and ears, now, more than ever. And I need the Thursday morning breakfast club ladies asking questions. The information you ladies have given me so far has been invaluable. And, I want you ladies to look out for Alice Portman. She's the most vulnerable person in Mount Penn right now. I'm not ready to get her full-time police protection just yet; in fact, I'm not sure she'd accept it, but I do want you to keep an eye on her."

"Do you have any idea who we might be dealing with?" Lillie Mae asked.

"No, but we do know what kind of person we're dealing with," Charlie said, absentmindedly moving his hand through his hair. "We're on to him, and he knows it. That makes him even more dangerous. Captain Alton is still doing research and new information is coming in daily. We'll get our man, Lillie Mae. I just hope we get him before someone else is hurt."

"There is something else I want you to do," Charlie said, a mysterious gleam in his eye.

"What's that?" Lillie Mae asked, skeptically.

"I want you to lie," he said, a grin forming on his lips. "Let me explain."

17

Lillie Mae looked out her bedroom window. It looked like it was going to be another warm spring day. Alice had called the night before saying she didn't need her help this morning, but wanted a ride to breakfast club. Lillie Mae agreed to stop by and pick her up at eight forty-five. Checking the clock on her night table, Lillie Mae saw it was just before seven, plenty of time for a first cup of coffee.

She had carried out Charlie's request, and she was proud of the work she had done. Now it was up to the others to do their bit.

By the time Lillie Mae and Alice arrived at the Mountain View Inn, the parking lot was full of familiar cars.

"Looks like we may be the last people here," Alice said, opening the passenger door of Lillie Mae's Toyota.

"Except for Clare's car," Lillie Mae said, stifling a sob. "Clare is always the first to arrive for Thursday morning breakfast. Do you think she'll ever return to breakfast club after everything that's happened?"

Alice sat back in the seat. "I don't know," she said. "I'm hoping she will."

"Clare used the breakfast club to escape Roger," Lillie Mae said.

"Breakfast club meant more to her than escaping Roger," Alice said. "She cares about us, too."

"I can't believe Roger is dead," Lillie Mae said, tears forming in her eyes.

"None of us can."

"But I hated him, Alice," Lillie Mae said, looking up at Alice with sad brown eyes. "For so many years, I hated that man for what he did to Clare. And now he's dead. Why do I feel so bad?"

"Because you care for Clare, and you know how miserable she and Billy are."

"Nothing is how we think it is." Lillie Mae wiped the tears away with a tissue she took from her purse

"Lillie Mae, Alice," Janet called, when the two ladies entered the restaurant arm in arm a few minutes later. "Come sit down and order your breakfast. I'm starving this morning. The rest of us have already ordered, but the waitress won't deliver our food until all the orders are in."

"Come sit by me, Alice," Joyce said. "I want to know how Alfred is doing. Carlos is missing the little guy."

Lillie Mae sat down next to Margaret, who had urged her to do so. "So good to see you this morning, Lillie Mae," Margaret said, softly as if they were in a conspiracy together.

"You're looking very well," Lillie Mae said.

"I am feeling so much better," Margaret said. "Just two more days and Sam and I will be leaving for California. I'm looking forward to the change of scenery."

A stout waitress hovered over Lillie Mae.

"Scrambled eggs and home fries, please, and rye toast," Lillie Mae said, holding her cup up so the young lady could fill it from the coffee pot she held in her hand.

"What kind of toast?" the girl asked, pouring the coffee into Lillie Mae's cup. The waitresses at the Mountain View seldom wrote orders down. Maybe that's why they were often wrong.

"Rye," Lillie Mae said.

"How do you want your eggs?"

"Scrambled," Lillie Mae said, rolling her eyes. This place never changes, she thought.

When she was settled with her coffee, Lillie Mae looked around the table at her friends and neighbors, ladies she'd been sharing breakfast with for so many years. Her eyes rested on Hester who was sitting at the far end of the table beside Mabel. Wearing a starched white blouse, her gray hair drawn back in a tight bun, Lillie Mae thought she looked ten years older than the last time she had seen her. I wonder if she's sleeping at night. I must ask her, she thought.

Mabel looked rested though. Her round cheeks, rosy, she smiled comfortably as she chatted with her mother. Working from her house and traveling less was good for her, Lillie Mae thought.

Even Margaret looks healthy this morning. Dressed in a neat pants suit, she was talking with Joyce. Joyce, usually the neat one in the group, looked unusually disheveled this morning, as if she had gotten up late and had scurried to get ready. Janet, sitting at the head of the table, Clare's usual place, looked as jolly as ever, her plump cheeks pink under her frizzy yellow hair. Dressed in a bright blue shirt with a duck outlined in rhinestones, draped her large chest.

"Where's Harriet?" Janet asked, looking around the table. "Does anybody know if she's coming today?"

"I'm sure she is," Alice answered. "She told me when she stopped by the other day that she would see me today. You know she's always at breakfast. It's not like her to be running late."

"Harriet is never late for anything," Janet said. "Does anyone have a cell phone I can use to call her?"

"I do," Mabel says. "What's Harriet's number?"

"Oh, Harriet doesn't carry her cell phone often, dear," Alice said. "I don't think I've ever called her on it. She'll show up in time, or we'll find out what happened when we get home."

"It just doesn't seem right that Clare's not here with us today. I keep thinking she's just late, and she'll walk through the door," Margaret said, looking toward the entrance. "Everybody seems almost too happy this morning. Clare's in jail, for goodness sakes."

"Yes she is," Lillie Mae said. "But things are looking up for her. Sid Firth is going to ask that the charge against her be lowered to manslaughter. If the charge is changed, Clare will be eligible for bail. If it all works out, and there's no reason it won't, she'll be home in a couple of days."

A loud laugh burst from the men's table across the room. Lillie Mae turned and saw Pete, Sam, and Carlos huddled together.

"I wonder what struck the boys as so funny?" Lillie Mae asked.

A tear escaped down one of Margaret's cheeks. "I can't believe how horrid everyone is being."

"They're just being human," Lillie Mae said, patting her hand. "Everything will be all right."

* * *

Breakfast was almost over when Harriet and Kevin came rushing into the dining room. Their daughter, Barbara, followed at a more leisurely pace.

"They're here!" Janet announced as Harriet and Barbara headed toward the ladies' table, and Kevin went to the back of the room to the men's table.

174

"Where have you two been?" Janet asked, a fork full of pancakes moving toward her mouth.

"It's a long, sad story." Harriet said, catching Lillie Mae's eye.

"One I'm sure she wants to tell you," Barbara piped in.

The ladies nodded and laughed.

Harriet pulled out the empty chair beside Janet and sat down. Barbara walked around to the other side of the table and sat by Mabel. "We had a flat tire on the old Merryville Road and we were there for ten minutes before someone stopped to help. You all know how Kevin feels about cell phones."

Everyone nodded.

"And fixing tires."

"And, I walked off without my phone today," Barbara said, looking up at the waitress. She motioned for a menu. "Of all days."

"Fortunately, Tim Harmon came by and changed the tire for us. He's such a nice young man," Harriet said, motioning to the same waitress.

"Well, you're here now," Margaret said, a huge grin on her face. "That's what's important."

"You're looking chipper today," Harriet said.

"I guess it's because I feel so good. And the news about Clare is good, too. Have you heard?"

"Yes, I heard that Clare may be out of jail in a couple of days," Harriet said.

Margaret's face dropped. "You did hear," she said, obviously disappointed.

"But tell me what you know," Harriet hastened to add.

Margaret, perking up again, spent the next several minutes happily telling Harriet all she had heard about Clare's situation.

The waitress appeared and Harriet, noticing Janet's breakfast, ordered pancakes and coffee. "Please bring the coffee as soon as possible," she said. "I've had a bad morning, and I'm in critical need of a caffeine fix."

Barbara ordered the same as her mother. The waitress left and returned quickly with cups and a pot of coffee.

"Now that we're all here," Lillie Mae said, standing up. "There are a few things I'd like to say to you."

The women immediately stopped talking and turned their attention to Lillie Mae.

175

"I know we're all thinking about Clare today and wish she were here with us."

Heads nodded.

"And, we all want her back with us very soon and believe that is going to happen."

Again all heads nodded.

"We're all very glad that Alice is with us today and looking so well. Would you like to say something?" Lillie Mae asked.

Alice smiled and shook her head.

"And Margaret is feeling much better, too. She's getting ready for her trip to California. We're very glad she's here with us today."

Eyes turned to Margaret who beamed, but said nothing.

"That's our good news. But we have plenty of awful news to share. Two men from Mount Penn are dead, and our dear Alice Portman was attacked in her own back yard since our last breakfast. Our good friend and neighbor, Clare Ballard, has not only lost her husband, but is in jail for a murder we know she didn't commit."

Lillie Mae scanned the room.

All smiles were gone.

"What's worse is the real murderer is still roaming free, and, until he is caught, we are not safe," Lillie Mae said in a loud clear voice that must have resonated through the restaurant.

The ladies turned to each other, but remained silent.

"We have to do something to change all this," Lillie Mae rallied. "Are you in?"

"The police are working hard," Hester interrupted. "Maybe we should leave it to them to do their jobs."

"The police are working hard, Hester, doing what they do best. But we can work hard, too, doing what we do best. And that's what I suggest we do."

"We've already made some progress, but now it's time for us to really get busy. We have to keep talking to each other—that seems to be working—but, we also need to talk to people outside our group, too. It's important for each of us to reflect on what we may already know. Think about what's happening around you. Focus on those things that don't seem quite right. Every piece of information, each feeling you have, could be important. Talk to the police. They want to hear from us."

Lillie Mae paused for her words to sink in.

"Are you all in?" Lillie Mae said in her best stage voice.

"Yes!" the women called out in unison, grabbing each other's hands.

"Are you committed to finding out who murdered Carl Lewis and Roger Ballard?"

"Yes!" The women stood up.

"Let's pledge to solve this crime by next Thursday," Lillie Mae said, throwing her arms into the air.

The women looked at each other. "I don't know if we can promise to do that," Joyce responded, meekly.

"But we'll try!" Janet said.

"Yes, we'll try!" the ladies shouted, all arms now in the air.

*   *   *

Lillie Mae noticed Mabel hovering near the exit as she and Alice approached the door.

"Lillie Mae," Mabel said, stepping in front of her.

"What's up, Mabel?" Lillie Mae asked. "We didn't have much chance to talk at breakfast."

"Patrick and I want to talk to you again as soon as we can. He has something else important to tell you. When's a good time?"

"I'm taking Alice home now, and then I'm going on to my house. Can you be there in fifteen minutes?"

"We'll see you then," Mabel said, pushing her purse up on her shoulder and running out the door.

Lillie Mae noticed her speeding out of the parking lot, as she helped Alice into the car.

"Wonder what that's all about," Alice said when she was sitting comfortably in the front seat of Lillie Mae's car.

"I suspect she took my little speech to heart," Lillie Mae said, opening her window just a bit so the fresh air could seep through the car. "I'll let you know after we talk."

Lillie Mae pulled into her driveway after having settled Alice into her house. She saw Patrick and Mabel walking toward her, coming from Hester's house next door.

"Thanks for seeing us," Mabel said, looking over her shoulder at Patrick. "We want your advice about something that happened yesterday."

"Come on in," Lillie Mae said, leading the way through her back door. "Go on in the living room. I'll be there in a minute. Can I get you anything?"

"No, thanks," Patrick said. Lillie Mae thought he sounded quite grown up.

When Lillie Mae walked into the living room a few minutes later, she found Patrick and Mabel sitting on the sofa, huddled in conversation. "What did you want to tell me?"

Patrick looked at his mother as if uncertain who was to speak first. "You go on," she said. "It's your story."

"I don't know if you can help or not, Lillie Mae, but Mom said I should talk to you," Patrick said. "It's about Jerry Foster, the guy driving the truck when we were busted."

"I know who Jerry is," Lillie Mae said. "I know his mother and father, too. Tell me what's bothering you, and I'll see if I can help."

"I went to see Jerry Foster yesterday afternoon," Patrick said. "It was the first time we'd talked since the arraignment. I tried calling him several times, but he didn't answer his cell phone. Once, when I called his house, his dad answered the phone. When I asked to speak to Jerry, he told me I couldn't, and that if I ever showed my face around their place, I'd be a goner."

"Is Perry Foster a violent man?" Lillie Mae asked.

"Nah," Patrick said. "Jerry's father has always been a good guy. Now, he hates my guts. Says I'm to blame for what happened to Jerry."

"I see," Lillie Mae said. "Go on."

"Jerry was out weeding his mom's garden when I got to his house. His dad and mom were gone, so it was just the two of us. Jerry's tone was none too friendly when he saw me. Told me to leave. He said if his Dad found me at his house, he'd shoot me first, then turn the gun on him."

"That's not good," Lillie Mae said, casting a glance at Mabel who was keeping remarkably quiet.

"Jerry wasn't serious. His Dad's not that kind of person. But, he is angry with Jerry, and even angrier with me."

178

"Dads can be like that," Lillie Mae said, remembering how angry her late husband had gotten at her oldest son John one time, for shoplifting. "Sometimes anger is their way of protecting their children."

"It worse than that, Lillie Mae," Patrick said. "Jerry told me he's being held prisoner in his own home. No TV, no friends, and his dad took his cell phone from him and hid it. He said his dad yells at him all the time and won't even let him leave the place to try and get a job. Jerry told me his dad said nobody would hire a felon anyway, so what's the use wasting their time talking to him."

"Jerry's father is very angry, that's for sure. But you haven't told me anything I need to be concerned about," Lillie Mae said. "What's bothering you, Patrick?"

"Jerry says he's being treated like a slave. His Dad gives him chores to do each morning before he leaves for work, and then checks on him like he's a schoolboy when he gets home at night. If Jerry hasn't finished the job his dad told him to do that day, he has to work late into the night to get it done. Everything has to be done to his father's satisfaction and he doesn't get supper until the work passes his approval."

"His father is certainly being harsh." Lillie Mae said. "But I suspect he's showing him what life would be like in prison."

"But, Jerry and I didn't do anything wrong," Patrick said sounding more like the young Patrick."It was a bum rap. I'm glad Mom and Grandma are more reasonable with me."

"I hope we did the right thing by you, Patrick," Mabel said.

"What do you want from me?" Lillie Mae asked, genuinely confused.

"I want you to talk to Jerry's father," Patrick said. "Make him see reason."

"Why would I want to do that?" Lillie Mae said, still confused.

"Because I told Jerry I talked to Charlie Warren, and I asked him to do the same thing. That's why I went up there. He said his father would never allow it."

"Why is that?" Lillie Mae asked.

"I don't know. He knew Roger Ballard was dead."

"How did he find that out?"

"He didn't say. I guess his dad told him. He told me when he found out Roger was dead, he got scared."

"Why was he scared?" Lillie Mae asked.

"Because Roger knew the truth about us. He may be the only person who knew for sure that we were innocent."

Lillie Mae paused to think. "Good point. Roger did know you were innocent. I wonder if that could be the reason he was murdered."

"Surely not," Mabel said.

"You're probably right," Lillie Mae said.

"There's something else, Lillie Mae," Patrick said. "Mother doesn't know this."

Mabel turned sharply toward her son.

"What is it, Patrick?" Lillie Mae asked.

"Jerry told me that he knows who asked Roger to send us up to Carl Lewis' place," Patrick said, his voice lowered, as if he didn't want anyone else to hear what he was saying.

"Who was it?" Lillie Mae asked, knowing the answer to this question was important.

"He wouldn't tell me," Patrick said. "He said he hadn't told anybody who it was, not even his dad, and he wasn't going to tell me." Patrick raised his eyes to met Lillie Mae's. She was certain he was telling the truth. "I asked him to talk to Charlie Warren, but he refused."

Lillie Mae stared at Patrick, but didn't speak.

"Will you talk to Charlie and ask him to go up to the Fosters?" Patrick pleaded. "I believe that Jerry knows the name of Roger Ballard's murderer, and if anyone finds out he knows, he'll be dead, too."

18

The phone rang in Lillie Mae's bedroom. Checking the clock she saw it was three thirteen in the morning. Not again, she thought, suddenly wide awake, thinking it might be Alice.

"Hello," she answered.

"Sorry to wake you, Lillie Mae. It's Hester here."

"Are you all right, Hester?" Lillie Mae asked, imaging the worst.

"Lillie Mae, I'm frightened! I'm not sure if what's going on is real or I'm dreaming."

"Settle down, dear," Lillie Mae said in her most soothing voice, which was not easy to affect that early in the morning.

"Something woke me," Hester said. "Made my heart race and my hands tremble."

"Do you want me to come over?" Lillie Mae asked, alarmed.

"No, I realized soon enough I had been awakened by a nightmare. I dreamed that I was in jail in chains, and people were shouting that I had killed somebody. Sid Firth was in the dream, standing in the corner laughing. Mabel was there, too, and she was very angry with me. I walked toward her, but the more I walked, the farther she was away. Patrick and his friend, Jerry Foster, were in the crowd, pointing and jeering at me."

"You poor dear. Go back to sleep, Hester, and everything will be fine in the morning," Lillie Mae said.

"I did realize it was just a bad dream, Lillie Mae. That's not why I called you. It's what happened next that caused me to wake you in the middle of the night."

"Go on," Lillie Mae said.

"I got up to get a glass of warm milk. I put on my robe and walked downstairs to the kitchen. I left the lights off, because I didn't want any of the neighbors to see that I was up in the middle of the night."

"What happened then?" Lillie Mae asked, sitting up on the side of her bed, phone still against her ear.

181

"I poured myself a cup of milk, and put it in the microwave. While it was heating up, I looked out the back window, and I saw something move. If nothing had happened around here lately, I wouldn't have given it a second thought."

"What was it, Hester?"

"I'm not sure. I looked again and thought I saw a dark figure walking down the hill. It could have been a deer or a bear, Lillie Mae, but I'm almost positive it was a person."

"Are you sure you don't want me to come over?" Lillie Mae said, her heart pounding now.

"No, I don't want you to go outside. Besides, I just looked out the window again, and I don't see anything. Whoever or whatever it was that was out there, is gone."

"You did the right thing to call me, Hester I will let Charlie Warren know in the morning what happened. Like you said, it's probably nothing, but Charlie told us to tell him about anything we think is suspicious. This certainly qualifies."

"Lillie Mae," Hester said, her voice very low, but still filled with terror. "You don't think it was the murderer, do you?"

"No, of course not, Hester. Don't be silly. Go back to bed. We will take care of this in the morning."

"Okay," Hester said, sounding relieved. "Thanks."

Lillie Mae sat perfectly still on her bed for a full minute after hanging up the phone. "What if it was the murderer," she said very softly, a cold chill running up her spine.

*　　*　　*

Lillie Mae tapped on Joyce's back door later that morning. Having trouble falling back to sleep after talking to Hester, she thought of Carlos and his nightly excursions and wanted to find out if he had been out romping last night, before she called Charlie.

"Lillie Mae," Joyce said, when she answered the door. "I'm glad you're here. Carlos and I are having a heated discussion, and you're just the person to mediate. Come on in, and have a cup of coffee with us."

Lillie Mae stepped back, surprised. "You want me to mediate your argument?"

"It'll be easy," Joyce laughed. "Come on in."

Lillie Mae followed her into the kitchen. Carlos sat at the breakfast table, a cup of coffee in front of him. Wearing reading glasses that had slipped down his nose, he looked like the absent-minded professor. Holding the front section of the New York Times completed the image nicely.

"Morning Lillie Mae," he said. "To what do we owe the pleasure of your company."

"I came to find out if you were out roaming the mountain in the wee hours last night," Lillie Mae said. "But Joyce has asked me to mediate your argument."

Carlos looked over the top of his glasses. "Joyce, that's not fair. Lillie Mae is sure to side with you."

"Lillie Mae is unpredictable," Joyce said, laughing. "She may just as well side with you."

"Get on with it," Lillie Mae said, losing her patience. "But, first, answer my question."

"No," Carlos said. "I did not go out last night and prowl around the neighborhood. Why do you ask?"

"No reason," Lillie Mae said, accepting a cup of coffee from Joyce. "Now tell me about this quarrel you're having."

Carlos looked at Joyce, then back at Lillie Mae. "I want to go on a short vacation, and Joyce doesn't. It's that simple."

"Things are never simple," Lillie Mae said. "Why do you want to go on a vacation now?"

"I was talking to Sam yesterday at breakfast, and he said that he and Margaret are flying to California in a couple of days to spend some time with Margaret's brother and his family. The trip sounded like such a fun idea, I thought Joyce and I might go somewhere, too."

"I asked him where he wanted to go?" Joyce said, buttering a piece of toast that she handed to Lillie Mae. She moved the butter dish towards Carlos. "He said he didn't know."

"I just want to get away from here for a while. A cruise would be nice. Sometimes you can get a really great price for when you sign up at the last minute. How does a trip to the southern Caribbean sound to you? No fuss, no muss, no hurricanes. Just miles and miles of clear blue water."

"Sounds pretty good to me," Lillie Mae said.

"Well, it sounds wonderful—of course, it does," Joyce said. "It's not the idea, it's the timing."

Carlos explained: "As I said, I was talking to Sam yesterday at breakfast, and he gave me the idea. I hate it around here right now. There is just too much stuff going on and Mount Penn doesn't feel right anymore. I'd like to go away and then come back and have everything settled. I didn't move to the mountains for drama. We had enough of that in the city. I moved here for peace. And all that's been disrupted. I don't want to ever hate it here,but this place is starting to make me feel uncomfortable. So, I want to get away for a while."

Joyce nodded her head. "I do understand what you're saying, Carlos. But I don't want to run away, and desert my friends as soon as the going gets tough. Clare needs our support now. So does Alice. She's seems fine, but she's not a young woman."

"We're not young, either. Are you saying you care more about your friends than you do about me?"

"Don't be silly. And don't try to use any of that psycho guilt on me. It's not going to work. You know that very well. What I'm saying is that I'd love to go on a vacation with you. I love the planning, the anticipation, and everything that goes into making it special. But I don't want to go on a cruise just to run away. Especially not now. You'll be fine, Carlos. All this nonsense here in Mount Penn will be settled before too much longer, and our lives will be back to the way they were before it all began."

"What do you say, Lillie Mae?" Joyce went on. "Should we go or should we stay?"

"I have no idea," Lillie Mae said. "Please don't make me decide."

* * *

Lillie Mae had just hung up the phone with Charlie when she heard a tap, tap on the window of her back door. Looking up, she saw Billy Ballard standing there.

"What a nice surprise," she said, when she opened the door. "You're looking a lot better than the last time I saw you, young man."

"I'm feeling a lot better," Billy said. "I doubt if I ever will get over Dad's death, but I'm not as crazy as I was, thank goodness. Maybe there's some hope for me and Mom, yet."

Dressed in an old pair of jeans and a flannel work shirt, Billy looked as if he had showered and shaved recently. He looked fresh and young.

"You've been through way too much, Billy," Lillie Mae, said fighting the tears that formed in her eyes. "But, you still should have lots of hope."

"I stopped by to see if you'd like to hike up to the hideout with me," Billy said, looking at Lillie Mae eagerly. "I want to give the place a good look around, and I'd like you to be there if I find what I'm looking for."

"Sure, I'll come along," Lillie Mae said, casting a look outside. "Besides, it's a perfect day for a hike. Let me put my jacket and boots on, and I'll be right with you."

A few minutes later, when they were outside, just feet from the trail, Lillie Mae suggested that they power walk.

"Love to," Billy said, a hint of a smile creeping onto his lips. "The exercise will do me good."

"Let's go, then," Lillie Mae said. "Whoever wins buys dinner."

"You're on," Billy said, smiling broadly now, obviously having picked up on the joke.

Twenty minutes later they were at the hideout. Lillie Mae, catching her breath, was first, but only because Billy let her win at the end, she knew. It was fun.

"Dinner's on me, anytime," she said, looking around.

Lillie Mae knew the hideout was up here in the woods, but hadn't seen it in years. A battered old shack with the door half hanging off its hinges, she could not understand its appeal, except that it was remote and offered some shelter. Large boulders surrounded it, as if it were a fort that needed protecting. Leaves and other debris blanketed the ground, along with cigarette butts and beer cans.

"What are we looking for?" Lillie Mae asked.

"I'm not sure," Billy said. "Any sort of evidence that proves my dad didn't kill Carl Lewis. I've got this crazy idea that the murder weapon might be here. According to Patrick, Dad told him this is where Carl Lewis was murdered. But, the police set up the crime scene closer to the trail, where you found the body, so I'm not sure if they even searched up here. "

"Let's do it," Lillie Mae said, stooping to pick up a piece of paper that she slipped into her jacket pocket. "Are we looking for a stick or a club?"

"I'm not sure. We'll know what we're looking for when we see it," Billy said, moving closer to the shack. "I'll search in here."

"I'll go around back," Lillie Mae said.

Lillie Mae, down on her knees looking closer at a large stick, heard a twig snap. Jerking her head up, she listened more closely. Hearing leaves rustle and another twig snap, she glanced over her shoulder. Suspecting a deer, she got up and walked a few feet toward the trail to check it out. She saw Sam Jenkins walking down the trail toward her.

"What are you doing here in the woods?" she asked Sam when he was close enough to hear. "I thought you hiked the road."

"Most of the time I do hike the road. But on days like today, I often go further into the woods. What are you doing here, Lillie Mae? You're popping up everywhere these days," he said, a smile covering his face.

"I'm here with Billy Ballard," she said. "We're looking for clues to connect this place to Roger's murderer."

"Sam," Billy said, coming around the side of the shed, his brows lifted in surprise. "I thought I heard voices. Good to see you." Billy's hand was outstretched to Sam, who shook it, then slapped him on the back.

Although Sam wasn't much more than fifteen years older than Billy, they looked generations apart. Both men were on the short side and slim, but that's all they had in common. Billy still looked like a kid, while Sam looked very grown up.

"How are you doing, son?" Sam asked. "I know your family's been through hell these last days. Is there anything Margaret and I can do for you?"

"I'm better," Billy said, stepping back a little. "But I doubt if I will ever get over the last couple of days. Dad is dead and Mom is in jail. I've been walking around in a daze, trying to figure out what happened. That's why Lillie Mae and I are out here. Somewhere, there's an answer to this mystery, and I think if we look hard enough, we'll find it."

"Let me help, too," Sam said. "Margaret will be fine without me for awhile. Tell me what you're looking for."

186

"Something that could be a murder weapon," Billy said. "We'll know it when we find it."

The trio searched the area together, finding lots of trash and cigarette butts, but not much else. Moving farther up the hill, Billy's foot hit on something. He reached down to pick it up.

"Look what I found!" Billy called out, after looking closely at the large, solid club hidden in the leaves. He carried it toward the others. "Doesn't that look like blood?"

He pointed at the top of the club.

Sam took the club from Billy. "Where did you find this?" Sam said, turning the club over in his hands.

"Just over there," he pointed. "It was under a pile of leaves. I almost tripped over it. Do you think this could be the murder weapon?"

"I think you should take it back with you and call Charlie Warren," Lillie Mae said, looking over Sam's shoulder. "It could be nothing, or it could be an important clue."

Sam looked at his watch. "I need to get back right away," he said. "I can take the club with me if you plan to stay here longer. I'll call Charlie."

"We can all walk back together," Lillie Mae said, brushing off her pants. "We can call the police from my house."

"Let's get started," Sam said, suddenly in a hurry. "This may be the breakthrough the police need."

"That would be wonderful, if it were true," Billy said, following Sam and Lillie Mae back down the trail towards Mount Penn.

*   *   *

Charlie and Lillie Mae had been standing on Dale Beaver's front porch for several minutes.

"Should I knock again?" Lillie Mae asked, raising her hand and forming a fist. "Maybe he has the TV on loud and can't hear us."

"I'm sure he's in there," Charlie said. "His truck's parked in front of the house."

Lillie Mae dropped her hand just as Dale opened the door.

"What can I do for you two?" Dale asked, showing mild surprise. "I was just on my way out."

'I'd like to talk to you," Charlie said. "Lillie Mae's here for support."

187

"Come in," he said moving out of their way so they could enter. "How are you going to support me, Lillie Mae?"

Lillie Mae noticed a brown duffle bag by the staircase. A tennis racket stood nearby. "Are you going somewhere?" she asked, ignoring his question.

"Just for the weekend," Dale said, with a shrug. "I'm going to visit a tennis buddy in Baltimore."

Lillie Mae could tell Dale was tired. His eyes were listless and red-rimmed. She suspected he might have done his share of crying over the last couple of days.

"Everything is folding in on me here, and I need some space, if just for the weekend," he said. "Hester Franklin is going to take over the music at church tomorrow. I'll be back home in the evening, since I've got to be in school on Monday. I've missed too many work days over this mess already."

"I won't keep you long," Charlie said, following Dale into the small sitting room just off the hall. Lillie Mae stayed a couple of steps behind the men.

"I heard you talked to Clare yesterday," Charlie said, sitting down on a straight back wooden chair. Dale sat in an identical chair just across from him. Lillie Mae opted for the sofa, feeling only slightly uncomfortable, passing between the two men to get there."

"I did," Dale said.

"How did it go?" Charlie asked.

"Not as good as I wanted it to," Dale said, his jaw tense. "Clare seemed in good enough spirits, though."

"Did she say anything to you about Roger?"

"No, we didn't mention his name, although Roger was right there with us the entire time," Dale said.

"So she didn't say that she killed him."

"Not yesterday," Dale said.

"Did you kill Roger Ballard," Charlie asked, his face as sober as Lillie Mae had ever seen it.

"You've asked me that question before," Dale said, dropping his head.

"I have," Charlie said. "And, you told me you didn't kill Roger."

Dale shook his head, an ironic smirk on his lips. "My answer's the same, Charlie. I did not kill Roger Ballard. Am I glad he's dead, might have been a more enlightened question."

Charlie took the bait. "Are you glad he's dead?"

"I was," Dale answered, dropping his head again. "But, now, I'm not so sure."

"Because …" Charlie said, drawing the word out.

"Because Clare and Billie are devastated. How could I possibly want people I care about to go through so much pain?" Dale brushed away a tear that moved slowly down his cheek.

"Is Clare protecting Billy?" Charlie asked.

Dale hesitated before answering. "At first, I thought that might be the case. But, I don't believe it now. Billy adores Roger. I've come to realize that. He was angry with him the night everything happened, but he never would have seriously hurt his father. Just look at him now. The kid is hurting. I've tried to reach out to him, but he wants nothing to do with me. He thinks Clare and I were closer than we ever were. We've both told him how our relationship was, but he won't believe us. I feel desperately sorry for Billy. His life will never be the same."

Charlie inhaled sharply, then turned and looked out the window. "Where were you before you showed up at Clare's house the night Roger was killed?"

"I met with several parents after school that day. I'll be happy to give you their names. They'll remember, I suspect, since most of them were not too pleased with me. Issues with their kids," he said, sitting back in his chair. "After the meetings, I stayed another hour catching up on the paperwork from the parent conferences, and then went to the Market Tree for dinner. When I finally got back to Mount Penn, I drove by Clare's house, and all the lights were on. Since that was unusual, I stopped in to see if something was wrong. You know what happened next."

"Did you think Roger might be there?"

"I didn't give it much thought, but I had noticed that the yellow Hummer he drives wasn't in the driveway."

"I see," Charlie said, pausing again as if thinking how to ask the next question.

"You were seen with Clare earlier that day up at High Mount."

"Yes, I had called Clare that morning and asked if she knew what all the excitement was about. She was as curious as we all were about what was going on. I asked her to ride along with me up the mountain, and she agreed."

"You've told me several times before that you and Clare were not having an affair, and yet several people have told me they've seen you together. This is the last time I'm going to ask you," Charlie said, his eyes meeting Dale's, "and I want you to tell me the truth. Were you and Clare having an affair?"

"Clare and I were not, and are not, having an affair, Charlie. I think she's the most beautiful, talented woman I know, who gave up everything for one of the biggest jerks that ever lived. And yes, I do love her, but she's never loved me. She made that very clear yesterday. That's why I have to get out of Mount Penn for a couple of days."

"I prefer that you didn't leave town right now, but I can't prevent you from doing so. Give me your cell phone number, just in case I need to get in touch with you."

Charlie stood, signaling that he was ready to leave.

Dale, standing as well, recited his cell phone number and Charlie punched it into his own phone.

Charlie reached out and touched Dale's arm. "I'm sorry, man, but I have to do my job." His voice filled with emotion. "I know you're going through a lot right now. You hang in there. Things will get better, I promise."

Dale nodded, but said nothing.

Lillie Mae patted Dale's arm, a sympathetic smile on her lips, as she followed Charlie out the door.

*   *   *

As Mabel Goody opened her back door, juggling a bag of groceries in one hand and the key in the other, she heard her name being called.

"Mabel," Lillie Mae yelled again. Mabel turned around, a bag still in her hand. "Do you have a minute?"

"Sure," Mabel said, "let me just take these groceries in, and I'll be right with you."

The trunk of her car still open, Lillie Mae picked up the last two bags, closed the truck, and followed Mabel into the house.

"What's up?" she asked, taking the bags from Lillie Mae.

"It's your mother," Lillie Mae said. "She had a bit of a fright last night. Did she call you?"

"I've been out most of the day and I haven't talked to Mother," Mabel said. "Is she all right?"

A loud pounding noise on Mabel's front door interrupted the conversation. "Who can that be?" Mabel asked, turning surprised eyes on Lillie Mae when the knocking continued.

Dropping the bag on the kitchen table, Mabel walked through the living room to answer the door, Lillie Mae keeping her distance behind her. Patrick, who must have heard the racket from his bedroom, rushed down the steps. Reaching the door first, Patrick opened it.

"What do you want?" Patrick said warily, seeing Perry Foster standing at the door.

"Listen, you punk," Perry threatened, taking a step toward Patrick. "You stay away from my house, you hear me."

Mabel appeared behind Patrick. "What's going on here?"

"This here is between me and your son, ma'am. I think it best you stay out of it."

Lillie Mae, hidden behind the door, could still see through the crack and would have sworn the man was blushing.

"Jerry and I didn't do anything," Patrick whined, citing what was now a familiar tale. "We were given a bum rap. Even the police believe we were framed."

As if reminded of why he had come, Perry turned his attention back to Patrick. "I don't want nobody snooping around my place. Charlie Warren or no Charlie Warren, you had no right to tell Jerry to talk to the police."

Perry's hands, now fists, pointed at Patrick.

"You wait just a minute," Mabel said, pushing her way between Patrick and Perry, her hands up to block Perry's fists. "You can't come onto my property and threaten my son."

"I'm saying the same thing as you, little missy. Your Patrick has no right to snoop around my place either and that's what he's done."

"What's going on up at your place, that you don't want the police to know about?" Mabel asked.

Perry turned his attention to Mabel. "I ain't hiding nothing from nobody. I just don't like police minding my business. They leave

191

me alone, I leave them alone. And that goes for my family, too. Your son has been getting my son into trouble. I have a right to decide who my family associates with, and who they stay away from."

"You can do whatever you like when you're in your own home," Mabel said forcefully. A foot shorter than her foe, she had moved within inches of him, her chin pointed toward his face. David and Goliath popped into Lillie Mae's brain.

"But this is my house, you lout!" she said boldly. "You better watch what you say, and what you do, or I'm calling the police on you now."

Perry Foster backed off the porch.

"You watch yourself, sonny," he said, his right index finger pointed at Patrick. "And stay away from my family or you'll be sorry."

"That's it," Mabel said as she moved to the end of the porch. "I'm calling Charlie Warren. You have just threatened my son on my property. That's against the law!"

"You better leave me and my family alone!"

Perry opened his truck door and jumped in.

"You don't have to fight my battles," Patrick said to his mother when Perry had driven off.

"I don't know when I've been so angry," Mabel said to Lillie Mae, ignoring Patrick for the moment. "That man has some nerve. I swear if I was a guy, I would have slugged him."

"Call Charlie," Lillie Mae said, picking up the phone. "Or I will."

"That's exactly what I'm going to do," Mabel said, grabbing the phone from Lillie Mae. "That man had no right to come here and threaten my family."

19

Lillie Mae was sitting at the kitchen table, drinking a cup of coffee and reading the Sunday paper when the phone rang.

"Lillie Mae here," she answered.

"Are you going to church this morning?" Hester asked, dispensing with the usual courtesies.

"Not today, dear," Lillie Mae said. "I want to check on Alice this morning. Why?"

"Mabel wants you to come to lunch at her house today," Hester said. "She told me to call you yesterday, and I forgot. She's says it's a thank you for being there for me the night before, and for insisting I talk to Charlie Warren. Can you come?"

"Sure," Lillie Mae said, grateful for the invitation. "What time?"

"Noon is good."

"I'll be there," Lillie Mae said, hanging up the phone.

Lillie Mae checked her watch. It was almost eight, plenty of time for a walk before going to Alice's house.

"Lillie Mae!" Alice called when she saw her friend walking up the steep hill from the park. "Come quick, please."

Alice was flushed.

"What is it?" Lillie Mae asked.

"Come into the house and I'll tell you what's happened," Alice said, taking hold of Lillie Mae's arm and guiding her up the steps to the porch. "I don't want to talk out here."

"What's so important?" Lillie Mae asked.

Alice guided Lillie Mae into the living room. Delighted to see the newcomer, Alfred jumped up, brushing her knees with his tail. "Settle down," Alice ordered, pointing a finger at the dog. "You know better than to jump on guests."

Lillie Mae reached down and petted Alfred who was sitting by her right foot.

"Let me get you a cup of coffee," Alice said. "I brewed a fresh pot right before I went to see Sam and Margaret. Go on in the living room. I'll be right there."

193

"Are you going to tell me what's up?" Lillie Mae asked, following Alice into the kitchen.

"Go on in and settle yourself, dear," Alice said, waving the back of her hand towards the room. "It's rather a long story. Give me a minute, and I'll be right there."

Alfred followed Lillie Mae into the living room, jumped up on the sofa when she sat down, and snuggled close to her. "Is everything all right?" Lillie Mae called, her hand resting on Alfred's head.

Alice walked into the room carrying a tray with two cups of coffee. "I don't know," she said, a crease forming between her eyes. "The strangest thing has happened."

"Tell me everything," Lillie Mae said.

"I went to see Sam and Margaret this morning," Alice said.

"And?" she asked.

"I took them the coffee cake you brought me the other day," Alice said. "I hope you don't mind. I wanted to take them something, and I haven't baked since my accident."

"No problem," Lillie Mae said. "I hope they enjoyed it."

"They did," Alice said you baked it, so they sent you their thanks."

Lillie Mae offered a brief smile and took a sip of coffee. "Go on," she said, putting the delicate cup back into his saucer.

"Margaret was looking so much better than the last time I saw her. This trip to California is like a tonic for her."

"Did Sam go for a walk while you were there?" Lillie Mae asked.

"He did," Alice said. "Why do you ask?"

"No reason. Go on with your story."

"Margaret gushed all over me," Alice said, laughing. "Like she usually does. Told me I was an amazing woman for being out and about so quickly after what happened to me. I told her I was running away from you."

"Running away from me?" Lillie Mae said.

"Yes, indeed," Alice said. "Said I was a bit bored and tired of all your fussing, so I ran away from you. That's when I told her you had baked the cake."

"I'm not sure I'm liking my role in all this," Lillie Mae said.

"That's not important," Alice said, swiping her hand in dismissal. "I just needed an excuse to visit them."

"I see," Lillie Mae said. "I'm the scapegoat."

"Exactly," Alice said.

"Let's get to the good part of this story," Lillie Mae said, shifting her legs and rousing Alfred who had fallen asleep beside her.

"Sam brought us the cake and some coffee," Alice said.

"Boring," Lillie Mae quipped.

"I know," Alice agreed. "But the coffee story is actually fun."

"Okay, I'll bite," Lillie Mae said. "But this better be good."

"The coffee smelled quite lovely, so I asked Sam if he bought it locally. 'Oh, no,' he said," Alice gushed, doing a respectable Sam imitation. "'I have it shipped special from the city. Margaret's picky about her coffee.'"

"He didn't?" Lillie Mae said, giggling.

"He did," Alice said. "And he was serious. I could barely contain myself."

"I'm still waiting for this story to get interesting," Lillie Mae said.

"You're going to have to wait a bit longer," Alice said. "Sam went out for a walk after practically begging Margaret, and Margaret and I did the usual chat thing while he was gone. She talked about her upcoming trip to California, and I talked about the attack and Alfred, of course, and before we knew it, almost an hour had passed. Sam came back from his walk flushed from the fresh air. I thought it a good time to make my excuses and leave."

"This is what was so urgent, that you had to tell me right away," Lillie Mae said.

'No," Alice said stretching out the word. "It's what happened next."

"Sam ushered me to the door with his usual bits of nonsense. Warning me to take care and stuff like that. I'm not sure what it was he said, but something triggered my memory."

"Yes," Lillie Mae said, prodding.

"When the door was closed, and I had walked down the back steps and around to the side of the house, I glanced up at Hester's house, and then it struck me. I remembered what was wrong, Lillie Mae. I knew right then why I had been attacked."

195

"Don't tell me yet," Lillie Mae said, up on her feet. "We're calling Charlie Warren."

* * *

"Mom, call Patrick to lunch," Mabel said, handing Lillie Mae a bowl of mashed potatoes to take to the dining room table. "Tell him we're just about ready to eat."

"Patrick, it's time for lunch," Hester called up the stairs.

"I'll be right down." Patrick shouted back.

Lillie Mae could hear the boy moving around upstairs as she turned to go back into the kitchen. "What else can I do to help?"

"You can carry the pitcher of iced tea into the dining room. Other than that, everything is ready."

"Are you hungry, young man?" Hester asked, when Patrick walked into the room a moment later.

"Starved." Patrick smiled at her and sat down at his usual place at the table. Lillie Mae thought that his arrest might have done the boy a world of good. He seems nicer, she thought. Wouldn't it be wonderful if something positive could come out of all this mess?

When Mabel sat down, Hester offered a short prayer. "Lord, give us the strength to get through this day. Thank you for this food and for our family and friends to share it with. Amen"

Amens resounded around the table.

"Everything is just delicious," Lillie Mae said, pointing to the bowl of mashed potatoes as a request for a second helping. "This is quite a treat for me."

"Well, you deserve it, dear," Hester said. 'You've been a big help to our family of late. It's the least we can do."

"You deserve a good meal, too, Mother," Mabel said. "You did a great job with the music and choir this morning. I was very proud of you."

"Way to go, Grandma," Patrick said, putting a fork full of pork into his mouth.

Hester glowed with the compliments.

Just as Mabel stood up to get the dessert, the telephone rang. She hurried into the kitchen to answer it. Lillie Mae could hear her talking low, but could only catch a couple of words. When Mabel returned to the room, she looked pale.

"Who was that on the phone?" Hester asked.

"I don't know."

196

Mabel scanned the trio of faces, her eyes wide.

"What do you mean, you don't know?" Patrick asked.

"Somebody with a strange voice said I was next." Mabel said, sitting back down at the table. "I couldn't make out if it was a man or a woman. The voice was muffled."

"Next for what?" Hester asked, confused.

"I have no idea." Mabel put her hands up to her throat. "My first thought was next to be murdered."

"It was probably Perry Foster," Patrick said. "He was so mad yesterday, I bet he's making crank calls today."

"Perry is stupid enough to make a crank call. Even though the voice was disguised, it had none of the inflections of Perry's voice. I really don't think it was him. But it could have been."

"What are you going to do?" asked Hester.

"I don't know."

"The same thing happened to Clare," Lillie Mae said, her voice low.

"What do you mean?" Mabel said, looking at Lillie Mae.

"Somebody with a weird voice called and threatened her."

"When was this?" Hester asked.

"The day before Roger was murdered," Lillie Mae said.

The phone rang again. Patrick rose to answer it, but Lillie Mae stopped him. "Let me get it," she said.

Picking up the phone after the third ring, she held the phone to her ear without offering a greeting. Hester, Mabel, and Patrick gathered around her.

"Who is this?" she asked.

"We're not scared of you!" Lillie Mae shouted into the mouth piece, and the phone went dead.

"We're calling Charlie," Lillie Mae said. "I know he's here in Mount Penn talking to Alice, so he can be here in a couple of minutes. Let's hope he can get a trace on this call."

* * *

Charlie and Lillie Mae left Mabel's house together.

"Are you headed home?" Charlie asked.

"Yes, for a bit," she said. "I have to do a couple of things before I walk down to the park this afternoon. I don't want to miss the festivities today. Opening day is often the best day of the year. And, my favorite band is playing at the pavilion this afternoon."

197

"Let me drive you, then," Charlie said, opening the door of his truck. "We can talk along the way."

Lillie Mae opened the door on her side of the truck and climbed in. "What's up?"

"We're almost done, Lillie Mae," Charlie said, starting the car. "Alice's information confirmed my suspicions."

"Does it put her in danger?" Lillie Mae asked, already sure she knew the answer.

Charlie hesitated. "Yes," he finally said. "Alice is a real trooper. She'll come through for us. All you ladies have surprised me. In the very best way."

"Do you think Mabel's in danger, too?" Lillie Mae asked.

"Yes, but for a very different reason than Alice," Charlie said. "Watch out for her, and Hester. I'll be here in Mount Penn full time until all this is settled, but I can't be everywhere at once. I need you and the other Thursday morning breakfast ladies to keep an eye on each other. You're doing great so far," he added glancing at Lillie Mae. "Keep calling me like you're doing just as soon as something comes up."

"Will do," Lillie Mae said, thinking she might be having too much fun under the circumstances.

"How about Clare?" Lillie Mae asked. "When will she be released?"

"Clare is still the official suspect in Roger Ballard's death. Believe me, jail is the safest place for her right now. If all goes as expected, she'll be free soon enough. But we need to keep a close watch on Billy and Dale. Assign someone to do that."

"Can you tell me anymore about the research the police are doing?" Lillie Mae asked.

"No," Charlie said, pulling his truck into her driveway. "I've probably told you way more than I should already. Just know the police are working hard, too, and it's all coming together. It won't be much longer now, Lillie Mae, and we will have caught ourselves a murderer."

Lillie Mae opened the truck door and stepped out. "I'll call you once everything's in place."

"Good," Charlie said, a small grin on his lips. "Let's get this show started.

*   *   *

198

Lillie Mae rapped on Alice's back door but there was no answer, nor any response from Alfred. She must have already left for the park, she thought. They hadn't really made plans to go together, after all.

Setting off down the hill Lillie Mae ran into Pete Hopkins just outside the park. "I fell asleep after lunch, watching the Orioles' game," he said, keeping in step with her. "Must have been the big lunch me and Janet had."

"Where is Janet?" Lillie Mae asked, looking around Pete.

"I left her snoring away on the daybed," Pete said, with a grin. "I didn't have the heart to wake her." Pete glanced over his shoulder as if he were about to share a secret. "We went off our diets today, you see. We went to the big buffet at the Mountain View Inn after church for lunch. I guess we both ate just a bit too much. The diets and all, you understand."

Lillie Mae smiled. "I do understand."

"I left her a note telling her I'd gone to the park to listen to the band. I'm sure she'll be over to join us before the festivities are over."

When Pete and Lillie Mae reached the pavilion they both looked around for neighbors and friends. "There's Sam," Pete said, pointing across the way. Sam must have heard him because he turned around and waved, then headed their way.

"Hi, Lillie Mae, Pete," he said. "It's certainly a lovely opening day, isn't it? Best I remember in years."

"Where's Margaret?" Pete asked, still scanning the crowd for familiar faces.

"She's home, napping," Sam said.

Pete laughed. "So's my Janet. But if she doesn't appear in the next half hour, I'll run home and wake her up. She'd be disappointed to miss all this."

"I'm going home to ask Margaret if she wants to come to the park, too," Sam said, stepping away from them. "Maybe we'll see you both later."

"Such a nice young man," Pete said, once Sam had moved on. "There's Alice, over there by the picnic table. She's got Alfred with her. Who's that young woman she's talking to, Lillie Mae?"

"It looks like our soon to be new neighbor, Rose Maynard," Lillie Mae said. "Let's go say hi."

Alfred jumped up as soon as he saw Lillie Mae headed his way. "Don't bark," Alice warned as Lillie Mae and Pete came up to them.

Lillie Mae stooped to pet Alfred on the head. "You've met Rose Maynard," Alice said to Lillie Mae. "And, Rose, this is Pete Hopkins."

Pete grinned like a schoolboy. "Nice to meet you," he mumbled.

"You'll meet Pete's wife Janet soon," Alice said. "She's one of the original members of the Thursday morning breakfast club. Rose is going to join us for breakfast just as soon as she's settled," Alice said, meeting Lillie Mae's eyes.

"And that date's getting closer," Lillie Mae said.

"It is," Rose said. "Just six weeks until the movers' come. I'm very excited."

"How's the work coming on your new place?" Lillie Mae asked.

"It's coming slowly, but the work that is done is good," Rose said. "All this takes time, I'm sure. This is my first house renovation, so I'm learning a lot. Maybe too much," she added, with a grin.

"Who's here today?" Lillie Mae asked, sure that Alice would know.

"I've talked to Carlos and Joyce earlier, and Harriet and Kevin were here for a short while. They stopped by the house after church, and we walked down here together. Kevin wanted to get home for the baseball game so they didn't stay long." Alice paused as if recalling other people she had chatted with. "I saw Patrick Goody, but just waved in passing, and Sam, of course."

"Here comes Janet now," Lillie Mae said, seeing Janet toddling across the park through the crowd, certainly in search of Pete.

Pete turned quickly and spotted his wife.

"Over here, Janet," he called.

But she was looking away and must not have heard him.

"I'll go fetch her," he said.

"I must go," Rose said. "It's been fun chatting, Alice. And, Lillie Mae, let's get together the next time I'm in Mount Penn. I work tomorrow you see, so I need to get back to Baltimore early. I hate driving in the city after dark."

"I would love a chat the next time you're here," Lillie Mae said, beaming. "Do stop by my house anytime when you're here. Everybody else in Mount Penn does."

When Rose had left, Lillie Mae turned to Alice. "So how did it all go," she asked, her voice just loud enough for Alice to hear.

"It couldn't have gone better," Alice said with a wink.

"Call Charlie when you get home, and give him a full report," Lillie Mae said.

"I'm going back to the house now. I'm tired and so is this little guy," Alice said, pulling on Alfred's lead to wake him up. He had curled up into a puppy ball and was asleep by her feet.

"I have some more work to do here," Lillie Mae said, her voice still low. "But I'll be in touch later."

"We'll talk soon," Lillie Mae said, raising her voice. "You rest this afternoon, dear."

"I will," Alice said, as she strolled away, Alfred following behind.

20

"What is it?" Lillie Mae asked, a bit out of breath when Hester opened her door. "You sounded frantic on the phone?"

"It's Mabel," Lillie Mae. "I've been calling her house all morning and no one's answering the phone."

"Maybe she's out for a walk or has gone shopping," Lillie Mae said, sitting at the breakfast table. "Why the panic?"

"Mabel said she was working from her home office today, I'm sure. She's never been one to go shopping during the day, especially on a workday. I have this feeling something's terribly wrong."

"Maybe she was on the other line when you called."

"No," Hester said firmly. "The answer machine came on. It wouldn't have done that if she was talking to somebody else."

"Maybe she was called out of town on business and didn't have a chance to let you know she was leaving town."

Hester paused to consider Lillie Mae's suggestion.

"That could be it," Hester said, sounding relieved. "When I called her cell phone before, she could have been on a plane. That would explain why she didn't pick up that phone either. Let me try her cell number again."

Hester punched in a number and waited. A few moments later she looked over at Lillie Mae. "She's still not answering."

"I don't think you need to worry. Mabel can take care of herself."

"Remember the phone calls, Lillie Mae," Hester said, her eyes huge as they met Lillie Mae's. "You're next, someone said. We have to go to Mabel's house and see what's going on."

"Okay," Lillie Mae said. "If it'll make you feel better, we'll go right away. I'll drive. You go get ready."

Lillie Mae watched as Hester changed her shoes, picked up her purse from the kitchen counter, then grabbed two sets of house keys off the key board by the back door.

"These are Mabel's keys," she said, holding up a set of keys. "To think nobody in Mount Penn locked their doors just a week ago."

Hester and Lillie Mae walked across Hester's backyard and got into Lillie Mae's car. She had locked her door, too, so she had her keys with her. In less than five minutes they stood on Mabel's front porch.

Hester knocked and waited for a few moments, then knocked again.

"Let's go around back and see if the car's in the driveway," she said, already off the porch and heading toward the back.

Lillie Mae had to agree that the house looked empty.

"That's Patrick's motorcycle," Harriet said, pointing to the large black machine sitting in the yard. "But Mabel's car is gone."

"Maybe Patrick's home but still asleep," Lillie Mae suggested.

"Let's go check," Hester said, taking Mabel's keys out of her pocket. A moment later the two ladies were standing in the kitchen.

"Something's wrong," Hester said, scanning the room. "Look at this place. It's a mess. Look at those dishes stacked in the sink. And the microwave door has been left open."

"It does look like she left in a hurry," Lillie Mae said, following Hester's hand with her eyes. Mabel was known for being a careful housekeeper.

"Patrick," Hester called out tentatively from the bottom of the stairs, but the house remained silent.

Hester walked into the living room. "Come here, Lillie Mae," she called. "Look at that."

A suitcase was lying on the sofa. It was empty except for a pack of matches, a remnant of another trip.

Lillie Mae walked to the back of the room where the office was set up. "Mabel's laptop is missing, too" she said, scanning the desk for clues. "It certainly looks like she packed up in a hurry and left."

Hester followed her into the Mabel's office. "Look Lillie Mae," she said, pointing to the phone. "Mabel has messages."

She picked up the phone.

"There are four new messages here," she said. "Three are from me."

"Are you sure she didn't try to call you?" Lillie Mae asked. She thought Mabel would have let her mother know if she had to go out of town, especially now with all that was happening in Mount Penn.

"I'm sure," Hester said, becoming flustered.

"Let's go upstairs," Lillie Mae said. "Who knows what we will find!"

Both ladies climbed the stairs to the second floor, neither one saying a word as they made their way slowly to the top.

Patrick's room was a mess, with clothes strewn all over the bed. Most were clean. He must have taken everything out of his closet before deciding what to take with him. Mabel's room wasn't as chaotic, but she had obviously packed in a hurry .

"Where could they have gone?" Hester asked, her face drained of color.

"Don't worry yet?" Lillie Mae said, her heart pounding so loudly she was afraid Hester might hear it.

"I'm sure it has something to do with those phone calls on Sunday," Hester said, sitting down on the bed, grabbing her own hand to keep it from shaking.

"Look Lillie Mae!" Hester pointed to the mirror. "There's a letter taped there."

"It's addressed to you," Lillie Mae said, pulling the letter off the mirror and handing it to Hester. "Read it."

Lillie Mae watched intently as Hester read the letter. When she was done, there was a slight smile on her face.

"Now you read it," Hester said, handing the letter to Lillie Mae.

Lillie Mae sat down on the bed beside Hester and read. When she was done, she looked directly at Hester. Both women had smiles on their faces.

"Let's get back to my house," Lillie Mae said. "And make some phone calls."

*   *   *

Hester and Lillie Mae sat at Lillie Mae's desk staring at the telephone.

"You make the first call," Lillie Mae said. "I'll put the phone on speaker."

Hester dialed the number from memory.

"Hello," Kevin said after one ring.

"Hello," Harriet said a moment later.

"Kevin, Harriet?" Hester said, looking at Lillie Mae and smiling.

"Kevin, hang up," Harriet boomed. "It's for me."

Hester and Lillie Mae heard the click on the other end.

"How are you doing, Hester?" Harriet asked, seeming to settle in for a morning chat.

"Not so well. I've had another terrible shock."

Hester and Lillie Mae's eyes met, and they both smiled.

"What's happened now?" Harriet said.

"Mabel and Patrick have disappeared," Hester said, slowly enunciating each word.

Lillie Mae nodded her approval.

"Disappeared?" Harriet said. "What are you talking about, disappeared? People don't just disappear?"

Hester told Harriet everything that had occurred that day. She told her about calling Mabel in the morning three times and getting no response. She told her about going to Mabel's house and finding evidence that she and Patrick had left in a hurry. She told her that she was frightened about what might happen next. The one thing she didn't tell her was that Lillie Mae was sitting beside her.

"Do you think they've been kidnapped?" Harriet asked.

"No, I don't think that. To be honest, Harriet, I think they've run away."

"Run away from what?" Harriet shouted. "What's going on over there, Hester?"

"I don't know, Harriet, but I'm afraid. What if they've done something terribly wrong? What if that's the reason they've run away?"

"Are you suggesting they might have committed murder?" Harriet asked, gasping.

"I don't know what they've done."

"Have you lost your mind, Hester? How could you suggest such a thing? You should be ashamed of yourself."

"Then, why did they leave so suddenly?" Hester asked, quickly.

"I'm sure I don't know," Harriet replied. "You know your daughter and grandson better than I do. But, if I thought about it I could come up with a dozen reasons."

"I wish I could think of one."

205

"Do you want me to come over to Mount Penn and stay with you?" Harriet asked. "Say yes and me and Kevin will be there in a flash. Kevin's not going to like it, but he'll come."

"No, I don't want you to come over here," Hester said, waving to Lillie Mae.

Hearing Harriet's relieved sigh from the other end of the phone, Hester turned to Lillie Mae and smiled.

"I'll be fine here," Hester went on. "I just needed to talk to someone. Get these worries off my chest. You're right, though. This idea of mine is crazy. I'm sure I'll hear from Mabel soon enough, and she'll have a perfectly good reason for leaving town."

Lillie Mae gave Hester the thumbs up.

"Now you're talking sensible." Harriet sounded relieved. "Call me when you hear something."

"I will." Hester paused for just a moment. "And thank you, Harriet for being there. I feel better already."

Hester replaced the phone gently back into its cradle.

"That should do it," she said, looking over at Lillie Mae, a small smile on her lips.

"You did good," Lillie Mae said.

"One more," Hester asked.

"Yes, one more. Make it Janet."

Hester dialed the number and waited. "I need to talk to Janet," Hester said when Pete answered the phone.

"I'll get her."

"What is it?" Janet said when she came on the line. "Pete said you sounded anxious."

"Something terrible has happened, and I'm worried, Janet. Mabel and Patrick have left town. They just packed up Mabel's car and left."

"Why in the world did they do that?" Janet said, her excitement streaming through the phone.

"I don't know. Maybe Mabel was worried about Patrick. Maybe Patrick was worried about his Mom. I don't think either one of them could have done anything so bad that they had to run away from town. I know they're innocent."

"What are you talking about, Hester?" Janet practically screamed. "Are you suggesting they might have murdered someone?"

206

"No, of course, not," Hester said quickly. "I'm sure it's nothing. I'm just an old woman with crazy thoughts. I'm sure there's a perfectly good reason why they've left town."

"Patrick and Mabel didn't murder anyone, Hester. Just settle yourself down and stop all the crazy talk. You'll hear from them later today. You've worked yourself up over nothing, dear. Now stop it."

"You're right," Hester said. "I'm sure I'll hear from Mabel today. What a silly idea I had. Listen, Janet I can't thank you enough for listening to me. I do feel better."

"You take care of yourself, dear, and if you need anything, please call."

"I will." Hester hung up the phone.

That's done," she said, turning to Lillie Mae. "I'm going home to wait for what happens next.

*   *   *

Billy and Lillie Mae waited outside Dale Beavers house, Billy knocking firmly on the door.

"Thanks for coming with me," Billy said, looking over his shoulder at Lillie Mae. "I'm not sure I'd have been brave enough to come by myself. But Dale deserves to know my news."

Dale swung opened the door. "What the hell?" he said, his voice groggy as if he had just gotten out of bed. His hair was disheveled and he was wearing a pair of ragged flannel pajama pants with a tattered robe on top. He looked as if he hadn't shaved in a couple of days.

"You look a mess," Billy said. "Lillie Mae and I saw your car and thought you were home. Can we come in and talk a minute?"

"If you don't yell at me," Dale said, opening the door wider. "I had a bit too much to drink over the weekend, and I'm feeling the ill effects of it. But, I might be coming down with the flu, too, for all I know. I'm not sure a couple of bottles of wine could make me feel this bad."

Dale eyes flickered between Billy and Lillie Mae, and then rested on Billy. "You're all spruced up. What's your story?"

"That's what I'm here to tell you," Billy said, casting his eyes into the living room. "Do you mind if we sit down?"

"Sure," Dale said. "But I'm not offering you anything to eat or drink. Sorry, Lillie Mae. Guess I wouldn't make a very good Thursday morning breakfast lady."

Determined to stay out of the way, Lillie Mae sat on the far side of the room.

"So, what's up," Dale asked, a suspicious glint in his eye.

"I've decided to go back to school," Billy said. "I'm not doing Mom any good right now staying here. Besides, I'm close enough if she needs me for anything. There's only a couple of weeks left in the term, and if I don't take my exams, I'll be out an entire semester. I've worked too hard for that to happen. I've talked to Lillie Mae and Charlie, and they agreed that going back to school is the best thing for me to do right now."

"Does your mother know you're leaving Mount Penn?" Dale asked.

"We talked to her last night. She seemed fine with my decision. But I wanted you to know, too. Even though you and my mother are having issues right now, I don't want to leave her high and dry. Would you stop by or call her when you get a chance?"

"Did you mention this arrangement to your mother?" Dale asked, stirring in his seat as if anxious to hear the answer.

"Not really, but I know it would make her happy to see you. She does like you, you know, regardless of what she's said in the past. She's just confused right now, and all she can do is push people away. But she needs people in her life, whether she realizes it or not, and I think you're good for her."

Dale looked down at the floor and scuffed his feet as if trying to come up with the right way to tell Billy what he was feeling.

"None of this is easy, Billy. I went away this weekend to think this situation over and figure out the best thing for me to do," Dale said, looking up to meet Billy's eyes. "I've cared about your mother for awhile now, but she's told me point blank that she doesn't return my feelings. I realize now that our relationship was only in my head. I resolved this weekend to give up the illusion. I'm going to live in the real world from now on, Billy. I have to, or I'll drop over the edge. Trust me, I've already done enough foolish things to get your mother's attention, and I've failed."

"It's too soon to give up," Billy said, standing up and walking over to Dale. "If you support Mom through all she's going through right now, you'll have a better shot at a strong relationship once all this drama is over. I know my mother, and I know what will make her happy."

Dale shook his head, but said nothing.

"It's not easy for me to talk to you like this," Billy said. "My dad is dead and I loved him. Whatever people think, he was a good dad to me. But Mom did not have it easy with him. I know that. I'm sure the only reason she and Dad stayed together was me."

Billy met Dale's eyes. "Mom's a wonderful woman and deserves better in the future. She is worth fighting for, Dale."

"I know she is," Dale said. "I have been fighting for her. What's hard is that what I'm fighting against is your Mom's past, her feelings for you, and her guilt. I'm not certain we'll be able to get through this, Billy. Your mom's a stubborn lady."

"You've got to keep trying," Lillie Mae said, unable to keep silent any longer.

"Listen, Dale, I've got to go if I'm going to make my last class today," Billy said. "I'm depending on you to help take care of Mom. Are you ready to go, Lillie Mae?"

"I'll do what I can, Billy. But I won't promise anything."

Dale reached out his hand to Billy who took it.

"I do appreciate you stopping by and talking to me, son. I'll consider everything you've said."

Lillie Mae stepped forward. Putting her hand on Dale's arm, she looked him squarely in the eyes. "Give Clare another chance," she said. "You'll be glad you did."

Dale stared at her.

"By the way," she added. "I hear Patrick and Mabel have left town in something of a hurry this morning. Any idea why they would have done that?"

"I don't have a clue," Billy said, seemingly unconcerned by the news and looking anxious to leave.

"This place is just crazy," Dale said. "What next? This is all too much for me. I'm going back to bed."

"Remember what I said about Clare," Lillie Mae said.

"I'll do what I can," Dale said, standing at the door watching as Billy and Lillie Mae left. Turning back as she reached the car, Lillie Mae saw him going back inside his house, his shoulders slouched. She thought that a good sign.

*   *   *

The phone was ringing when Lillie Mae walked into her house.

"Lillie Mae, here," she answered, checking the caller ID.

"It's working, Lillie Mae," Hester said, her voice filled with excitement.

"Tell me who you've heard from."

"Joyce and Margaret called me, and apparently they'd talked to each other. Margaret got a call from Janet and Harriet, too. Margaret also said she tried to reach you, but you weren't home."

"How about Alice?" Lillie Mae asked.

"Everybody called Alice, but she's not answering her phone. "Do you know if she's out?"

"No," Lillie Mae said. "But I'm not worried. I'll call her later."

"So, Mabel's little scheme is working," Hester said.

"Yes, I think it is," Lillie Mae said. "What's everybody saying?"

"Gossip has it that Patrick murdered Carl Lewis and Mabel murdered Roger," Hester said, sounding rather proud of herself. "Although no one really believes it. That's what they're telling me."

"Good," Lillie Mae said. "Call me again if anything new happens."

"I will," Hester said, hanging up the phone.

*   *   *

Lillie Mae was down on her knees in her backyard pulling weeds out of the flowerbed when a shadow fell over her. Letting out an involuntary scream, she looked over her shoulder and saw Charlie standing over her.

"Hi there," he said casually.

"You scared the living daylights out of me, Charlie Warren. I must have been deep in my own thoughts, because I didn't hear your truck pull up."

"Sorry, Lillie Mae. I didn't mean to scare you. I just stopped by to talk. I guess I should have called first."

Lillie Mae stood and brushed off her knees. "Don't worry. I've recovered."

"Can we go inside and talk? It's important."

Lillie Mae pulled off her gardening gloves.

210

"Sure, plenty of time for you, Charlie," she said, as she led the way into the house. "I'll get us a glass of iced tea. I've been outside working since Billy dropped me off, so I could use a break."

Once inside Lillie Mae pointed Charlie to a kitchen chair while she went to the sink to wash her hands and fix the iced tea. "Do you like lemon in your tea?"

"No, plain is just fine."

She brought the drinks to the table and sat down opposite him.

"Okay, what's up, Charlie? I know you don't have time for social calls just now."

"So, Billy got off to school?" Charlie asked, seeming to stall for a few moments.

"Yes," Lillie Mae said. "You were right to suggest it. He needs to be away from here for the next couple of days."

"What did Dale say when you told him?" Charlie asked, sipping the tea.

"Dale thought it was a good idea. He's sick though," Lillie Mae said. "He looked awful when I saw him and thinks it might be the flu. I'm actually worried about him. For lots of reasons."

Charlie nodded his head. "I'm worried about him, too. I'll stop by his place when I'm done here. I have a question or two for him anyway."

"So, what's next?" Lillie Mae asked, a gleam in her eye.

"Alice and I have been talking most of the morning, and we have a plan," Charlie said.

"And?" Lillie Mae asked impatiently.

"That's why I'm here. To tell you what I want you to do next."

"And," Lillie Mae said again.

Charlie spent the next half hour explaining the plan.

21

"Who's here?" Hester asked, jumping up from the kitchen table to look out the back door window after hearing a car drive up.

"Oh, my goodness," she said to Lillie Mae who had stopped by for a cup of coffee and a catch-up chat early that morning.

"Who is it?" Lillie Mae asked, seeing the look of surprise on Hester's face.

"It's Harriet and Kevin." Hester openede the door to the new arrivals. "Of all times for a visit."

"Come with us," Harriet said, grabbing Hester's arm. "Kevin and I are going over to the Mount Summit Cafe for breakfast, and you're coming with us."

"I've had my breakfast," Hester said, resisting Harriet's pull. "Besides Lillie Mae is here."

"You're both coming then," Harriet said, glancing back at Kevin who was still sitting in the car. "Kill two birds with one stone as they say. No back talk either. I've had enough of that for one morning, thank you very much."

Harriet opened the car door and waited for the ladies to get in.

No one said a word as Harriet drove her reluctant crew to the café. Kevin sat sulking on the passenger side, his head down, mumbling to himself. Lillie Mae assumed he was there under duress as well.

"Pretty day," Lillie Mae finally said, hopeful of breaking the ice. The floodgate opened.

"Pretty enough," Harriet ranted. "I'm so worried about you folks in Mount Penn, I can't even appreciate the weather. The place is falling apart, and it was my home for a long time. It's just tearing me apart. Kevin feels as I do. We have to do something to get things back the way they were."

Kevin mumbled under his breath.

"But why talk to us?" Hester asked. "We're already doing everything we can to get things back to normal."

"I want to know what's going on with Mabel and Patrick. I don't believe for a minute that they ran away from home or murdered anybody. And, I don't believe you think they did either. You'd be far more upset if you did. I know you, Hester Franklin, and I know how you react under crisis. I suspect you, Ms. Lillie Mae Harris, have something to do with this."

"Actually, I don't," Lillie Mae said. "I'm completely innocent this time."

Harriet drove the car into the restaurant's parking lot. Kevin jumped out and opened Hester's door, taking her hand to help her out. Harriet did the same for Lillie Mae.

"I'm sorry, Hester," Kevin told her in a quiet voice. "I asked Harriet not to interfere in your business, but you know Harriet once she gets a bee in her bonnet. But her heart is good."

"I appreciate her concern, Kevin, but I don't know what I can tell her," Hester said. "It will all be fine, I promise."

Harriet came around the car, Lillie Mae in tow, grabbed both of their arms and led them into the restaurant.

"We'll take the booth by the window," Harriet told the hostess when she walked up to them with her hand full of menus. When they were settled in the booth and had ordered coffee, Harriet looked Hester straight in the eyes.

"Now tell me what's going on," she demanded. "I'm no fool, so don't try to treat me like one."

"You know what I know," Hester said, stalling.

"Balderdash. Out with it, Hester. You're wasting my time. What are you not telling me?"

Hester turned to Lillie Mae who nodded.

"This was all Mabel's idea," Hester said. "She had a run in with Perry Foster, the father of the boy Patrick was in jail with. The next thing we knew, Mabel was getting strange phone calls."

"The same person who had been calling Clare, we think," Lillie Mae said.

Harriet's eyes strayed between the two women. "Keep talking," she said.

"Mabel was spooked. I suspect she and Patrick decided to go away for a couple of days to let the dust settle. That's all."

"If that's the case, why did you spread a rumor that they might be the murderers?" Harriet asked, her hands flying into the air.

"That was Mabel's idea," Hester said. "She said she was told to stir a pot. I have no idea what any of this means, so don't ask me

213

any more questions, Harriet. Mabel said to call around to the Thursday morning ladies, and tell them she and Patrick had left town in a hurry, and I was afraid they were running away because they were guilty of something. I never said the word murder, although I might have inferred it."

"Stir the pot," Harriet said. "Who would have asked her to do such a thing?"

"She didn't tell me," Hester said.

Kevin, still slumped in the corner, eyed Hester, but stayed quiet.

"Now, don't you dare tell anybody what I've done," Hester pleaded. "If Mabel finds out I told you, she'll be upset with me. This was all to be hush-hush."

"Oh, I won't tell a soul." Harriet had a mischievous glint in her eye as she looked over at Lillie Mae. "I promise."

*   *   *

Lillie Mae sat at her desk putting the last touches on an article on plant invaders and their role in shaping the mid-Atlantic region, when the doorbell pealed.

"Who now?" she asked, looking out her front window.

Dale Beavers waited there, his back toward the door.

"You look a lot better than the last time I saw you," Lillie Mae said after opening the front door and taking a moment to check Dale over. Dressed in a pair of khakis and a blue and green plaid shirt, he was cleaned-shaved, and his short blond hair was styled in fashionable disarray.

"Come in and tell me what's brought on this amazing transformation," she said, opening the door wider.

"I went to see Clare this morning," he said, a hint of a dimple appearing in his left cheek as he followed Lillie Mae into the house.

"I suspected as much." Lillie Mae said. "And it went well?"

"Yes," he said. "Very well."

"Come sit down," she said. "Coffee or tea?"

"No, thanks," he said, plopping onto the sofa.

"So," Lillie Mae said, sitting down opposite him. "Tell me everything."

Dale settled back on the sofa as if preparing to stay for awhile.

214

"The visit didn't start off well," he said. "I almost didn't stay. I hated the wait before I was allowed in to see Clare, but I stuck it out."

Lillie Mae nodded.

"Honestly," Dale said. "I wouldn't have gone to see Clare at all, if Billy hadn't asked me to. You know how discouraged I had become with our relationship." A smile appeared on his face. "But, I'm glad I did."

Lillie Mae beamed, but stayed quiet.

"I knew things were going to be okay as soon as I saw her. The smile on Clare's face when she looked at me, Lillie Mae, was more than I could have hoped for. 'I'm so glad you came,' were the first words out of her mouth."

"That's wonderful, Dale." Lillie Mae was truly happy for the young man. "What else did she say?"

"Just that she and Billy had made up and that he understands about us. He's rooting for us were her words."

"So am I," Lillie Mae said.

A loud knock sounded on Lillie Mae's back door.

"Who's that?" Lillie Mae asked "Wait here, Dale," she called over her shoulder.

"Charlie," she said, opening the back door. "What's up now?"

"I've got to talk to you," he said, rushing into the room.

"Dale's here," she said, a warning in her eyes. "Do you want him to leave?"

"Yes," Charlie said.

Lillie Mae went back into the living room.

"Dale, I'm sorry, it's Charlie. He needs to talk to me right away. Do you mind coming back later?"

Dale jumped to his feet.

"I'm good, Lillie Mae. Don't worry. I told you what's most important. Clare and I have a chance now," he said, heading toward the door.

"Give me a hug," Lillie Mae said, as they reached the door.

Dale welcomed her into his arms. "I'm so happy for you both," Lillie Mae said.

"Thank you for all your encouragement," Dale said, as he walked out the door.

"I'm back," Lillie Mae said, coming into the kitchen. "Coffee?"

215

"Please," Charlie said. "It's been a rough morning."

Lillie Mae poured him a cup, and then joined him at the table.

"We're getting close," Charlie said, taking a sip of the black coffee. "But there's been a new development, and we might have to deal with some fallout. I need you to come with me. Captain Alton has approved you being there."

"Where?" Lillie Mae asked, her eyes huge.

"We're going to arrest Perry Foster. Me and Paul Lowman."

"When?"

"This afternoon. I need you to come with me, now," Charlie said impatiently.

"Why me?" Lillie Mae asked, stepping back.

"Because his family might need some support and you're the best person to give it. Besides, you were there when Perry came to Mabel's house and made a scene. Mabel filed the complaint, you see."

"Shouldn't Mabel be there?" Lillie Mae asked, trying to get out of going.

"No, we want you. Besides, Mabel's not in town. Are you coming?"

"Okay," Lillie Mae said. "I'm committed to seeing this through, and I promised to do what I could, but I want my life back, too. Let me get my purse."

Her purse slung over her shoulder, Lillie Mae and Charlie walked out the door.

"Are you expecting trouble?" Lillie Mae asked, settling herself in the front seat of Charlie's truck.

"Not really," Charlie said. "But, we never know. Foster has a temper."

"The club that Billy and Sam brought to you," Lillie Mae said, suddenly remembering it. "Did it mean anything?"

"It's exactly what we expected to be found," Charlie said, looking at Lillie Mae out of the side of his eyes. "All the pieces of the puzzle are falling into place, Lillie Mae. It won't be long now, I promise."

* * *

Sergeant Paul Lowman was waiting for them at the turn around area just down the road from the Foster house. Lillie Mae and Charlie got out of Charlie's truck, both opening their own doors

216

and stepping down. Lillie Mae crawled into the back seat of Paul's police car, Charlie got into the passenger's side.

"Lillie Mae," Paul said. "I'm Paul Lowman."

"I remember meeting you the day Carl Lewis' body was found," Lillie Mae said.

"You're only along because Charlie thinks it's important for you be here. But this is an official arrest, so you'll need to stay well out of the way."

Lillie Mae nodded.

"She knows the ropes," Charlie said. "I'll vouch for her."

"Good," Lowman said. "This is all extremely unconventional."

"It is, but our town is unconventional," Charlie said.

Lowman nodded. "You've said that before. This better work," he said, glancing in the rear view mirror at Lillie Mae who was huddled in the corner of the car trying to disappear. "What are we going to do with her once we've arrested Perry?"

"We'll drive her home and then I'll come back later for my car. What's the plan for Foster?"

"We'll wait for him to pass by us, and then we'll follow him to his home," Lowman said. "We've been watching him for a couple of days, and his life is like clockwork. He goes to work every day at six forty-five in the morning and comes home at four fifteen in the afternoon. He has dinner at five and is at the local bar by seven, back home by nine, and in bed by nine-thirty. Each day is the same."

"Sounds like the man has a routine," Charlie said.

Lowman looked at his watch.

"Perry's big shiny red truck should come by any minute now," he said, yawning. "Sorry, I've been here awhile."

Charlie looked into the side mirror.

"Here he comes," he said, glancing at his watch. "Right on time."

Lowman waited for Perry to pass, then pulled out and followed him slowly up the hill and into his driveway.

"What's up?" Perry asked, his voice leery, when he climbed out of his truck. Lowman and Charlie were out of the police car, walking toward him. Lillie Mae had opened the back door so she could hear, but stayed seated.

217

"Perry Foster, I need to take you into headquarters for questioning," Paul Lowman said, his hands out in front of him.

"What the hell for?" Perry's face turned scarlet. "I ain't done nothing."

"Then you have nothing to be concerned about," Charlie said.

"Why can't you talk to me here?"

"You know why," Lowman answered, his voice stern and uncompromising. "If you don't cooperate, I'm going to have to put you in handcuffs."

"Are you harassing me?" Perry clenched his fist and gritted his teeth. "I've got my rights."

"Calm down," Charlie said. "Mabel Goody has filed a complaint against you. If you come with us peacefully, everything will work out. If you resist us, you're going to be in a lot more trouble, Perry. I suggest you do as Sergeant Lowman asks."

Lowman backed up a few steps, and then turned to face him.

"Mr. Foster, if you don't agree to come with us to the station, I will have to put you under arrest for resisting an officer. As I said before, I think you know why we're here, and I think it would be best for you all around if you cooperate. Where is your son?"

"What's my son have to do with this?" Perry asked, his face still bright red.

"We understand you're holding him prisoner in your house," Lowman said, glancing at the porch as if to draw the boy out.

"Who told you that pack of lies?" Perry yelled. "My son got himself into trouble. I'm just trying to keep him out of any more trouble until his trial. I think you people have it out for me and my family. I'm going to file a complaint myself."

"You do that, Mr. Foster. But, first, you're coming with us. Do you want to let your wife know where you're going?"

Lowman moved forward.

Sarah Foster walked out onto the porch.

"What's going on here?" she asked, looking at her husband.

"These cops are taking me into Antioch for questioning," Perry said.

"No!" she screamed, looking at Charlie, and then back to Perry. "You can't take my husband!"

"It'll be okay, honey," he said, his eyes clouding over.

Sarah rushed down the steps.

"No!" she repeated.

Perry opened his arms and she ran to him. "What have you done?" she sobbed, holding him tight.

Charlie and Paul stood back to give the couple some space.

"It ain't serious," Perry said. "I'll be back before you know it."

"But you haven't had your supper."

"It'll be okay this time," he said, hugging her to him again. "I won't be gone long. I'll probably miss dinner, but I should be back by bedtime. Now don't you worry, sweetheart. Everything will be fine."

Jerry Foster came out onto the porch. "What's going on? I saw the police car in the driveway. Has something happened?"

Perry explained to his son that he was going to be taken to the Antioch police station for questioning. He didn't say why.

"Dad didn't do nothing," Jerry said, his faced gone white when he heard the story. "Why are you picking on him?"

"We have to talk to your father," Charlie said, turning to Jerry. "It's just routine, son. You stay calm, hear. And, take care of your mom."

Jerry walked over to his mother and took hold of her arm.

"It'll be okay, Mom" he soothed, still looking sideways at Charlie.

Lillie Mae watched the family drama play out.

"I think we should be going now, Mr. Foster," Charlie said, his hand resting on Perry's elbow, guiding him toward the car.

Perry Foster pulled away from Charlie and went to his wife, then leaned down and kissed her. "You take care of your mother," he said to Jerry, patting him on the back before following Paul and Charlie to the police car.

Calmed down, Perry looked sad and confused.

"Should I call a lawyer," Perry asked Charlie on his way to the car.

"You can decide once we're at the police station," Lowman answered, opening the door.

Looking into the back seat of the car, Perry noticed Lillie Mae.

"What's she doing here?" he asked, more perplexed than angry when he saw her huddled in the far corner of the car.

"Ignore her," Charlie said.

Perry got into the car, glanced at Lillie Mae again, then dropped his head as he sat as far away from her as possible. No one said a word during the ten-minute ride back to Lillie Mae's house.

"Guess you didn't need to come along after all," Charlie said as he walked her to her door.

"Guess I didn't," Lillie Mae said in a low voice as Charlie turned to go. "But, I'm glad I did. I actually learned a lot today."

Looking over her shoulder she saw Perry sitting in the back of the car, his head hanging as if defeated. The car drove off, headed down the road toward the Antioch police station.

*   *   *

Alice and Lillie Mae sat in Lillie Mae's living room each with a glass of wine. The sun had started to set, and they were enjoying what they believed was their last bit of peace for awhile.

"This is it," Alice said, looking at her friend, her hands kneading in her lap.

"This is it," Lillie Mae said, taking a sip of wine. "How do you feel?"

"Nervous," Alice said. "But not scared."

"Who do we call first?" Lillie Mae asked, eying the phone that was sitting on the table between them.

"Hester," Alice said. "She should be easy."

"I'll put it on speaker," Lillie Mae said, dialing the number. "Don't tell Hester you're here with me."

Alice nodded.

"Hester, it's me Alice," Alice said, when Hester answered the phone after just one ring.

"Mabel and Patrick are back," Hester blurted out. "I just got off the phone with Mabel. You're the first person to know."

"Did they tell you where they went?" Alice asked.

"No, just that they were home and fine," Hester said.

"That's good news. You must feel so much better."

"I do," Hester said, then paused for a moment. "Why are you calling me?"

"It's Alfred," Alice said, sounding distressed. "He's gone missing."

"No," Hester exclaimed. "When?"

220

"He's been gone about two hours and I'm frantic," Alice said, shivering on her end of the phone. "I'm checking with all the neighbors to see if anybody's seen him."

"I am so sorry, Alice, but I would have called you right away if I had seen Alfred," Hester said, sounding truly worried. "Let me check around, too, and see what I can find out."

"Thanks, Hester," Alice said. "Anything you can do will be greatly appreciated."

"I'll call you later, dear," Hester said.

Both ladies hung up.

"That went well," Lillie Mae said. "Interesting the way she told you the story about Mabel and Patrick."

"Who's next?" Alice said, seeming to be enjoying herself.

"Sam and Margaret," Lillie Mae said.

"Sam, this is Alice," Alice said a few minutes later after punching in the familiar number. She had changed her voice to one that was low and eerie.

"What's wrong, Alice?" Sam said, his voice full of concern. "You sound terrible. Are you sick?"

"No, no," she said, mimicking a sob. "It's Alfred. He's gone missing. I called to see if you had seen him on one of your walks today. I'm calling all the neighbors, but I thought I might have the best chance with you."

"Oh, you poor dear. I didn't see him, or I would have brought him back to you," Sam said, sounding distressed.

"What could have happened to him?" Alice sobbed. "I can't believe someone would have taken him. He was out in the back yard playing, as he does each afternoon. When I went to call him, he wasn't there. And the gate was standing wide open. The gate is never opened, and even if it is, I don't think Alfred would run away."

"I was planning one last walk before Margaret and I have to go to the airport. We're taking the redeye from D.C. to Los Angeles tonight, but we have plenty of time before we have to leave. I'll call for him as I walk. Please don't be too distressed, Alice. I'm sure someone will find him and bring him back to you. Nobody would hurt Alfred."

"Oh, thank you, Sam," Alice said, sounding more like herself . "You're right. We'll find Alfred. I knew I could count on you to help."

"Two down," Alice said, when she had hung up the phone. "Janet and Pete next?" she asked.

Lillie Mae, making notes in a notebook, nodded.

"Pete here," Pete said, after just one ring.

"Pete, it's Alice. Alfred is missing," she rushed to say.

"Oh, my gosh," Pete exclaimed. "Tell me what happened."

Alice repeated what she had told Sam. Pete echoed her words to Janet who must have been standing next to him.

"No," Janet said a moment later, after taking the phone from Pete. "Carlos and Joyce are missing, too."

"What?" Alice said. "What do you mean Carlos and Joyce are missing?"

"I've been calling their house all afternoon, but no one answers," Janet said. "I'm going to send Pete over there to check right now. He can look for Alfred at the same time."

Alice heard a pause on Janet's line. "That's Sam for Pete," Janet said, a moment later. "I'll let you go. The men can go in search of Alfred together."

"Keep me informed," Alice said.

"I'll call you as soon as I know something," Janet said and hung up.

"Anybody else?" Alice asked Lillie Mae.

"That's good for now. You go home and wait for the results. I'll be down later," Lillie Mae said, standing up and stretching. "We've done a good evening's work."

22

"You two are finally here," Lillie Mae said when she answered the knock at her back door and saw Kevin and Harriet Peterson standing there. "Where have you been?"

"Sam called and told us about Alfred gone missing, so we knew right away the next horrible thing was about to happen up here on the mountain. We high-tailed it over here as quick as possible, but had to make a couple of stops along the way."

"She forced me to come, Lillie Mae," Kevin said, in a whiny voice. 'I'd rather be anywhere else."

"You'll be glad you came along when this is all over," Lillie Mae said, tossing him an encouraging smile.

"We stopped by Joyce and Carlos' place first, but nobody was home," Harriet said. "Janet and Pete were gone, too, but there was a sign on their door saying they were out looking for Alfred."

"Good," Lillie Mae said, nodding her head enthusiastically. "Looks like everything is getting in place."

"What about Sam and Margaret?" Lillie Mae asked.

"No one's home there either," Harriet said. "They've probably left for the airport."

"I see," Lillie Mae said. "Was it tonight they were leaving for California?"

Harriet laughed. "Now, you're just being funny."

Lillie Mae smiled.

"Did you speak to Hester?" she asked.

"We talked earlier. She told me all about Mabel and Patrick's adventure. As far as I know they're at their house. We didn't stop by to check."

"I'm sure they're home and glad to be there," Lillie Mae said, glancing at Kevin who was staring out the window as if looking for somewhere to escape.

"Too bad they weren't the real murderers," Harriet said. "It would have saved Kevin a heck of a lot of anguish."

"That's not funny," Lillie Mae said, throwing a black sweater over her shoulders. "Mabel and Patrick did what they were told to do. Odd as it was."

"We're all doing what we're told to do," Kevin said, turning to face the ladies. Harriet and Lillie Mae looked at him as if surprised to find out he could talk.

"Think of it as being in a play," Lillie Mae said, checking her outfit in the hall mirror. "Are you two ready to go?"

"Ready," Harriet said, bouncing with enthusiasm.

"Ready," Kevin said, his voice full of doom.

"Then let's get this show on the road," Lillie Mae said, opening up the back door and checking to make sure there was no one was around to see them.

*   *   *

Alice's eyes sprung wide-open as the shuffling noise from downstairs signaled that the night's expected guest had arrived. Someone must have shut off the electricity at the breaker, because all at once the house went black, and the furnace went still making the house eerie quiet. Alice let out a deep sigh, but there was no other noise, save for the ticking of the old-fashioned alarm clock on the night stand.

A loud creak broke the silence. Someone was coming up the stairs, taking each step one by one. A second pair of steps followed the first, confirming there were at least two intruders in the house. Alice lay huddled in her covers, waiting for what was to happen next.

She only had to wait a moment to find out. The bedroom door flew open, letting in a cold draft of air from the hall. Two darkly clad figures entered the room.

"She's in here," a man whispered. "What do you want me to do?"

"Kill the bitch," the other man said, his voice low and raspy. "You should have killed her the first time you had the chance, but you and your soft heart thought scaring her would be enough. You were wrong, as usual, and now you have to clean up your mess."

Time stood still for a brief moment, then everything seemed to happen at once. The larger of the two intruders, a hammer in his hand, lunged at Alice. She screamed and rolled out of the way, then picked up a pillow and threw it at him. Surprised, the intruder

224

jumped back, but only for a second. Raising the hammer again, his arm cast back high over his head, he was beginning to lunge forward when John Alton jumped out of the closet, grabbed his arm and bent it behind his back, bringing the culprit to his knees. Paul Lowman, also dressed in black, too and carrying a gun, came through the bathroom door.

"Stop or I'll shoot!" he shouted, his gun thrust forward.

"Run, you fool!" the now familiar gruff voice man said. "Nobody will shoot us here. There are too many people around."

"This fellow's going nowhere!" John Alton said forcefully as he cuffed the culprit's wrists and threw him in the closet, locking the door behind him.

"You stupid fool, " said the man with the gruff voice. "You've left it all up to me again." The wiry figure ran toward the open bedroom door, a gun visible in his hand, but John Alton beat him there. Reaching out to grab him, John tripped over the assailant, who's arms and legs were flailing, and they both fell to the floor. There was a scuffle, and then a gun fired.

Alice screamed.

"I've got him!" John Alton called, then he screamed. "He kicked me! My God, the bastard kicked me!"

Just then, the light in the bedroom came back on, and Lillie Mae, standing by the door, saw the chaos in the room. John Alton was lying on the floor, curled up in pain. The assailant had kicked John in just the right spot to get the maximum effect.

A small figure, trembling and out of control, but with a gun in his hand, rushed toward her.

"Watch out, Lillie Mae!" Alice screamed.

Lillie Mae looked into the eyes of a black-clad figure, a ski mask hiding his face. A gun pointed straight up at her head. Terror doesn't begin to describe how she felt at that moment.

"Stand clear, you cow, or you're dead!" the man said, pushing Lillie Mae aside, and rushing down the steps. Paul Lowman, from where he stood behind Lillie Mae, raised his gun, but didn't shoot. Instead, he raced down the stairs after the attacker, who stayed too far ahead of him to reach out and grab.

Lillie Mae, still too frightened to take a step forward, watched. Charlie Warren stepped out of the shadows at the bottom of the steps and pointed his gun at the attacker.

"Stop or I'll shoot!" Charlie called out, but it was too late. A gun fired, and Charlie was down on the floor, wrenching in pain. The culprit rushed past him into the living room.

"Stop that man!" Lowman called out as he reached the bottom of the stairs. "Hurry, before he gets away!"

Another voice, more timid, shouted, "I've got him!"

Paul Lowman turned on the lights and saw Kevin Peterson holding the masked man, who was kicking and spitting in an effort to get free. The gun that had been flung during the scuffle was lying on the floor about six feet away. Harriet stood over it, her foot on the handle.

Taking the wriggling form from Kevin, Paul Lowman cuffed him quickly, then forced him down on the floor in a sitting position.

John Alton came hobbling down the steps, slowly, Alice and Lillie Mae at his heels. Harriet was standing over Charlie, who was still on the hallway floor, blood all over his arm, struggling to get up. Lillie Mae and Alice joined Harriet, and the three of them helped Charlie to his feet.

Kevin still stood over the culprit, who was writhing and hissing.

Paul Lowman yanked the prisoner, now in handcuffs, around and pulled off the ski mask.

Sitting there, spewing profanities, was Margaret Jenkins.

*   *   *

News spread quickly that the murderers had been caught and identified. Calls were made and plans were formed to let the Thursday morning breakfast ladies, who were not already there, know to gather in Alice's living room before dawn to rehash the events of the night before.

An ambulance had arrived to take Charlie Warren to the emergency room shortly after Captain Alton, who had recovered quickly from Margaret's kick, and Sergeant Lowman had left with Sam and Margaret Jenkins, taking them to the Antioch police station. They were to be handed over to federal agents who were waiting there to arrest them.

That left Lillie Mae, Harriet, and Kevin at Alice's house. The women were in the kitchen getting ready for the onslaught of neighbors. Kevin was resting on the sofa.

226

"Kevin deserves his nap," Harriet said. "He was very brave last night."

Lillie Mae and Alice agreed.

Charlie called from the hospital about four in the morning to let Lillie Mae know the wound to his arm was just superficial.

"I'll be ready to come back to Alice's house, as soon as someone can get here to pick me up," he told her. "The doctor's almost done wrapping me up and tells me, after that, I'm free to go."

Lillie Mae looked at Kevin who had just walked into the kitchen.

"Will you go pick up Charlie at the hospital and bring him here?" she asked sweetly.

Standing up straight, he looked briefly at Harriet, as if considering. "I will," he said, his voice firm and crisp.

Being a hero is good for the man, Lillie Mae thought. In former days, his first inclination would have been to say no.

"Kevin's on the way," she said into the phone. "Are you sure you're going to be all right, Charlie?"

"Perfectly sure," he said. "Tell Kevin to come quickly, please. I want to get back to Alice's house to tell all of you what's going on with Sam and Margaret."

"Hurry," Lillie Mae said to Kevin as he scurried to leave. "Charlie's waiting for you. The sooner you get him back here, the sooner we'll find out what's going on."

Pete and Janet were the first to arrive at Alice's house soon after Kevin had left. Lillie Mae had called them in the wee hours of the morning to tell them what had happened. Janet had agreed to call around to the Thursday morning ladies and have them at Alice's house early enough to hear what Charlie had to say, then they'd all go to the Mountain View Inn for Thursday morning breakfast.

Janet brought some sweet rolls with her and was in the kitchen with Harriet readying the food, while Lillie Mae and Alice rested in the living room.

"Someone's at the door," Alice called from the front room when she heard the knock. "Can someone get it?"

"I will," Pete said.

"It's me and Carlos," Joyce called through the screen door just as Pete opened the door to let them in. "We've brought Alice a precious present."

A yelp signaled the arrival of Alfred.

Alice was up in a jiffy and out in the hallway. Alfred, who had wiggled his way out of Carlos' arms jumped up on Alice, planting kisses all over her face when she bent to greet him. Now in her arms, his tail flew every which way.

"How was my little man?" she asked, her nose buried in his neck.

"He was the perfect companion," Carlos said. "He took to the motel better than Joyce and I did. He moped for you, of course, but other than that he was the perfect little dog."

"He seemed to know he was coming home this morning," Joyce said, her arm inside her husband's. "He was completely calm, sitting on the back seat of the car, as patient as can be the entire ride here. As soon as we pulled into the driveway, he let us know he was pleased to be home, barking and wagging his tail. He hasn't stopped yet."

"Yoo-hoo," Hester called through the open screen door. "Mabel and I are here and we've brought a coffee cake."

"Come in," Alice invited, Alfred still in her arms. "Joyce and Harriet are in the kitchen with Janet, getting the food together."

"How are you doing?" Hester asked, taking Alice and Alfred into her arms. "You are so brave. I would have never been able to do what you did."

Janet walked into the hallway with a tray full of goodies and handed them to Lillie Mae.

"OK everybody," Lillie Mae called, carrying the tray into the living room. "Come sit down if you want coffee and pastries and a good story. Alice is going to tell us what happened last night."

Janet followed Lillie Mae into the front room carrying the coffee and tea tray. Joyce was right behind with cups, sugar, and cream. Harriet brought up the rear with another tray of pastries.

It took everyone a few minutes to get settled. Pete and Carlos, who had been out on the porch while the ladies were getting the refreshments in order, came back into the house, and found seats by their wives.

"Are you ready to tell us what happened last night?" Lillie Mae said to Alice when the group was assembled, coffee and cakes in hand.

"Yes, do," came assorted voices from around the room.

"You tell them," Alice said, looking at Lillie Mae. "It was mostly your idea."

"It was no such thing. It was Charlie's idea, but he got it from you. I only did as I was told to do, and that wasn't very much. This is your story, Alice. You tell it."

Alice leaned down and petted Alfred who had not left her side since arriving back home. "To tell the truth, it was all rather exciting," Alice said. "But scary, too."

Lillie Mae watched as Alice paused to look around the room. She had to check herself from giggling when she saw the expressions on her neighbors' faces. She thought them all adorable as they eagerly awaited her friend's tale, so refreshing after the horrors of the night before.

"I drank a cup of warm milk and took a nice hot bath," Alice said, beginning her story, "just as I do most every night, then crawled into bed and read. Charlie had told me to stick as close to my routine as possible. So at eleven, I turned off my light sure I wouldn't fall asleep. But I did. I know this sounds silly, but I didn't hear Lillie Mae or Charlie arrive, nor any of the other police officers. I knew they were coming, of course, but I slept through it all."

"Harriet and Kevin came with me," Lillie Mae said, picking up a piece of cake from the tray.

"Yes, that true," Alice said, catching Harriet's eye. "I don't think I knew they were going to be here, did I?" Alice said, looking at Lillie Mae.

Lillie Mae shook her head, and Alice continued.

"As I said before, Lillie Mae and the police must have gotten into place quietly because I didn't hear a thing until later when I was roused awake by a shuffling noise downstairs. To be honest, I'm not certain I would have noticed that noise either if I hadn't known I might be having company in the middle of the night. I guess I'm too used to Alfred alerting me to any danger."

"You are so brave," Janet said, picking up Pete's hand.

229

"Thanks, Janet, but I don't think I've ever been so frightened in all of my life," Alice said, shivering as she remembered. "I certainly didn't feel brave at the time. I curled under the covers and prayed that everything would work out as planned. I remember taking a deep breath, closing my eyes, and pretending to be asleep.

"Then I heard someone coming up the steps. The electricity was off by then, so the noise was deafening, at least to me, which didn't help my nerves at all. My body was trembling so badly, I don't know how I stayed in the bed. I clinched my fist and turned my face into the pillow, just trying to get control over myself. When the door opened, I could feel the draft from the hallway drift into the room. I was shivering so much by then, my teeth were rattling."

Hester grabbed Mabel's hand and closed her eyes.

"I heard someone whisper that I was in the room. I didn't know at the time if it was a man or a woman, but I know now that it was Sam Jenkins. Then Margaret said . . ." Alice paused, and a tear escaped down her cheek. "This is hard, because it's so awful. You tell them, Lillie Mae."

"Margaret said this time we'll kill the bitch," Lillie Mae said, catching her own words on a sob.

"How horrible!" Joyce said. "Can you image someone saying something like that about Alice?"

"Awful," Janet said, shaking her head.

"That's not all," Lillie Mae said. "Then, Margaret said that they should have killed Alice when they had the chance the first time. It was Sam who had spared her."

"How could Margaret be so awful?" Janet asked, a tear forming in her eyes. "She was a Thursday morning breakfast lady."

"Goes to show you can't trust strangers," Hester said, then immediately felt bad as her eyes caught Joyce's. "I don't mean you, dear."

"I was terrified," Alice said, picking up the story again. "I screamed when I heard the door open. I couldn't help myself but it must have been the scream that unsettled Margaret since she knew then I was awake. Everything happened so fast after that. Margaret had ordered Sam to kill me and he was prepared to do just that. With a hammer in his hand, he lunged toward me, but I twisted to get out of the way, then threw a pillow at him.

"No!" Janet said, squeezing Pete's hand. "This is all just too horrible."

"My screamed forced John Alton and Paul Lowman out of hiding, surprising Sam," Alice said.

"Where was Charlie?" Pete asked.

"He was downstairs, but we'll come to that later," Lillie Mae said.

"What happened next?" Joyce asked.

"Margaret was furious. She screamed at Sam to hit Alice, but it was too late. John Alton had already tackled Sam, handcuffed him, and locked him in the closet," Lillie Mae said, her face reddening as she relived the scene.

"I was hiding under the covers again, praying," Alice said. "Most of the action was above me."

"What happened next?" Hester asked.

"Margaret was acting even more erratic," Lillie Mae said. "John Alton grabbed her. She was having none of that. She turned on him, her hands flailing, and she squirmed out of his hold. Then she kicked him in his man parts and he let out this piercing scream. Things were going terribly wrong."

"Oh my goodness!" Hester exclaimed. "What next?"

"I peeked out from under the covers," Alice said, "and saw Lillie Mae standing at the bedroom door. The night light in the hallway had come back on by then and I could see Margaret running toward her with a gun—and I screamed a warning."

"Who turned the electricity back on?" Lillie Mae interrupted.

"I did," Harriet said. "I knew where the fuse box was."

"The next part of the story is yours, Lillie Mae," Alice said. "You tell it."

Lillie Mae nodded.

"Paul Lowman saw Margaret rushing toward me, her gun pointed at my head. Although he had his gun out, he didn't shoot because he was afraid he might hit me," Lillie Mae said. "I'm not sure why, and I don't really care because I'm here to tell this story, but Margaret made some snide remarks then pushed me aside and ran pass me, down the steps. Maybe it was because she spotted Charlie at the bottom of the stairs with a gun in his hand, pointed toward her. Who knows what was going in that woman's mind by then. When Charlie took a step toward her, she turned her gun on him and shot.   He fell to the floor."

" No!" Mabel said. "Is Charlie OK?"

"Fortunately, Margaret's aim was dismal," Lillie Mae said. "The bullet hit him in the arm and the wound is superficial. Kevin should be back with Charlie shortly and then he will tell us his part of the story."

"What happened next?" Mabel asked.

"Kevin happened," Lillie Mae said.

 Everyone turned to look at Harriet. She was beaming.

Lillie Mae continued. "Kevin had been standing in the dark wings the entire time, according to him, just trying to stay out of the way, when Margaret ran pass Charlie, who was collapsed on the floor by the steps. Margaret was headed toward the door. In a move that must have surprised Margaret, Kevin jumped in front of her and grabbed her arm. Swinging her around, he squeezed her arm tight enough that she dropped the gun."

"I had run to Charlie when he was shot," Harriet interrupted, "but still watched what was going on in the living room. When Margaret dropped the gun, I hurried over to it, and just stood there until I was sure Kevin was safe."

"Good for you," Joyce said, smiling at Harriet.

"Paul Lowman handcuffed Margaret while Kevin held her, and then torn off her mask," Lillie Mae said. "We were shocked when we discovered the villain was Margaret Jenkins. Even now I find it unimaginable.The evil look in that woman's eyes when Paul Lowman unmasked her will haunt me for a very long time."

"John Alton, who had kept me calm while we waited upstairs, thought it time for us to make our way slowly down the steps," Alice said. "He held me steady since I was shaking like a leaf. By the time we reached the bottom, I was thankful that the excitement was over and we all had survived. "

"You were amazing, Alice," Joyce said, her eyes filling with tears.

"Maybe foolish is a better description," Alice said, hugging Alfred tightly.

*   *   *

When Charlie and Kevin walked into Alice's living room a few minutes later, everyone in the room stood and applauded. Mabel let out a loud bird whistle and Lillie Mae joined in. Alfred was up dancing and barking as the crowd welcomed their heroes home. Charlie, his arm wrapped in a sling, smiled and waved his good arm. Kevin, lowering his head and blushing, raised his arm as well. The crowd cheered even louder as the two men found seats and sat down, Charlie beside Alice, and Kevin beside Harriet.

Kevin's blush reddened deeper when Harriet leaned over and kissed him.

"Way to go," hailed from all corners of the room.

Joyce and Janet rushed back from the kitchen with fresh trays of pastries and coffee. When everyone was served and settled in a comfortable place, Alice spoke.

"Tell us everything, Charlie," she said. "Who were Sam and Margaret Jenkins?"

"We've known them for years," Janet said, close to tears. "They've been a part of our community. Our neighbors. Margaret is a member of the breakfast club. How could these dear people be murderers? How could they be as awful as Alice just described?"

"People are not always who they appear to be," Charlie said. "That is certainly true of Sam and Margaret Jenkins."

"Amen," Pete said, nodding.

"Let's go back to where the story begins," Charlie said, tossing a smile at Pete. "The police have known forever that Carl Lewis dealt recreational drugs out of his trailer off the High Mount road in Mount Penn. Nothing hard, mostly marijuana. We raided his place off and on over the years, but it was always clean. He was smart and either kept the drugs somewhere else, or more likely someone tipped him off as to when we were coming. Although we raided him often enough, we never found a hint of drugs at his place. He was a small time dealer, so we didn't brother with him too much, but we did keep our eye on him. All that changed recently."

"What do you mean, changed?" Mabel asked.

"There had been a tip to the Antioch police that a big drug deal was going to go down locally. That's why there was a roadblock the morning drugs were found in the back of Jerry Foster's truck. The one Patrick was in."

Mabel nodded but stayed silent.

"Paul Lowman and I questioned Carl Lewis than searched his place later that morning although, as before, it was clean. The man was obviously scared, but he refused to talk to us. We suspected then that he had gotten involved with the wrong people and was in way over his head. People much higher in the food chain than he was even aware existed. We didn't have enough to arrest him, so we left him go. In hindsight, that was probably a mistake."

"In our own Mount Penn," Janet said. "Well, I never."

Charlie continued: "We found out soon enough that Carl had reason to be scared. A large amount of drugs that he was responsible for had been confiscated by the police. Someone had to pay, and when he looked around he knew that someone was probably going to be him. I guess it was the fear that drove him to make the next big mistake. Carl Lewis decided to seek out the man he thought might help him, Sam Jenkins."

Charlie paused. "Can I have a glass of water?" he asked.

Joyce, who was standing by the door, rushed into the kitchen. A few moments later she was back with the water. Charlie accepted it with a nod and a smile when she handed it over to him.

Charlie took a sip and continued to talk.

"Lillie Mae told me that she saw Carl Lewis driving up and down the street the day Jerry and Patrick were arrested," he said. "She watched him get out of his truck and walk up and down the street before crossing it. We can only guess he was trying to decide whether or not to confront Sam. He must have decided to do it, because he walked over to Sam's place and knocked on the door. But Sam wasn't home, or wasn't answering."

Charlie looked over at Lillie Mae, who nodded.

"We believe that Carl Lewis either knew or suspected that Sam Jenkins was his supplier. Although any dealings with someone at that level would had been done over the Internet or through the mail, apparently something must have pointed Carl to Sam. He had seen Sam Jenkins walking around his place often enough. He probably thought Sam was just a minor player, too.

"We can only surmise at this point, but we believe that when Margaret Jenkins heard that Carl Lewis had been to her house, she was livid. There had never been anything to connect the Jenkins with the drug business before. If they were to continue to be successful, they had to remain inconspicuous. We believe Carl

Lewis knew he had screwed up and should have never gone to the Jenkins' place. He might have thought he had lucked out because they weren't at home when he stopped by. But news travels fast in a small village. The next day he was dead."

"But I thought Roger Ballard killed Carl Lewis," Janet said. Pete grabbed her arm to shush her, but she just smiled at him.

"We never seriously believed that Roger killed Carl Lewis. We knew Roger had had a fight with him, but we didn't think he killed the man," Charlie said, addressing Janet's question. "Roger was angry because he was afraid he might be made the scapegoat for the latest operation. He knew Carl Lewis dealt drugs, but he believed he was a small timer, just like the rest of us. Roger never had anything to do with Carl's drug business."

Charlie took another sip of water. "Besides dealing in drugs, Carl Lewis fenced stolen goods. Roger sometimes bought those goods. He and Carl had been working together for years, but as I said, it was all small-time. We believe Roger was genuinely as surprised as Patrick and Jerry when the drugs were found in Jerry's truck. But we know he got angry and confronted Carl Lewis."

"Carl told Roger he had used unsuspecting couriers for years to move the goods from one place to another, if necessary, and this was the first time someone had been caught."

"How do you know all this?" Joyce asked, stunned by what she was hearing. "Carl and Roger are dead."

Charlie glanced at Mabel.

"Actually, much of this information came from Patrick. He told me what he and Roger had talked about the night he got out of jail. Patrick goaded Roger into a fist fight when they first met, but once that was over, the two men settled down and talked. Roger convinced him that he had not killed Carl Lewis and it was then, Roger told him much of what I'm telling you now. Patrick said that Roger was scared that night and he swore that he had never had any drug dealings with Carl Lewis or anyone else. We believed Patrick, because drugs weren't Roger's style. But, Roger admitted to Patrick that he was buying fenced goods from Carl Lewis and he didn't want anyone to find that out. With the water project certain to be approved, Roger was out to make big bucks for his plumbing business. If he was caught using stolen goods, he'd lose his license, and his business would go under just when the biggest opportunity of his life was about to drop in his lap."

"When did Patrick tell you all this?" Mabel asked, obviously surprised. "It wasn't when he and I talked to you."

Charlie smiled for the first time since he had started to speak. "He came to talk to me again, without you. It was after his run in with Jerry Foster. He said he hadn't told me everything he knew before, and he wanted to come clean. Jerry filled in the gaps later."

"I see," Mabel said."Go on."

"The timing was what was worrying Roger," Charlie said. "So, he went in search of Carl Lewis. He must have been steaming when he finally found him up at the hideout. It was probably Roger who picked the fight with Carl. And from the looks of the bruises on Roger, it must have been a real slugging match. But once the fight was over, the two men settled down and talked. Carl must have told Roger what was going on and that he was planning to meet someone that afternoon to negotiate. Carl didn't tell Roger who it was. But when he found Carl's body the next day, Roger became terrified. Justifiably, I might add."

"Why did Roger stop by Sam Jenkins' house if he didn't know that it was Sam that was involved with the drugs?"

This question came from Harriet.

"I can't answer that question," Charlie said. "He may have heard that Carl Lewis had been at Sam's house, and he was curious. If that is the case, it was that same curiosity that got him murdered."

"I was the one who told Sam that Carl and Roger had been at his house," Lillie Mae said, the color draining from her face.

"You weren't the only person who saw Carl Lewis and Roger Ballard at the Jenkins' house. Sam probably heard about their visit from several folks. It's a small village, Lillie Mae, and neither Carl nor Roger, were discreet. Everyone knows everyone else's business here. You know that. You don't need to feel guilty. It's not your fault these two men are dead."

"Why didn't Roger go to the police?" Alice asked.

"As I said, he was scared that he would have too much explaining to do. I could be wrong, but I don't think being murdered, even after he found Carl Lewis dead, entered his head. He was scared that he was going to be outted, not murdered."

"Who made those strange phone calls to Clare?" Lillie Mae asked, remembering them all of a sudden.

"It was probably Margaret, but it could have been Sam," Charlie said, turning toward Lillie Mae. "I'm sure their goal was to flush Roger out of hiding. They were using Clare and Billy to find Roger."

"So, how did Roger die, and why did Clare confess?" Harriet asked.

"Those are interesting questions," Charlie said. "And you asked them in exactly the right order. Let me explain."

Charlie took another sip of water before continuing.

"Clare honestly believed she had killed Roger. Thank goodness you all knew her better than she knew herself and believed in her. Here's what happened."

Lillie Mae suspected Charlie might be hamming it up when he paused again to take another sip of water. Then she saw him wince, and felt bad. His arm must be bothering him.

"When Clare talked to Billy earlier that day, she had told him some things about his dad that he hadn't known. I'm not sure what that was, and it really isn't important for us to know the details, but whatever she had said stressed him. It was the next bit of information that made him angry."

Charlie took a deep breath and continued. "Clare did her best to convince Billy that she was not having an affair with Dale Beavers. He had confronted her that morning after Dale had called and then showed up at their house to drive his mother up the mountain. She told me that, and so did Billy. Her efforts to deny it didn't budge him. She felt she had to set Billy straight, so she told him how her life had been with his father. Billy was torn. He told me that, too.

Billy confronted his father that night. Clare had called Roger and after explaining the situation to him, he agreed to meet with Billy in the park. After Billy left to go talk to his dad, Clare thought better of it, so she followed him. When she caught up with them Billy and Roger were fighting. Worried that someone would get hurt, she picked up a large stick. and yelled for them to stop. Ashamed, Billy turned and ran away. Clare stayed to talk to Roger.

Roger and Clare were both angry and they argued. When he approached her, he raised his hand as if to slap her, and she hauled off and hit him with the stick. He fell and she ran. Roger got up and chased her out of the park, catching her at the bottom of their yard. She hit him again, and he fell again. She ran into the house as quickly as she could, without looking back. When she and Dale Beavers discovered him dead, she thought it was her blow that had killed him."

"But it wasn't?" Alice asked, her eyes big and blue and questioning.

"No, Sam Jenkins had been following Roger, too, staying in the shadows. We're not sure when or where he first found Roger, but we know he must have been nearby as everything played out in the park. It all couldn't have gone better for him had he planned it.

"Well, I'll be," Janet said.

"Clare had only stunned Roger," Charlie continued. "We believe that when Roger was getting up off the ground, Sam stepped out of the shadows and slammed him in the back of the head with a club he'd been using as a walking stick. It was almost too easy. Later when Clare found Roger dead, she was so distressed she didn't even notice that Roger was lying in a completely different position than he had been when she left him."

"This is crazy," Kevin said under his breath. "All this stuff happening in Mount Penn. It just doesn't seem possible."

"When did you suspect Sam and Margaret Jenkins?" Carlos asked.

"Earlier than you might think," Charlie said, turning to face Carlos. "John Alton was in charge of research, and he discovered early on that Margaret Jenkins was not at the hospital when she claimed to be. In fact, there was no record of a Margaret Jenkins ever being at any hospital in the area. That was our first clue that all was not what it seemed. When we checked deeper into their histories, we found out quickly that they were not who they said they were. Sam Jenkins had never worked for the government, they had no known relatives, and until they arrived in Mount Penn, they had no past. But we still had no proof they were involved in the Mount Penn murders. All we knew was that they were not who they said they were, so we had nothing to link them with either the drug business or the crimes. But, they were definitely suspicious. We had to draw them out, if we were going to catch them."

"What made you think they would come after Alice?" Harriet asked.

"Somebody had attacked her once before, you see. We suspected it was probably the murderer. It certainly looked like whoever attacked Alice was just trying to scare her. Not do her real harm. The mystery was why attack Alice at all. It wasn't until later that she realized why she had been attacked. Do you want to tell them what you remembered?" Charlie said, inviting her to continue the story.

"I couldn't for the life of me remember what had struck me as so odd the first time I visited Sam and Margaret after they got back from what I thought was their emergency trip to the hospital," Alice said. "It was on another visit, when I looked into the living room, that I remembered. Sam and Margaret have a mirror that faces their back wall and casts a reflection of the living room into the front hallway. What I had seen that first time was a reflection of someone in the mirror. I realized later that it had to have been Margaret. But how could it be her, if she was confined to her bed? Whoever's reflection I saw had to be up and moving. I knew then why I had been attacked. I talked to Charlie and he agreed."

"Sam and Margaret were high on our radar a long time before Alice came to us," Charlie said. "But her information helped us confirm that we were on the right track."

"So, how did you get Sam and Margaret to risk attacking Alice again," Pete asked.

"I'm glad you asked that question, Pete," Charlie said.

Pete sat up straighter, a huge grin on his face. Janet reached over and patted his hand.

"It was actually Alice's idea," Charlie said. "But, we're getting ahead of ourselves. It was Mabel and Patrick who started stirring the pot, so to speak. Their job was to confuse the suspects."

"Mabel and Patrick," Joyce said, incredulously. "What do they have to do with all this?"

"Actually quite a bit," Charlie said, looking at Mabel and smiling. "Hester played a role in all this, too."

"Way to go, Hester," Carlos said, standing up and moving behind Hester. When he patted her on the head, she blushed, and then smiled.

"It was after Mabel got a couple of crank phone calls that I thought of a plan," said Charlie. "Perry Foster was upset with Patrick because he had gone to see his son, Jerry, a couple of days earlier. Jerry had told Patrick that he was being held as a virtual prisoner at his home by his parents and all visitors were off limits. This turned out to be untrue, but that's not the point. The Fosters were at work when Patrick stopped by to talk, but Sarah Foster had left work early that day, and had passed Patrick on his way down the hill. She confronted Jerry when she got home, and he admitted that Patrick had been there. When Perry found out, he got angry and showed up at the Goody house. Mabel was home, and she and Perry got into it."

"Then Perry did a stupid thing that worked out for us. He made a couple of harassing phone calls to Mabel. When she called me about them, I got an idea. Patrick and Mabel should leave town for a couple of days, and we'd put out a rumor that they might be the murderers. Mabel left Hester a note where she knew she would find it, letting her know what was going on. Hester made a few well-placed phone calls, and the rest is history."

"How did that help?" Carlos asked, confused.

"Sam and Margaret felt safe—at least for a while," Charlie continued. "They were already planning on leaving town to set up their next business deal, but they breathed a little clearer. They also began to make mistakes."

"Why did you arrest Perry Foster if you didn't think he was guilty of anything?" Lillie Mae asked.

"Another good question," Charlie said, turning to face Lillie Mae again. "To keep him safe. We were afraid he might be set up by the real murderers. Once Mabel and Patrick returned to Mount Penn, the real murderers would be looking for someone to blame. Perry Foster was a likely candidate. We also wanted to find out who Jerry believed murdered Carl Lewis. Patrick had told us that Jerry was scared, and might be willing to talk. We knew we'd need Perry in jail, if we wanted to get information from Jerry."

"What did Jerry tell you?" Mabel asked.

"He told us he had seen Carl Lewis and Sam Jenkins talking," Charlie said.

"So, he did know," Hester asked.

"He suspected, and of course, we know now he was right," Charlie said. "The good news is that Perry Foster has been released from jail, along with Clare."

Everybody cheered.

"But the story's not over," Charlie said, regaining center stage. "We arranged for Sam to overhear Alice tell Lillie Mae that she had remembered what had been bothering her."

"When was that?" Pete asked.

"Actually, you were there Pete. It was on Sunday, down at the Mount Penn Park."

"Well, I'll be," Pete said.

"We thought Sam would act before Alice had a chance to talk to anyone else. We knew the time was ripe for something to happen."

"That's when Charlie put forth this final plan," Alice said. "I was to let our friends and neighbors know that Alfred was missing. Actually Carlos and Joyce had taken him to Baltimore with them for the night so he was perfectly safe. Charlie thought Sam was planning some action, and that would take advantage of Alfred being gone. Sam had been lucky before and never doubted that this was another stroke of luck for him. Sergeant Lowman and Captain Alton were to stay upstairs with me during the night, and Charlie would be downstairs. Lillie Mae was to be upstairs, too, in case I needed something. It was her idea that Harriet and Kevin come along."

"Only because Harriet insisted on being part of it all," Lillie Mae said. "A good thing, too, since it was Kevin who grabbed Margaret and held onto her."

Everyone turned to Kevin again and smiled.

"It was a very dangerous thing to do, and it wasn't in the plan," Charlie said. Then he smiled at Kevin, too. "But, it did work out in the end."

"I can't believe Margaret would go along with Sam's evil ways," Joyce said. "I never liked her very much, but I always thought she was a good person."

"Margaret ran the operation," Charlie said. "Sam was just her stooge. But they were into this business together big time. We found all this out yesterday afternoon when we had a visit from a representative from the White House Office of National Drug Policy, a part of the National Institute on Drug Abuse."

"No!" Joyce said, looking around the room. Shocked expressions were on everyone's face.

241

"You're kidding," Lillie Mae said, hearing this piece of information for the first time.

"I'm very serious, actually," Charlie said. "They knew a big operative was working in this part of the country. They just didn't know who was running it or where it was being run from. They had a code name and according to them they were close to catching the guy. I'm not sure that was true. They were certainly excited enough when they received our call. According to them, their operative, which turned out to be Margaret, was just getting into distributing Fentanyl, a potent painkiller. Fentanyl mixed with heroin has become a drug craze in the United States, and Margaret wanted to control the distribution of this new product on the East Coast. There have been a number of deaths from this lethal drug combination, but for some strange reason, the deaths only increase the demand for the stuff. Apparently, Margaret was involved in smuggling clandestine Fentyanyl into the country from Mexico. She was building a pipeline through Chicago to the east coast. This was a big business, and there was big money involved."

"I can't believe all this," Alice said. "It's too much. This is Mount Penn, not some big city."

"Drugs are everywhere," Charlie said, shaking his head. "It's a huge business driven by huge demand and huge profits. I know it's crazy, but sadly, it's true. That's why Margaret insisted that Carl Lewis and Roger Ballard be murdered. She was livid that two small town punks could interfere with her latest business venture. She knew they didn't know much, but they knew just enough to be dangerous to her. But like many big time criminals, she was stupid in the end. And she underestimated us country bumpkins."

Alice started to cry. "And she wanted me dead."

"She was a woman without a heart," Lillie Mae said, hugging Alice.

"She was worse than that. Power and money were what drove her. But it was her arrogance that finally did her in. She and Sam will be spending the rest of their lives behind bars as a result. She's the type that will spill the beans on others once she's in prison, so she's even a bigger catch, the federal guys told us."

"She underestimated the Thursday morning breakfast club ladies as well," Lillie Mae said, a big grin on her face. "We were right when we thought Clare was not capable of murder."

242

"Yes, but we were wrong when we thought none of the ladies could be murderers," Harriet said. "Maybe we really are the Thursday Morning Breakfast and Murder Club."

"Look," Joyce said, pointing outside. "The sun's coming up and it looks like it's going to be another beautiful spring day. It feels like a new beginning for Mount Penn. Let's go home and get ready to meet at the Mountain View Inn for Thursday morning breakfast."

###

Author Acknowledgements

This novel was written while spending summers in the Maryland mountains in a small village not unlike Mount Penn. Just as it takes a village to raise a child, it takes a community to build a book. I'd like to thank some of those people who served as my community during this project.

First, I'd like to thank my son, Todd, an author, publisher, and now my agent, to whom this book is dedicated, for his efforts in making all this happen. His patience and gentle prodding keeps me moving forward. I'd like to thank James L. Dickerson, my first literary agent, who believed in the project enough to offer to publish the book when he opened his own publishing house. His guidance along the way has been a huge source of encouragement and a fountain of information.

Thanks to my son, Brian Stauffer, who managed my online presence, designed and built my website and my author pages, and my twitter logo. Also thanks to Kelsey McBride, a terrific publicist, and Rachel Simeone, my social media coach, for all your guidance and support.

I'd like to thank Lynette Hanson for being an amazing copy editor. She taught me so much including why authors gush about their editors. Not only did we work well together, but we had lots of fun in the process.

I'd also like to thank all my early readers, especially Paula Roberge, who has read each of my books, and has given me the special privilege of knowing what it feels like to have a number one fan. Sharyle Doherty has offered me unfailing support during my writing years and I thank her. Thanks also to Cheryl Bomar who continues to encourage me, and Matilde Vaida, who's belief in me is a constant inspiration. Also, thanks to Don and Bernie Harkin, and my adopted Irish family, who keep me sitting on top of the world.

Thanks also to my brother, Al Morningstar, who has paved the way to authorship for me with his own example, and his wife, my sister-in-law, Jane, who inadvertently gave me the idea for this book.

Printed in Great Britain
by Amazon